Praise for **VANISHED!**

2018 EDGAR AWARD NOMINEE

★ "As in *Framed!* (2016), fast brain- and footwork saves the day at the last moment, but watching Florian wow everyone . . . with Holmes-style connecting of dots along the way is just as satisfying. A splendid whodunit: cerebral, exhilarating, low in viole~~nce~~, methodical in construction, and occasionally hilariou~~s~~." —*Kirkus Reviews*, starred review

Praise for **FRAMED!**

2017 EDGAR AWARD NOMINEE
2016 PARENTS' CHOICE AWARD WINNE~~R~~

"Mystery buffs and fans of Anthony Horowitz's Alex Rider series are in for a treat. . . . With elements of Alex Rider, James Bond, and Sherlock Holmes stories, this is likely to be popular with mystery and action/adventure fans." —*School Library Journal*

"What stands out is the portrayal of Florian's and Margaret's intelligence, their close friendship, and athlete Margaret's sports prowess. Refreshingly, the adults aren't portrayed as completely clueless; they are respectful of the kids' crime-solving abilities, even though the preteen sleuths, as they realize themselves, are not infallible. Young readers will enjoy this first caper in a projected series." —*Booklist*

"The real draws here are the two resourceful leads' solid, realistic friendship, bolstered by snappy dialogue, brisk pacing, and well-crafted ancillary characters—not to mention behind-the-scenes glimpses of the FBI. More escapades are promised in this improbable but satisfying series starter." —*Kirkus Reviews*

"Florian resembles a young Sherlock Holmes, and together he and Margaret use the TOAST technique to prove that things are not always as they first appear. This book will grab readers from the first page with its witty characters and nonstop action."
—*School Library Connection*

"TOAST—the Theory of All Small Things—leads to a great big, hugely fun, ginormously exciting thrill ride of a mystery!"
—Chris Grabenstein, *New York Times* bestselling author of *Mr. Lemoncello's Library*

"*Framed!* is an enormously fun, deviously clever novel. It has everything you could possibly want in a book: intriguing characters, surprising plot twists, an excellent mystery, action, suspense and plenty of humor. I wish I'd written it myself. Florian Bates is a fantastic protagonist, a worthy—and dare I say smarter—successor to Sherlock Holmes and Encyclopedia Brown. I look forward to many more adventures with him." —Stuart Gibbs, *New York Times* bestselling author of the Spy School series

"Clever, touching, and a ton of fun—Florian is my new favorite twelve-year-old spy!" —Wendy Mass, *New York Times* bestselling author of *The Candymakers* and the Willow Falls books

"Florian Bates is awesome! I want him to be my best friend and solve the mystery of all my missing stuff." —Liesl Shurtliff, author of *Rump: The True Story of Rumpelstiltskin*

"This book is a delight from beginning to end. Lots of twisty clever fun with a healthy dose of danger. Move over, Encyclopedia Brown—Florian Bates is on the case!" —Lisa Graff, author of *A Tangle of Knots*

"*Framed!* is a captivating mystery where relatable characters string you along to a surprise ending. Readers will have fun picking out the little clues and piecing them together to solve the big case. Ponti has created a fascinating story that will make you value the power of simple observation." —Tyler Whitesides, author of the Janitors series

BY JAMES PONTI

The Framed! trilogy
Framed!
Vanished!
Trapped!

The Dead City trilogy
Dead City
Blue Moon
Dark Days

VANISHED!

A FRAMED! NOVEL

JAMES PONTI

ALADDIN

New York London Toronto Sydney New Delhi

ALADDIN

An imprint of Simon & Schuster Children's Publishing Division

1230 Avenue of the Americas, New York, New York 10020

First Aladdin paperback edition April 2018

Text copyright © 2017 by James Ponti

Cover illustration copyright © 2017 by Paul Hoppe

Also available in an Aladdin hardcover edition.

All rights reserved, including the right of reproduction in whole or in part in any form.

ALADDIN and related logo are registered trademarks of Simon & Schuster, Inc.

For information about special discounts for bulk purchases, please contact Simon & Schuster Special Sales at 1-866-506-1949 or business@simonandschuster.com.

The Simon & Schuster Speakers Bureau can bring authors to your live event.

For more information or to book an event contact the Simon & Schuster Speakers Bureau at 1-866-248-3049 or visit our website at www.simonspeakers.com.

Cover designed by Laura Lyn DiSiena

Interior designed by Laura Lyn DiSiena and Steve Scott

The text of this book was set in Jansen.

Manufactured in the United States of America 0318 OFF

2 4 6 8 10 9 7 5 3 1

The Library of Congress has cataloged the hardcover edition as follows:

Names: Ponti, James, author.

Title: Vanished! / by James Ponti.

Description: First Aladdin hardcover edition. | New York : Aladdin, 2017. |

Series: A Framed! mystery ; 2 | Summary: In Washington, D.C., twelve-year-old Florian Bates, a consulting detective for the FBI, and his best friend Margaret must uncover the truth behind a series of private middle school pranks that may or may not involve the daughter of the President of the United States. |

Identifiers: LCCN 2016041962 (print) | LCCN 2017013550 (eBook) |

ISBN 9781481436335 (hc) | ISBN 9781481436359 (eBook)

Subjects: | CYAC: Mystery and detective stories. |

United States. Federal Bureau of Investigation—Fiction. | Practical jokes—Fiction. |

Preparatory schools—Fiction. | Schools—Fiction. | Washington (D.C.)—Fiction. |

BISAC: JUVENILE FICTION / Mysteries & Detective Stories. |

JUVENILE FICTION / Action & Adventure / General. |

JUVENILE FICTION / Humorous Stories.

Classification: LCC PZ7.P7726 (eBook) |

LCC PZ7.P7726 Van 2017 (print) | DDC [Fic]—dc23

LC record available at https://lccn.loc.gov/2016041962

ISBN 9781481436342 (pbk)

for ro stimo

finder of clues, solver of mysteries,
champion of writers

1.

The Zodiac

MIDDLE SCHOOL IS HARD.

Solving cases for the FBI is even harder.

Doing both at the same time, well, that's just crazy.

Trust me, I know. My name's Florian Bates, I'm twelve years old, and along with my best friend, Margaret, I'm a consulting detective for the Bureau's Special Projects Team. We assist the FBI, the same way Sherlock Holmes helped Scotland Yard; only Sherlock never had to close a case *and* write a book report on the same night.

He also didn't have to deal with all the other seventh-grade headaches like locker room bullies, nine o'clock curfews, or figuring out what to wear. All he had to do was put on his coat and deerstalker hat. Instant detective.

Me? It seems like I'm always dressed for the wrong occasion. Like when we had to interrogate a witness while I was still in my soccer uniform. Or the time I was wearing my I'M WITH CHEWBACCA T-shirt and we ended up going undercover at the reception for the French ambassador. (In case you're wondering, "*Que la Force soit avec toi*" is how you say "May the Force be with you" in French.)

So when we arrived at the harbor patrol's maintenance-and-repair yard it shouldn't have been a surprise that I was the only one wearing a double-breasted blazer and herringbone tie. My mistake was that when I dressed for the symphony, I forgot to factor in the possibility of racing down the Potomac in a police boat. (I know, you'd think I'd learn.)

The boat was Marcus's idea. He oversees the Special Projects Team and it was a good plan except for one little detail: None of us actually had access to a boat. That meant we had to borrow one.

Margaret and I waited outside the harbormaster's office while he went in to see if he could get the duty sergeant to help us out. The stench of diesel was overwhelming, engine grease was everywhere, and when I saw my reflection in the window, I noticed my tie was crooked.

"What are you doing?" Margaret asked when she saw me fidget with it.

"Trying to straighten the knot," I explained. "It's a Windsor. It's supposed to be perfectly centered."

She gave me a look. That Margaret "you've got to be kidding me" look. "We're standing on a wharf surrounded by gas and grime and you're worried about your tie being crooked. Why don't you try to relax? No one's going to notice."

"Technically it's not a wharf," I corrected. "We're standing on a *dock*. And the dock is part of a *marina*. A wharf is an entirely different thing."

"Seriously?" she replied, shaking her head. "That's your takeaway from what I just said? Correcting my vocabulary?"

I gave her a sheepish smile and apologized. Then I tried to follow her advice and relax. But it wasn't easy. I'm not that good at relaxing on a normal day when nothing's going on, and this was no normal day. We were baffled by a missing persons case that was on the verge of making headlines across the world.

That morning we'd boarded a school bus for a field trip to the Kennedy Center for the Performing Arts. At the time, our biggest worry was finding a seat just the right distance from the bullies in back and the chaperones in front. Then one of our classmates disappeared into thin air. That might have been okay if it had been a magic show, but like I said, we were there for the symphony. So it was bad. And if the press found out, it would get even worse.

Suddenly bullies and chaperones didn't seem like such a big deal. We had a case to solve and we weren't having much luck figuring it out. Each clue seemed to lead us further away from the answer. And now, on top of that, I had an additional obstacle to overcome.

"Can I be honest with you?" I asked Margaret.

"This far into the friendship and you don't know?" she said. "You can always be honest with me. In fact, that's all you can be."

That made me smile.

"Okay, so here's the deal," I replied. "I'm not exactly *comfortable* when it comes to boats."

She gave me a curious look. "What does 'not exactly comfortable' mean?"

"They terrify me," I admitted. "They have ever since I saw that movie about the *Titanic*."

"You know it's at least eighty degrees today," she said. "I'm pretty sure we're not going to run into any icebergs."

"I'm not worried about sinking," I explained. "It's just that I got . . . seasick."

"You got seasick *watching* a movie?"

I nodded reluctantly.

"Were you at least on a boat while you were watching it?"

"No. We were home. I'll skip the vivid details, but we ended up having to rent one of those industrial-sized steam cleaners for the carpet and couch."

My thoughts wafted back to the salami sandwich and jalapeño-flavored tortilla chips that began the day in my lunch bag, and I wondered if they would soon be reintroduced to the world.

"Well, you might not have to worry about it," Margaret said, looking through the window into the office. "I think Marcus is striking out in there."

Even though we weren't inside, it wasn't hard to guess what the problem was. The harbor patrol was part of the Metropolitan Police Department, and Marcus was with the FBI. Those two groups are very protective of their turf and almost never work well together.

"Think we should help out?"

She asked it like a question, but considering she didn't wait for me to answer before she opened the door and went inside, I didn't really have much of a chance to say no.

The sergeant was big with ruddy skin, chubby cheeks, and a mustache that looked like it belonged on a walrus. He stood behind a counter similar to the check-in desk at a hotel and looked as though his patience was gone.

"But this is an emergency," Marcus said, frustrated.

"You keep saying that," replied the cop. "But I haven't heard a thing about it on my radio." He nodded to the police scanner on his desk.

"That's because we're trying to keep it contained to the FBI and Secret Service," answered Marcus. "We haven't involved the local police yet."

The sergeant flashed a smug smile. "There, you just said it yourself. You don't want to involve the local police. Well, unfortunately for you, these boats belong to the local police. So have a nice day."

Despite my dread of seasickness, I knew we needed the boat, so I tried to help out.

"What if Frankie was missing?" I asked, interrupting. "You'd want us to look for him, wouldn't you?"

The sergeant turned his attention to me and shot me with a laser stare.

"Or imagine your daughter, Maddie, went camping with her Girl Scout troop and got lost in a national park."

"How do you know about my kids?"

I ignored his question. "How would you feel if the park rangers wouldn't help the police who were trying to rescue

6

her because they were from different agencies? How would you feel if they did to you what you're doing to us right now?"

By this point he was really angry, his fat cheeks turning crimson. "I said, how do you know about my kids?" he demanded.

"The nameplate on your desk says you're Frank Bergen Sr.," I explained. "That means there's a junior. I know you call him Frankie because that's how he signed the drawing you taped to the window over there. I know your daughter Maddie's in Girl Scouts because you've got five cases of Girl Scout cookies marked 'Maddie B.' stacked behind your desk so you can deliver them to your coworkers."

He started to say something, but I just kept talking.

"I don't know your kids at all, but I know you're the kind of dad who tapes his son's pictures up at work and tries to help his daughter sell cookies. It's the best kind of dad to be. That's why I know that eventually you're going to give Agent Rivers the keys to a boat so we can try to rescue my friend. I just don't know if you're going to do it soon enough for us to make a difference."

For a moment the room was silent except for the sound of the sergeant taking a deep breath while he considered what I'd said. His nostrils flared as he inhaled and he studied me for a moment before begrudgingly slapping a set of keys down onto the counter.

"If there's so much as a scratch . . ."

"There won't be," Marcus said as he snatched them up. "You're a good cop, Frank. And a good father. Thank you."

"Just do me a favor and find the kid," he said.

"That we will," Marcus said as he grabbed a pair of dingy orange life vests from a rack and handed them to us. "That we will."

We followed Marcus outside and had to hurry to keep up. "That was great work in there, Florian," he said, taking quick long strides. "Our boat's at the end of the dock."

I looked out at the water and felt a wave of uneasiness. "We're sure this is the best way to go, right?" I asked, hoping it sounded more like a question of strategy than a fear of barfing.

"Yes, for two reasons," he said. "First of all, it's our only chance to get close to the bridge without anyone noticing us."

This was the part he hadn't mentioned to the police officer—or anyone in the Bureau, for that matter. The FBI and Secret Service were on the case, but we weren't. A Child Abduction Rapid Deployment (CARD) team was in charge and they didn't want any help from us.

Our problem was that we were pretty sure they had it wrong.

"Secondly, they're going to put the bridge under surveillance and check all the roads and sidewalks leading to it," he said. "So they'll have everything fully covered up there. But I don't think they'll be checking the river traffic, and if you're right, that's where we need to be."

I gulped, realizing my theory had set this little adventure into motion, and wrestled my way into the life vest. The boat didn't have one of those clever names like *Oh, Say Can You Sea* or *When You Fish Upon a Star*. Instead, it was just called *MPDC-4*. But what it lacked in creativity, it made up for in stability. I was relieved by how solid it felt beneath my feet.

"You know, this isn't so bad," I said as I plopped down on a thickly padded seat. "It's actually kind of comfy."

"Too bad it's not ours." Marcus chuckled. "We're taking the Zodiac."

"The what-iac?"

"The Zodiac," he repeated. "It's the boat tied to the back of this one."

"You know," Margaret added as she pulled me back up by my life jacket and turned me toward a small inflatable tied to *MPDC-4*. "The teeny-tiny one."

Up until that point the only zodiac I knew was the collection of astrological signs like Capricorn and Aquarius. But apparently it was also the name of the world's most terrifyingly inadequate water vessel. My horoscope: rough seas ahead.

"Shouldn't we take one of the ones with, you know, sides?" (I was no longer concerned with sounding scared.)

"Remember the part about us trying not to attract attention?" Marcus said. "If the CARD team sees a boat with police markings invade their crime scene they'll go nuts. This one's completely unmarked. Besides, it's a whole lot faster."

"So you're telling me it's supersmall *and* superfast?" I said, trying to force a smile. "That's just . . ."

"Super?" joked Margaret.

I started to climb down into the Zodiac, but Marcus took me by the shoulders and stopped me. "You don't have to go, Florian. I mean it. You can stay right here and I'll have someone give you a ride home. In fact, it might be a good idea for both of you to stay. Even without the markings, there's a decent chance they'll spot us. And if they do there's no telling what kind of trouble there'll be for encroaching on someone else's case. Especially a case so big."

"No way," I answered. "We have to solve this case fast. The second the press finds out, the whole situation will explode and our job will be much harder. Besides, that's not just anyone who's missing—it's someone I consider a friend. I'm going to follow the clues wherever they lead. Even if it means I have to take a submarine or ride in a helicopter."

"Me too," said Margaret. "Besides, if any one of us is getting in trouble, then all of us are."

He didn't say it but I could tell he was happy with our responses. We were in every way a team.

Once we were on board, Marcus untied the boat, maneuvered it out onto the river, and opened the throttle to full speed. As we raced toward the Key Bridge, the wind made it so my tie flapped in the air and kept slapping me in the face. I was too busy double clutching the safety rope that ran along our seat to do anything about it, so Margaret leaned over and tucked the tie into my life vest.

"You okay?" she asked, her voice barely audible over the whine of the engine.

I almost answered, but stopped when I realized that I wasn't sure if words or lunch would come out. Instead I just nodded and gripped the rope tighter.

"Look for anything suspicious," Marcus shouted so we could hear him.

"You mean more suspicious than the three of us?" Margaret responded.

There was so much mist spraying my face, I had to close my eyes as I tried to picture the crime scene in my head. A thirteen-year-old had disappeared despite being surrounded by dozens of people. There were no signs of foul play, no signs of anything out of the ordinary. The only clue we found was a sticky note with three words written in pen: HELP KEY BRIDGE.

The boat slowed down and I opened my eyes to see the Francis Scott Key Bridge come into view. Spanning the Potomac between Washington and Rosslyn, Virginia, it looked much bigger from the river than it did from the land. Whenever we drove over it in our car, it just seemed like a road that happened to pass over water. There were no towers or cables holding it up. But from this vantage point, you could see the six massive arches supporting it.

Marcus continued to slow the engine until we were basically floating along with the current. He turned on his walkie-talkie and clicked through the channels until he heard some agents communicating up above.

"They're up there," he said. "Let's hope they won't notice us."

"What are we looking for?" asked Margaret.

"Anything suspicious," he replied. "On the water or along the riverside."

He nodded to the jogging-and-bike path that ran along the water.

We saw a couple of kayaks and a man riding a stand-up paddleboard, but none of them was suspicious. A pair of sightseeing cruisers approached. One was named the *General*

Washington and the other the *President Jefferson.* Both were decorated with red, white, and blue banners, as well as signs that advertised STAR-SPANGLED TOURS.

I scanned the decks of the first one but saw only tourists taking pictures. When it passed us, our boat started bobbing up and down in its wake and my stomach gurgled even more. I closed my eyes and tried not to give the second boat a show. (Imagine dozens of tourists snapping pictures as I puked over the edge of the Zodiac.) I focused all my mental energy on my stomach, trying to calm the storm inside me. Trying to ignore the motion and my sense of uselessness. Trying to block out everything.

And that's when I noticed the music playing over the speakers on the boat. My mind was so busy concentrating on my seasickness that my subconscious brain was free to identify that something was out of place.

I looked up at Marcus and Margaret and asked, "Why's a sightseeing boat in the capital of the United States and named after an American president playing the British national anthem?"

They both gave me a confused look.

"What are you talking about?" she asked.

I worried I might be hallucinating. "Don't you hear the song?"

They listened for a moment and Margaret began to sing along:

> *My country, 'tis of thee,*
> *Sweet land of liberty,*
> *Of thee I sing.*

"No, no, no," I said. "Those aren't the lyrics. The song is 'God Save the Queen.'" Having grown up in Europe, including three years spent in England, I was quite familiar with it. I started to sing the version that I knew:

> *God save our gracious Queen!*
> *Long live our noble Queen!*
> *God save the Queen!*

Marcus smiled when he realized why I was confused. "I forgot that they both have the same tune," he said. "The Americans kept the music and wrote new lyrics to give it a completely different meaning."

I don't know if it was the dizziness, my stomach, the case, the clues, the music, or all of it. But in that moment I felt a surge moving up through my body. I couldn't tell if I was going to get sick, if my head was going to explode, or if I was going to solve the mystery right then and there. It just bubbled up through me. And then . . .

"I need to get off the boat," I said urgently.

"What's the matter?" asked Marcus. "Are you going to get sick?"

"No," I answered, my nausea instantly cured by my realization. "I told you I'd follow the clues wherever they lead, and they're not in the water."

"How do you know?" asked Margaret.

"It's complicated," I replied. "But the first thing you have to understand is that 'God Save the Queen' changes everything."

2.

Capital Crimes

Nine Days Earlier

BEFORE THE FIELD TRIP, THE SEASICKNESS, AND "God Save the Queen." Before I was looking for a missing teenager, I was trying to find a moon rock. It had been stolen from a safe inside NASA headquarters, just a few blocks south of the US Capitol Building. Despite some significant clues, I was struggling to solve the case. I'd narrowed the list of possible suspects down to two, but the evidence pointed equally at both. That meant one was guilty, one was innocent, and I was stumped.

Stumped!

Me? Florian Bates? That's not supposed to happen. I'm

the one they call Young Sherlock. The seventh grader who helped the FBI recover four masterpieces stolen from the National Gallery of Art. The twelve-year-old who figured out how spies were passing secret messages in the doughnut shop across the street from the Russian embassy. (Amazingly, it had to do with where they placed the apple fritters in the display case.)

I closed my eyes and tried to clear my brain of everything except for the evidence, but it was hard to focus with Margaret staring at me so relentlessly. Even with my eyes shut, I knew that's what she was doing. Still, just to make sure, I opened the left one ever so slightly to check. That's when she pounced.

"Have you solved it?" she asked eagerly.

"No," I admitted. "But I'm close. Very, very close." (Detective tip #1: Repetitive adverbs are often a dead giveaway that someone's lying.)

"That's good," she said. "Because time's running out."

"I know that," I snapped, doing a bad job of hiding my frustration. "Just give me a second."

"Okay, but that's all I can give you because—"

Bzzzzzz.

The buzzer sounded and she cackled with glee.

"Your time's up and it's my turn!" She grabbed the dice

and began shaking them in her hand. "I am finally going to win this game."

She rolled a pair of fours and was deciding which direction to move when Mom arrived with Marcus. We were in the basement room we called the Underground and the doorway was low enough that he had to duck as he entered.

"You've got company," said Mom.

"Hey, Marcus!"

"I hope I'm not interrupting."

"Not at all," said Margaret. "You've arrived just in time to watch me beat Florian."

She moved her token eight spaces and placed it in front of the Supreme Court Building. "Clue card, please."

"There's no guarantee she's going to win," I told them as I handed her one of the blue cards. "I'm only a turn or two away from solving it."

"Which is going to make it that much more painful when I beat you." She jotted something from the card onto her notepad and in true Margaret fashion covered it with her spare hand to keep me from seeing what she was writing.

Marcus tried to make sense of our Frankenstein's monster of a board game. We'd cobbled it together with buzzers, dice, tokens, and pads raided from other games. A sightseeing map of Washington was taped to a Scrabble board and there were three stacks of index cards marked: CLUE, SUSPECT, and EVIDENCE.

"What are you playing?" he asked.

"It's called Capital Crimes," answered Margaret. "We invented it."

"You invented your own mystery game?" he said, shaking his head.

"We've tried playing Clue, but Florian wins it too quickly," she answered. "So we had to come up with something more complicated."

"It's good," I added. "But it's still got a few kinks."

"He's only saying that because he's losing," she retorted. "He doesn't know what I know, that the moon rock was stolen by George Washington, who hid it in the House of Representatives."

She stood up and delivered a triumphant "Boom!" before doing a victory dance.

I let her have a moment of glory before breaking the bad news. "Sorry, but George couldn't have done it."

"Of course he did," she said as she started listing off clues from her pad. "It was stolen by a president, from Virginia, who—"

"Was short," I interrupted, showing her an Evidence card. "George was six foot two."

She sat down and stared at the card, shaking her head in disbelief.

"How'd I miss that?" she muttered, rechecking her notes.

I gleefully snatched the dice off the board and was about to roll when I noticed something and stopped abruptly. "Let's call it a draw," I suggested.

"Why would I agree to that?" asked Margaret. "I'm about to—"

"Because Marcus is here to talk about a real mystery," I interrupted. "And those are way more fun than fake ones."

She turned to look at him more closely and her eyes opened wide with anticipation. "Deal. It's a draw."

"Whoa, whoa, whoa," Marcus said. "How do you know I'm not just paying a friendly visit? What makes you think I'm here on business?"

"Your shoes," I answered.

"And your belt," added Margaret. "We could go on if you'd like."

"What's wrong with my shoes and belt?"

"Even though it's Saturday afternoon, you're wearing dark dress shoes with rubber soles and a belt thick enough for a holster and walkie-talkie," I pointed out.

"That means you're on duty," explained Margaret. "And if you're on duty and you come by here . . ."

"That means you want to talk about a case," I finished.

Margaret and I shared a low-key but confident fist bump. (Elbow high, no eye contact, no blowing up.)

He laughed. "Okay, I guess you guys are pretty smart."

And this is where Margaret went a bit too far by boasting, "Can't get anything by us."

"Is that so?" he asked. "Then how come neither one of you knew that James Madison stole the moon rock?"

It took a second to realize he was talking about the game and another to see that he was probably right. I opened the case file and shook my head when I read the solution.

"How could you possibly know that?" I asked, stunned. "You've never even seen the game before."

Marcus flashed a playful grin. "There were eight presidents from Virginia. Five were tall, two were average height, but James Madison was five foot four. He's the only suspect who fits your profile."

"You memorized the heights of the presidents?" Margaret asked in disbelief.

He winked at her and whispered, "Boom."

We went upstairs to the living room, where Dad was riveted by the Notre Dame football game. After a brief negotiation with my mom, he muted the TV and we all listened as Marcus explained the particulars of the case.

"First of all, I apologize for interrupting your weekend," he said. "But we've got a situation that we need to move on quickly."

"What is it?" I asked, tingling with excitement. "Bank robbery? Counterfeit ring? Please tell me it's international espionage. That's my favorite."

"Middle school pranks," he answered, completely deflating the moment.

"Oh," I said, slumping.

"Two weeks ago some lockers were vandalized at Chatham Country Day School," he continued. "Then last week someone hacked into the school e-mail server and crashed the whole system."

I waited for more, but that was it. "I'm confused," I said. "What do you want us to do?"

"Go undercover and figure out who's behind it," he answered.

I really wanted to sound enthusiastic, but it seemed so very . . . small.

"Why does the FBI even care?" I asked. "Shouldn't this be handled by the principal or a dean?"

"Normally, but . . ."

"CCD is anything but normal," interjected Margaret.

"Exactly," he said.

I turned to her, still confused.

"Chatham Country Day is the most prestigious prep school in the District," she explained. "Its student body includes the children of some very powerful people."

"Including Lucy Mays," Marcus added.

"You mean the Lucy Mays who's the president's daughter?" I asked as I began to grasp the magnitude of the situation.

"The one and only," he said. "To make matters worse, she's at least circumstantially connected to both pranks. We don't know if she's the target, an innocent bystander, or maybe even the perpetrator. But whatever's going on has to stop before it escalates and turns into something news-worthy."

"Yes! Yes! Yes!" exclaimed my father.

I thought it was a pretty enthusiastic response. Then I noticed that Notre Dame had just scored a touchdown and realized he was reacting to that, not the conversation. Mom gave him a dirty look and he sheepishly turned off the tele-vision.

"Sorry."

"All three of Admiral Douglas's children went to Chatham," Marcus said, referring to the director of the FBI. "So the headmaster called him directly and asked for help as a personal favor."

"What about the Secret Service?" Mom asked. "Aren't they supposed to be with the first family at all times? Can't they tell you what's happening?"

"It's true they're always with her," answered Marcus. "But they can't help us."

"Even if they know, they wouldn't tell," added my dad.

Marcus nodded. "That's right. Their sole job is to protect her. If they turned her in every time she did something wrong, she'd try to hide from them, which would jeopardize her safety. The Secret Service is well named. They keep secrets."

"So, I'm still a little unsure how we fit into this," I said.

"With the children of so many powerful people at the school, if there was a hint that the FBI was investigating, it would become an instant scandal," he answered. "So the admiral thought the perfect solution would be for you two to go undercover and figure it out. Once you give us the information, we'll pass it along to the school and they'll handle everything. Low-key. No news reporters."

"So we're going to pretend to be students at Chatham?" asked Margaret. "Of all the places . . ."

"Why do you say that?" I asked.

"Because I hate them," she said. "I play a lot of those girls in soccer. They're all stuck-up and mean."

"All of them?" I asked. "Think you might be exaggerating just a bit?"

"Well, I haven't met each one individually," she said only half jokingly. "But I still feel pretty confident in my assessment."

"How long will this take?" asked Mom.

"Hopefully just a week or two," said Marcus.

"That's a lot of school to miss," she replied. "Remember the policy we agreed on with Admiral Douglas. Florian can help save the country, but not if it hurts his academics. He can't miss that many days."

"That's the best part," Marcus informed her. "They have an International Baccalaureate program just like the one at Deal Middle School. The schoolwork will transfer back and forth. These two will hardly miss a thing."

"Great," I said sarcastically. "I'd hate to miss any homework."

"Okay, I just remembered something," Margaret said. "I may have a conflict. I have to be at Deal Thursday after school."

"Since when?" I asked.

She looked a little embarrassed as she answered, "Since I signed up to audition for the school talent show."

I couldn't believe it. "How is this the first I'm hearing about this?"

"I was waiting to see if I got picked," she said. "I thought I'd surprise you."

"I'll make sure you get to the audition," promised Marcus.

"Then I'm in," answered Margaret.

"Me too."

"But if any of those girls gives me attitude," she added, "I'm giving it right back to them."

Marcus laughed. "I'd expect nothing less."

3.

The Headmaster

WITHIN THIRTY MINUTES OF ARRIVING ON CAMPUS, I knew more about the history of Chatham Country Day School than I did about any of the five schools I'd actually attended. For example, I knew that:

Colonel John Rees Chatham founded the school in 1866 after serving in the Civil War as a field surgeon.

The campus sat on twenty-three picturesque acres nestled alongside Rock Creek Park in the Forest Hills neighborhood of Washington, DC.

The "foundation of a Chatham education is the honor code each student signs at the start of every school year."

I knew these things because they were all featured during the five-minute welcome video that played on a continuous loop in the Founder's Room, which is where Marcus, Margaret, and I were kept waiting until the headmaster could meet with us.

The video was impressive the first time or two we saw it, but by the fifth viewing we pretty much hated everything about the school.

"I told you they were stuck-up," Margaret commented as a pair of recent grads talked about how Chatham prepared them for the Ivy League.

I looked over at Marcus and noticed his jaw was locked into his "simmer face," the tight-lipped expression that usually meant he was trying to keep his frustration from boiling over into anger.

"Something wrong?" I asked.

"No," he said unconvincingly as he exhaled. "It's just that you'd think they wouldn't keep the FBI waiting so long. Especially since *they* asked *us* for help."

Unspoken but understood was the fact that from the moment we arrived, it had been obvious we were less than they'd been expecting. I'm sure the headmaster told his assistant that three FBI agents were coming. She was anticipating men in suits with crew cuts, not Marcus and a pair of kids. Even the request for us to wait in the Founder's Room, instead of staying in the outer office, seemed like an insult. As if they wanted to keep us out of view until they figured out how to get rid of us.

In addition to the video, the room featured oak-paneled walls covered with photographs of graduating classes going back more than a century, shelves teeming with ancient yearbooks, and for some unexplained reason, a display case featuring the fossilized jawbone of a giant ground sloth. (The only fossil at Deal was the cafeteria lady who deep-fried the tater tots.) The inscription on the case read, "*Megatherium* sample collected by Col. J. R. Chatham, on loan from the Smithsonian Institution." I was trying to make sense of it when the headmaster's assistant finally came to get us.

"Dr. Putney can see you now," she said.

We were ushered into an impressive office with antique furniture and a small sitting area. It was nothing like the principal's office at Deal, but Putney was the headmaster of an elite prep school. People paid a lot of money for their kids to attend and I'm sure they expected a certain level of formality.

Putney was built like a runner, tall and lean, with a hawk's nose. He wore a crisp white shirt with a burgundy tie. The reading glasses perched on the top of his balding head gave him the air of a professor.

"Welcome," he said as he motioned toward the sitting area. "My name is Dr. Putney and I'm the headmaster here at Chatham Country Day."

The greeting was polite but hardly warm.

"I'm Special Agent Rivers," Marcus said firmly. "And this is Florian Bates and Margaret Campbell." Then he added, "Did you have any luck reaching Admiral Douglas?"

The man gave Marcus a quizzical look. "What do you mean?"

"That's why we had to wait so long, right?" Marcus said. "Because you were trying to reach him to ask why he sent us."

"I am sorry you think that, but I assure you I did not try to call Admiral Douglas," he said with a smile.

(Detective tip #2: When people lie, they often try to cover it by using formal speech like Putney did twice in this sentence. He said, "I am" instead of "I'm" and "did not" for "didn't." Liars also tend to add terms like "I assure you.")

"But since you bring it up, I must admit I am confused," he continued. "When I spoke to the admiral over the weekend, he led me to believe he was offering the help of the Special Projects Team."

"That's correct," said Marcus.

The headmaster waited to see if there was more to the

answer but there wasn't. Then he looked at the three of us and asked, "Will they be coming soon?"

"We are the Special Projects Team," Marcus replied with a smile. "And I'm certain he informed you that our role must be kept a secret from everyone. Including your staff, faculty, and the board of trustees."

He eyed us again.

"Then I really am confused. I assumed that the team might consist of some forensics specialists to discreetly look for evidence or maybe a computer expert to figure out who hacked our server."

"Forensic evidence can only help if we can fingerprint your entire student body," Marcus said. "Do you think their parents would be okay with that?"

"Well, no," he admitted. "But . . ."

"And as for a computer expert, for that we'd need access to all of your internal files, accounts, and records storage."

"Well, there are privacy concerns . . ."

"More important, you're not looking for a criminal mastermind or a cyber thief. You're looking for a kid, or perhaps a group of kids. So that's what we've brought you. The quickest way to find out who's been pulling pranks at your school is to let Florian and Margaret go undercover as visiting students."

"Undercover?" He practically choked on the word. "You're not infiltrating a street gang. This is a prestigious prep school. We can't just have them snooping around and interrogating people. Our student body is very special and—"

"So is theirs," Marcus interrupted again.

"I beg your pardon?" he asked, confused.

"Their student body at Alice Deal Middle School," he said. "It's also very special."

"Of course."

"In fact," Marcus continued, "so is the student body at every school in Washington. For example, Duke Ellington School over on Eleventh Street Northwest. That's where I went."

"I'm sure it's very nice," Putney said condescendingly.

"I also went to Harvard," added Marcus. "And Georgetown for my PhD."

"I didn't mean to imply . . . ," Putney said, backpedaling.

This is when I came to his rescue. (Detective tip #3: If you help someone when you don't need to, they'll be more willing to help you later.) I appreciated Marcus standing up against the headmaster's snobbiness, but I needed Putney to like us, to want us to be there. It was the only way we were going to be successful.

"Agent Rivers, I think Dr. Putney just meant that many of the students here are in a unique situation because their parents hold very public positions in the government. It's important that what happens during this investigation doesn't get swept up into that."

"Exactly," he exclaimed. "That's all I was saying."

"You have nothing to worry about, Dr. Putney," I assured him. "We're discreet. We'll approach it the same way you approached your church mission. Just like when you went to Brazil and adapted to their customs, we're guests and will respect the customs and traditions unique to Chatham while we do our work."

Marcus shot me a wink.

"Y-y-yes," he stammered, trying to make sense of what I'd just said. "But how did you know that?"

"How did I know what?" I asked. "That you went on a mission? Or that it was to Brazil?"

"Both," he replied.

"TOAST," I said.

"Toast?"

"The Theory of All Small Things," answered Margaret. "The idea is that little details often give away much bigger pieces of information than you think. When you add them up, you have an indisputable truth. That's how we're going to find who's responsible for the pranks. Florian and I are going to use TOAST."

He looked back and forth at us like we were speaking a foreign language. "What *little details* could possibly tell you that I took a mission to Brazil?"

"On the wall beside your desk are your college diplomas," I explained. "They're from Brigham Young University. Over ninety-eight percent of the students at BYU are Mormon. And roughly a third of all Mormon men go on a mission."

"Okay, but that means two-thirds don't," he said as a challenge. "What makes you think I did?"

"You're featured in the welcome video not only as the headmaster but also as a graduate of Chatham Day," I replied. "But there's a six-year gap from your high school graduation until the date you received your bachelor's. That's four years of college with two years left over for your mission."

"As to Brazil," Margaret said, picking up without missing a beat, "that was easy. There's a picture of you on the far bookcase when you were about twenty years old. You're standing in front of the giant Christ the Redeemer statue, which is in Rio. There's also a picture of your family on your desk. It looks like a vacation shot and in it you're wearing a yellow-and-green jersey. Anyone who plays soccer knows it's the jersey of the Brazilian national team. I'm guessing you became a fan while you lived there and you've continued ever since."

He sat for a moment flabbergasted, unsure what to say. That's when I decided to really show off. "We're here to help. We understand you can't have another embarrassment like you did with Alexis Fitzgerald."

And just like that, the color drained from his face.

"The Wicked Witch of Wall Street?" asked Marcus, unsure where I was heading but delighted by the potential. "The woman who was arrested for stealing millions of dollars from charity? What does she have to do with Chatham?"

"She paid for the new gym, didn't she?" I asked Putney. "With some of the money she stole."

He let out a slow, pained breath.

"We had absolutely no idea where she got it," he said defensively. "And we're repaying it to the charities with interest. It's just going to take a little time."

"Rich private-school kids playing in a gym paid for with money stolen from the homeless," said Marcus. "It's funny how I never heard about that."

"Almost nobody has," he said, looking at me. "Who told you? Admiral Douglas?"

"Never," I answered. "The admiral *keeps* secrets. He doesn't share them. You're the one who told me. Or at least your assistant did, when she made us watch *Welcome to Chatham* over and over again."

I let him sweat that for a moment.

"There are two abrupt edits in the video," I explained. "Visually they're fine, but the music skips both times. I had the same problem once when I was trying to make a short movie on my computer. It's really hard to re-edit a video after you've added the music. Once you know that, it's obvious something was taken out. The two cuts are where sound bites from Alexis Fitzgerald's interview ran, right? All you had to do was clip her out. Except you forgot to have the credits redone. She's the only person mentioned in the special thanks who's not in the video. Of course no one ever looks at the credits. Well, almost no one."

"But how did you know she donated the money for the gym?" he asked.

"When we walked by it on the way to your office, I noticed the name above the entrance is off center. It says Tate Gymnasium, but there's way too much room over to the left. It was designed to read Fitzgerald Gymnasium. That's the problem with chiseling names into marble. It's hard to fix a mistake."

"And you figured out all of that while you were waiting in the Founder's Room?" he asked.

"Actually, I figured out more than that," I said ominously. This is when he gulped.

"I looked her up in one of the old yearbooks and realized both of you were in the same class. That got me thinking. I bet you're the one who called her up when you were trying to raise money for the gym. Just like you called the admiral to solve this problem. And while you've been able to keep the story of her involvement out of the press, the board of trustees knows it was you. They blame you. That's why you can't have another mistake. That's why you need us to make this problem go away."

There was silence in the room for a moment.

"Don't feel bad," Marcus said. "He does that a lot." He turned to Margaret and asked, "What do you call it again?"

"Getting toasted," she replied.

"That's right." Marcus smiled and turned back to Dr. Putney. "You just got toasted."

4.

Loki

ONCE WE WERE DONE WITH OUR TOAST DISPLAY, Dr. Putney was an entirely different person. The snobby headmaster with an attitude had been replaced by a much humbler man with a problem.

"Why don't we start over?" he said apologetically. "How can I help you?"

"First of all, tell us about the two incidents," replied Marcus.

"Of course," he said. "Two weeks ago someone put super-glue into the mechanisms of five lockers, totally ruining them. It's the type of prank you'll see at schools, but not typically at Chatham. Still, I wouldn't have been too concerned if it weren't for the fact that one of the lockers belonged to Lucy Mays."

Margaret and I shared a look at the mention of the president's daughter.

"Do you have any idea who might've done it?" asked Marcus.

"None," he said. "There are too many possibilities. It happened near the library in the main hallway. And since none of the girls went to their lockers between lunch and the end of the day, there's a two-hour window during which it could have taken place."

"All the lockers belonged to girls?" asked Margaret.

"Yes," he said as though he hadn't considered that this might be important. "Do you think that matters?"

"At this point we don't know what does or doesn't matter," said Marcus. "But I'm curious to know if the girls are part of the same friend group."

"I can't help you there," he said. "The social lives of middle school girls are more complicated than Russian literature. Besides, other than Lucy, the only one of the five I know well is Victoria Tate."

"Tate, as in the name on your gymnasium?" I asked.

"And the name on our library. The Tate family is a thread deeply woven into the fabric of Chatham Country Day. In fact, Moncrieff Tate is chairman of the board of trustees."

"We saw him in the video," Margaret said. "I love that name—Moncrieff Tate. He sounds like a law firm."

"He's Victoria's grandfather," he replied. "She's the fifth generation to attend Chatham and the queen bee of the middle school."

"Queen Victoria," grumbled Margaret.

Putney laughed. "That's exactly what they call her."

"We'll need the names of all five girls," said Marcus.

Putney pulled out a legal pad and started writing them down.

"And what can you tell us about the computer hack?" I asked.

"That happened last Thursday night," he answered. "Someone got into the server and flooded the system with spam until everything crashed. Our tech expert doesn't think any grades or records were accessed, but we're still checking that."

"Any idea how the hacker got into the system?" asked Marcus.

"More than an idea," he replied. "We know it was accessed through Chat Chat."

"What's Chat Chat?"

"Its official name is the Chatham Day Chat Forum," he replied. "But everyone calls it Chat Chat. It's an internal messaging system for students and faculty. It started as a project in a coding class a few years ago and really caught on. Now everyone uses it to post notes, bulletins, homework assignments, pictures, whatever."

"In other words your school has its very own social media network," Margaret said with a mixture of envy and admiration.

"Well, we did," he replied. "We've had to take it off-line until we can put in some security safeguards to prevent any future hacks."

"And only students and faculty could access it?" asked Marcus.

"That's right," he said. "The app only works if you have a Chatham e-mail account."

"So for both pranks we're looking for people at the school," reasoned Marcus. "The lockers were vandalized during the school day, and the computer was hacked through a closed system."

"Actually," Putney said. "I think they were both pulled by the same person."

"What makes you think that?" asked Margaret, echoing my own thoughts. "Superglue in a locker sounds pretty caveman compared to computer hacking."

"I'd think the same thing except for this." He crossed

over to his desk and opened a drawer. "The lockers were vandalized the same day the National Junior Honor Society announced its new members. They made the announcements by placing a sign on the locker of each inductee. This is the tag from Lucy's locker."

He pulled out a small piece of blue poster board with gold glitter and placed it on the table in front of Margaret. Marcus and I leaned over to look at it too. WELCOME TO NJHS, LUCY MAYS was written across it. But someone had used a marker to change it from "Lucy" to "Loki."

"Loki?" asked Margaret. "Like Thor's brother?"

"He's Thor's brother in the movies and comic books," I said. "But in Norse mythology Loki is the trickster god who loves to create havoc."

"Of course you'd know that," Margaret said, shooting me a look.

"He's right," said the headmaster. "And that's exactly what our Loki is doing. Creating havoc. When the server was hacked, the junk mail we all received read, 'Have a Nice Day!' And was signed, 'Loki.'"

"So you have a trickster named Loki," I said, thinking out loud. "What's his motivation? Maybe he doesn't like the five girls. Maybe he's angry about something that's happened to him and wants to disrupt school."

"Don't assume Loki's a *he*," said Margaret. "It could be a girl. I told you the girls here are . . ." She stopped when she realized she was about to bad-mouth the school in front of the headmaster. "Well, I'm just saying it could be a girl."

"Have you ever had pranks like this before?" asked Marcus.

"Harmless pranks used to be common," said Putney. "Back when I was a student they were practically a tradition. But there haven't been any since I came back as the head-master seven years ago."

"So we need to figure out what triggered their return," said Marcus. "Something had to get the ball rolling."

"It could be the honor society," I offered. "Maybe some-one didn't get in and was jealous because Lucy did."

"Then why attack the other lockers or the e-mail server?" asked Margaret.

"To cover his or her tracks," I said. "So the motivation wouldn't be obvious."

"That's possible," said Marcus.

"Ms. Stewart is the faculty sponsor," said Putney. "I'll ask if anyone was angry about not getting selected."

"When you talked with Admiral Douglas, you said there were connections to Lucy Mays regarding both incidents," said Marcus. "I know her locker was one of the five, but how is she connected to the computer hack?"

"We were able to track the hacker's path back to a Chat Chat group page set up for the school orchestra," he replied. "Lucy's quite an accomplished cellist. She's in the orchestra and would have had access to that page."

"Okay," said Marcus. "That's a pretty loose connection, but we'll need those names too. Anyone who's part of the orchestra."

Next we spent thirty minutes going through class schedules figuring out how Margaret and I could go undercover without falling behind in our schoolwork. (Thanks, Mom!) Putney opened up Lucy's schedule on his computer and Marcus handed him a copy of our records that he'd gotten from Deal Middle.

"Impressive scores," he said, admiring them.

"I told you they were special," Marcus said proudly.

The headmaster looked at my file and then up at me. "You lived in Paris?"

"Yes," I said. "London and Rome too. My family moves a lot."

"How's your French?"

"Maybe not fluent still, but close."

"Excellent," he replied. "Lucy takes an immersive French

class over in the upper school. Everyone else is in high school, but I can slip you in. The rest of your core classes are the same, so you can stay with her throughout the day."

"What about Queen Victoria?" asked Margaret. "Can you put me with her? If she's the alpha girl at the school, then she's the best way to learn all the dirt."

Putney pulled up her schedule on his computer and compared it to Margaret's. "Yes. That'll work just fine. You take all the same courses except for music."

"Great," said Marcus, much happier now that we were all working together.

"I understand your need for secrecy," Putney said. "But we have to inform the Secret Service about anything involving Lucy. I have a very close working relationship with them and it's essential that I maintain it."

"I've already spoken with them," replied Marcus. "And as soon as we're done, I'm going to have a meeting with the head of her protection detail so they know exactly what we're doing."

"Excellent," said Putney. Satisfied with the plan, he called his assistant on the intercom. "Ms. Caldwell, can you please send for Lucy Mays and Victoria Tate and have them report to my office?"

"Yes, sir," came the response.

Putney turned back to Margaret and warned, "One thing about Victoria. She's . . . I guess the most delicate way to say it would be . . . assertive."

"Yeah." Marcus chuckled. "I'm not so worried about that with Margaret."

I couldn't help but laugh.

"What do you call it again?" the headmaster asked while we waited for the girls to arrive. "The technique you used to figure out I'd been to Brazil and that Alexis Fitzgerald paid for the gym."

"TOAST," I said. "The Theory of All Small Things."

He nodded as he contemplated this. "It's really something."

"You've only seen the appetizer," Marcus assured them. "Wait until they show you the main course."

Lucy Mays was the first to arrive. Even though I'd seen her countless times on television and in magazines, I was surprised by how completely *normal* she looked. She was a little taller than me and her brown-blond hair was pulled back in a ponytail. She wore the school uniform of a plaid skirt and white polo and had her backpack slung over her shoulder like millions of seventh graders around the world. The only visual clue that marked her as different was the Secret Service agent standing a few feet behind her who was no doubt carrying a weapon, had been trained in deadly martial arts, and was prepared to sacrifice her own life to save Lucy's.

"You wanted to see me, Dr. Putney?"

"Yes, please come in," he said. "I'd like to introduce you to Florian Bates and Margaret Campbell. They're top students at Alice Deal Middle School and are going to spend a couple weeks here as part of a new IB exchange program."

"Welcome to Chatham," she said to us.

"Florian's in your French class, and since it's in the upper school, I was wondering if you could show him how to get there and be a host for him today."

"Of course," she said.

She turned to me and said, "Hi, I'm Lucy."

"Florian," I said. "Nice to meet you."

She was introducing herself to Margaret when Victoria Tate arrived.

Queen Victoria offered a startling contrast to the president's daughter. Unlike Lucy, who did everything she could to blend in, Victoria had pushed the boundaries of her uniform and the dress code to ensure everybody knew she was special.

She'd rolled her skirt at the waist to make it shorter, popped the collar of her shirt to stand out, carried a designer bag instead of a backpack, and wore boots that Margaret later discovered were available only from a boutique in Paris.

Putney explained the situation to her and asked her to be Margaret's host. Unlike Lucy, who'd introduced herself to both of us, Victoria just gave us the once-over. Her face was expressionless until she looked Margaret in the eyes. She held the look for a moment and then said a single word.

"Beast."

"I beg your pardon," Margaret replied, stepping closer so that she loomed over her. "What'd you call me?"

"Save the outrage," she said. "It's a compliment."

"Really?" Margaret said, her anger building. "Because it doesn't sound like one."

"You play center midfield for DC Dynamo, right?"

This caught Margaret by surprise. DC Dynamo was the best girls' soccer team in the District and she was their star player. I'd seen her almost single-handedly win the city championship and realized that Victoria may very well have been using the term as a compliment.

"Yes, I do," replied Margaret, the hint of a smile forming on her face.

"I knew I recognized you," she said. "We call you the Beast because you're unstoppable. I've had nightmares about you. We all have."

By now the smile was fully formed.

"I guess that's okay."

"Are you transferring to Chatham?" Victoria asked, suddenly excited.

"No, I . . ."

"You *have* to come here," she said. "With you on our team, we'd be unbeatable. We'd win the district every year."

Margaret gave me a smirk that suggested the girls at Chatham might not be so bad after all.

5.

Lucy Face

IT WASN'T UNTIL MEETING HER IN THE HEAD-
master's office that it dawned on me that I'd never actually
heard Lucy Mays speak before. Like almost everyone else on
the planet, I knew her from pictures. There was the famous
one of her in a bright blue overcoat at her father's inaugura-
tion and the one that was all over the news when she yawned
during a speech by the German chancellor. But mostly she
was just the kid in countless images of the first family getting off Air Force One or walking across the White House
lawn. That's why I was surprised to learn she spoke with a
Southern accent.

"We better hurry," she said when the bell rang. "We can't

be late for Madame Thibault or she will be *très énervé*," she added, using the French for "very angry."

"*Allons-y*," I replied, meaning "Let's go."

I thought this was a great start: her talking to me in French, and me responding in kind. I figured by the afternoon bell we'd be *bons amis*. Turns out I figured wrong. Not only did we not become good friends but our little French exchange was pretty much the conversational high point of the day.

I soon realized that although Lucy was the most well-known thirteen-year-old in the world, it was difficult to actually get to know her well. I tried asking questions to open her up, but she always responded with short answers that revealed virtually nothing. Some examples:

"What do you think of Chatham?"

"It's pretty good."

"Are the kids here friendly?"

"Most of them."

"Are you part of any clubs or teams?"

"Just the orchestra."

I began to wonder if one of her father's campaign advisers had instructed her to always give three-word responses. There were dozens of similar exchanges. Each time I waited for more, and each time she just kept walking toward the next class. Fast.

She always walked fast. At first I thought this was because she was worried about being late for French, but as I followed her throughout the rest of the day, I noticed she never slowed down to socialize.

Not only that but she always kept to the far left side of the hallway with her backpack on her right shoulder like a buffer. This put her against the natural flow of students but also made it so that she saw the faces of the people approaching her and limited their interactions to the fleeting moments when their paths crossed.

"Hey, Luce," someone would call out in passing.

"Hi," she'd answer with a nod as she kept moving.

These exchanges were almost always followed by what I dubbed "Lucy Face." It was the expression people made the moment they were out of her view. Some smiled, others rolled their eyes, and more than a few whispered comments to their friends. But virtually everyone reacted in some noticeable way. And since I was an anonymous kid walking a few steps behind her, no one bothered to hide those reactions from me.

Lucy Face made it hard for me to identify potential suspects. I was looking for someone acting odd around her, someone who might be Loki or at least point to a connection between her and Loki. But since almost everyone acted a little bit odd, there was nothing particularly suspicious about any one person.

I found my first candidate by turning that thinking upside down. Her name was Becca Baker and, unlike everybody else, she had virtually no reaction to the first daughter. Even though they sat beside each other in French class, Becca never once looked her way. When Lucy did a recitation and the rest of the class naturally turned to listen, Becca kept her eyes locked on the board as if she were specifically not looking at her.

This hardly made her guilty of anything, but it was different and I was desperate for suspects. I sat right behind Lucy, so I had a good angle to study Becca without being obvious. She had a small black instrument case that held either a flute or a piccolo, and there was a Stanford University logo on her backpack. Among the books I saw in her bag was a well-worn copy of *Bulfinch's Mythology*, and I could tell she was a germophobe because she used hand sanitizer at least three different times, even though she hadn't touched anything.

The two observations that stood out the most were the instrument, because if she was a member of the orchestra she would have had access to their Chat Chat group page, and the book, because if she was a fan of mythology it might explain the choice of Loki as an alias. Although neither of these was particularly incriminating, I still tried to sneak a picture of her as we left class. I pretended to be texting but right as I went to snap the photo, she turned and all I got was a shot of the back of her head.

I didn't find any suspects in gym class while we did laps around the track. Lucy ran with a quiet focus and I tried to keep up. But whenever I got almost close enough to say something to her, she picked up her pace and lost me. I couldn't tell if she was intentionally avoiding me or just having fun seeing if I'd continue trying to catch her. Eventually I got tired and walked the last ten minutes. As I did, I couldn't help but notice that everybody else either jogged or walked in little groups, talking to each other to pass the time. Only Lucy ran by herself.

It made me kind of sad. It seemed like she was friendly with everybody but friends with no one. All eyes were constantly watching what she did, yet she had no way of knowing what was going on behind those eyes. And as much as I hated to admit it, I was the worst offender. I was an undercover agent literally sent to spy on her.

By the time we were walking across the patio toward lunch, my sense of guilt had reached a breaking point. I had to do something. And for some reason, I decided the thing I had to do was embarrass myself.

"One time I rode a roller coaster and got so scared I started crying," I blurted out.

I'm certain she heard me, but she didn't react. She just kept walking. I didn't care. I was committed.

"It was pathetic," I continued. "You know those souvenir pictures they sell when you get off the ride? In mine, everyone else has their arms up as they scream but I'm just blubbering like a baby."

She stopped and gave me a curious look. But since she still didn't say anything, I just kept talking.

"And whenever I enter a public restroom, I try to identify the best place to hide in case there's some sort of zombie apocalypse. I figure the undead will check the toilet stalls and supply closets, so I look for a way to use the sink to climb up into the ceiling tiles. They'll never think to look there."

Finally she broke her silence. "And you're telling me this because . . . ?"

"Because it must get old meeting strangers who know all about you, but who you know nothing about. So I thought I'd just tell you some of the most embarrassing things about me to try to even things out a little."

She tilted her head and studied me for a second. I couldn't read her well enough to know if my "confession" had been a stroke of genius or just the latest in a lifetime of awkward social encounters.

"Are you done?" she asked.

"That should be enough for now."

She nodded and we resumed walking toward the cafeteria.

"Oh, I almost forgot," I added. "I'm terrified of frogs because they can jump in six different directions, which makes it impossible to predict how they might attack you." I punctuated this with a little shiver of fear.

She kept walking, but I could see her working out the math in her head. Finally she stopped again and turned back toward me.

"Forward, backward, right, left, and up," she said, counting them off with her fingers as she listed them. "That's five. What's the sixth direction?"

"Backward, up, and at an angle all at one time," I answered, simulating the maneuver with my hand. "Just like a ninja. It's the most terrifying of all because you think you're safely behind him and then . . . boom . . . frog attack."

It was the first time I saw her real smile all day. "You're not normal, are you?"

Five words. I was making progress.

"No," I replied. "Not even close."

Her posture changed. Just a little, but enough for me

to notice. "Okay, some tips for cafeteria survival," she said, looking toward the door. "The pizza's pretty good. The burgers are okay if you cover them with enough ketchup. But be wary of anything else. Especially if they're serving fish sticks. Here they call them 'Neptune Nuggets' to sound cute, but the rumor is that the Food and Drug Administration told them they can't be called fish sticks because what's inside them doesn't meet the legal definition of fish."

"Good to know," I said. "I'll play it safe and stick with pizza. What about you?"

"No lunch for me today. I'll be locked in a practice room with my cello. We've got a big performance next week and I have to practice, practice, practice. I'll meet you back here when the bell rings. We've got sixth-period algebra together."

"Great. I'll be right here."

"See you then." She turned to walk away and made it a few steps before she looked back over her shoulder and gave me a warning in French. *"Attention aux grenouilles."*

I smiled and replied, "Don't worry, I always keep a lookout for frogs."

6.

Saved by the Bell

THE CHATHAM CAFETERIA LOOKED NICER THAN
the one at Deal, but it still had that same stomach-
churning lunchroom smell familiar to students around
the globe. I guess there are some things even expensive
tuition can't cover up. I got a slice of pepperoni pizza and
was looking for a place to sit when I heard a voice from
behind me.

"Solve it yet?"

I turned to see Margaret carrying her lunch box.

"Not even a little bit," I admitted. "In fact, I feel like I
know less now than I did when we started."

"What's the matter with you?" she joked. "First I beat

you at Capital Crimes and now you're stumped again. You're losing it, Bates."

"Correction. You did not beat me at Capital Crimes. We called it a draw and then Marcus solved it with a ridiculous guess. But today, this was hard. Really hard."

"What's Lucy like?"

"Nice, I think. She's quiet so it's hard to know for sure. I couldn't get her to open up about anything. I got so desperate I even told her the story about crying on the roller coaster."

"Awww, I love that story," Margaret said. "If you'd like, I can bring in the souvenir photo so you can show it to her."

"I'm still not happy you bought that," I replied.

"Are you kidding? Me triumphantly raising my hands and screaming my head off. You bawling your little eyes out. It's like my favorite picture ever," she answered. "Where is she, anyway?"

"Practicing her cello," I said. "Which means I'm free for lunch."

"Great. Come sit with Tori and me," Margaret said.

"Who's Tori?"

"Victoria Tate."

"*Queen Victoria* is now *Tori*?" I said incredulously. "This morning Chatham girls were evil and now you're BFFs?"

"I'm working on a case, which means I'm totally committed

to doing whatever it takes to solve it," she said defensively. "Besides, she's not a complete monster."

"So says the Beast," I joked.

"I'll never admit it to anyone except you, but I kind of love that nickname. There are girls I've never met who are terrified of me. It just makes me all warm and fuzzy thinking about it."

Tori and three of her friends were sitting in the middle of the cafeteria as though they were the center of the universe and everyone else at the school orbited in their gravitational pull. They smiled when they saw Margaret coming but gave me a suspicious look when they realized I was heading toward them as well.

"Mind if my friend joins us?" Margaret asked, putting them on the spot.

"Any friend of yours is a friend of mine," Victoria said with a phony smile. "What's your name again?"

Inexplicably, I decided this would be a good time to do a James Bond impression. "Bates. Florian Bates." (Yet another addition to that lifetime of awkward social encounters.)

She somehow managed to laugh and roll her eyes at the same time. I sat down and quickly scanned the faces of the other kids at the table. There were two girls, Mallory and Lauren, whose job it seemed was to pay constant attention to Victoria, ready to laugh at any joke she told or agree with any observation she made. There was also Gunther, tall with sharp features, who looked more like a fashion model than a middle schooler. He spent the entire lunch texting at a ridiculously fast speed. At one point I thought his thumbs might explode.

"I was just telling everybody how great it would be if you transferred to Chatham," Victoria said to Margaret.

"You simply must come," said Mallory.

"It would be epic," added Lauren.

Gunther stopped texting for a second, looked up, and nodded.

"Thanks," she said. "But I like it at Deal."

They looked at her as if she were telling a joke and waited for the punch line. Certainly she couldn't mean it. How could anyone like Deal more than Chatham? It was right around then when I felt the jab in the side of the head.

"Outta my seat," a voice commanded.

I looked over my shoulder and saw a boy I'd noticed during a couple classes. Since he had his lunch tray in his hands, he was using his elbow to get my attention.

"Get out of my seat!" he said more emphatically. "What's the matter? Are you deaf?"

"They said it was okay for me to sit down," I answered.

Then I motioned to an empty seat at the end of the table. "Why don't you sit there?"

"Because that's not my seat," he said. "This is."

Victoria and her friends snickered and it occurred to me they knew this would happen when they said it was okay for me to sit down.

"Fine," I answered. "I didn't know. I'll move."

Margaret gave me a look but I signaled that it was all right as I picked up my tray and moved to the end of the table. This put me next to Lauren, who cringed as if my lack of cool might be contagious.

"Tanner, this is Margaret and Florian," Tori said, introducing us. "Margaret is an absolutely amazing soccer player, and Florian . . ."

She paused, unsure what to say about me, and Tanner happily filled in the gap.

"Follows Lucy Loser around like a puppy," he sneered. "You training to be the new White House dog?"

"Tanner?" she scolded, although her expression indicated she thought it was funny. "They're guests."

"I didn't invite them. Besides, he can take a joke." He turned to me. "You can take a joke, can't you?"

I'll be honest. At this point, I officially hated him. He was just a bully. But I worried Margaret was going to get in his face and I didn't want that. We were undercover and didn't need to attract any extra attention.

"Sure," I said as I tried to force a laugh. "I always like a good joke."

Over the next ten minutes, I quietly studied the group at the table. I would've been hard-pressed to believe that Mallory, Lauren, or Gunther was a criminal mastermind, although if Victoria was one I had no doubt they'd do whatever she told them.

If she was the queen of the middle school, then Tanner was definitely the king. He was good-looking, was bigger than most kids our age, and had perfectly shaggy hair. I noticed cuts on the knuckles of his left hand and wondered if he'd gotten them by pounding undersized seventh graders such as me.

He obviously hated Lucy, always referring to her by the oh-so-clever "Lucy Loser" nickname. Mostly he talked about lacrosse. There was nothing particularly interesting during the conversation until Victoria asked, "You ready for the algebra test?"

"What algebra test?"

"Next period. We have a unit exam."

"No we don't." He checked his phone. "Ms. Curtis always sends a reminder on Chat Chat."

I couldn't help myself. I laughed. Unfortunately I laughed loud enough for him to hear.

"What's so funny?" he said, his anger suddenly focused on me.

"Chat Chat's closed down because of the e-mail hack," I said. "I know that and I don't even go here."

Now he was mad and embarrassed.

"He's right," said Tori. "It's been closed down for days. We have a test in twenty-five minutes."

Mr. Cool suddenly looked panic-stricken. "I can't bomb a test," he said. "I'm already on academic probation. If my grades drop I won't be able to play lacrosse."

Apparently this was devastating news because Lauren and Mallory both gasped audibly. It may have been impolite, but I just happily chomped away on my pizza while he had his panic attack. He glared at me like he wanted to say something, but he had a more pressing issue on his hands. He had virtually no time to study for a test he needed to pass. He got up and hurried out of the cafeteria without saying anything else.

There were a few more comments about how terrible it would be if he couldn't play lacrosse, as if his playing were a gift to humanity, but soon the conversation returned to convincing Margaret to transfer schools. (No surprise that no one tried to convince me to do likewise.)

I scanned the cafeteria, looking for anyone or anything noteworthy as I finished my pizza. When I was done, I got up to leave.

"Where are you going?" asked Margaret.

"I think I'm going to go look for some TOAST," I said with a sly smile.

"That sounds *really* interesting," mocked Victoria, happy to see me go.

"Wait up," said Margaret.

The others were stunned. They couldn't believe she would pick me over them. "But we were going to tell you some more about Chatham," Victoria whined.

"You can tell me some other time," Margaret said as she stood and followed me toward the patio.

She waited until we were far enough away so that they couldn't hear us before asking, "Are we really looking for TOAST? Or were you just doing that to mess with them?"

"Can't it be both?"

We laughed and once again I was reminded how lucky I was to have Margaret as my best friend. We got library passes from a teacher on cafeteria duty and headed for the main academic building.

"Why are we going to the library?"

"I want to see if we can find the five lockers that were

ruined," I replied. "Dr. Putney said they were in the hall near there."

"I know exactly where they are," she said. "Tori told me all about it."

Margaret led me to a bank of yellow lockers stacked two high. We could tell which ones had been superglued because they had new silver latches that were brighter than the others. None of the five had locks.

"Tori said they had to drill the doors to get out their stuff, and all the girls were given new lockers down in the ninth-grade hall."

"Do you know whose locker was whose?" I asked.

"No," she answered. "But I do know that Tori and Lucy picked ones that were side by side, so these must be them."

She pointed at the only pair of adjoining lockers with new handles. There was no lock on either so I opened them to look inside. Both were empty.

"They've been fixed," I said. "So why haven't the girls moved back?"

"Because they don't want to," she answered. "Their new lockers are twice the size. Besides, they think it's cool to be in with the older kids."

"Any idea if the other girls who were affected are friends with Lucy and Victoria?"

"Actually, I don't think the two of them are really friends with each other. You heard how many times Tanner called her Lucy Loser and Tori never defended her."

"But you just said they picked out lockers side by side," I reminded her. "Doesn't that mean they're friends?"

"I think they want to appear to be friends," she said. "But I get the feeling that they're very competitive with each other. Tori mentions her all the time. She's obsessed. She always says positive things, but her voice is loaded with snark. They're probably more like *frenemies*."

"What are frenemies?"

"You know, friends and enemies at the same time?" she said. "Haven't you heard that term before?"

"No. It doesn't make any sense. You're either friends or you're enemies. You can't be both."

She shook her head. "You're such a boy. Girls are far more complex than that. Lucy and Tori are the two most important girls in the seventh grade, so they have to have some sort of relationship. They're like global superpowers, but on a middle school level. They work together but they're competitive. Friends. Enemies. Frenemies."

"Okay, sometimes you and I are competitive," I said, thinking about the intensity of our board games. "Does that mean we're frenemies?"

"No way!" she exclaimed. "We're *besties*. That's completely different."

I considered this for a moment. "How is it possible that I can speak three languages yet barely comprehend the vocabulary of girls?"

"It's a mystery, but luckily you've got me to help figure things out."

Something inside the left locker caught my attention. "What's this?" I pointed to a spot on the back of it where three stripes had been painted. Each was about four inches long. There were two purple stripes with a green stripe in the middle. Underneath that was written "How How."

"I don't know," said Margaret. "Decoration of some sort?"

"Seems like an odd way to decorate your locker," I said. "Normally you'd put up pictures or something. And 'How How'? That doesn't make sense."

"I feel like I saw those colors somewhere else today," she said.

I looked at them for a moment and replied, "So do I."

We thought about it but couldn't remember where.

"So do we have any suspects?" she asked.

"I don't know, how does Victoria look? Could she be the one?"

"Why would she bother?" answered Margaret. "She practically owns the school. She's got minions waiting on her hand

and foot. Why mess with that? I can't imagine what she'd gain by being Loki. Besides, why would she damage her own locker? She couldn't know that she'd get a better one as a result."

"Classic misdirection," I reasoned. "Make yourself a victim and no one suspects you. It's the perfect cover."

"So maybe that's what Lucy did," she suggested. "You followed her most of the day. Any signs that she's Loki?"

"None," I replied. "Like I said, she's just quiet."

"There wasn't anything even the slightest bit suspicious?"

"I don't know if I'd call it *suspicious*," I said reluctantly.

"Aha," said Margaret. "You've been holding out a piece of TOAST."

"I wasn't holding out," I said. "I just noticed something over by the library that didn't seem important but might be worth looking into."

"What is it?" asked Margaret.

"Lucy was always in a hurry," I explained. "She never stopped in the hall. She never went to her locker. And she always made it to class well before the bell rang."

"Okay, so she's punctual," said Margaret.

"Exactly," I said. "But on three separate occasions she made a point of walking past the library even though it wasn't the most direct path."

Margaret seemed underwhelmed by this observation.

"You know, Florian, not everyone shares your obsession with shortcuts and route efficiency."

We reached the library entrance and I studied it.

"You're right," I said. "But I think *she* does. So why did she make a point of coming this way? What was she looking for? She never stopped. She just walked along here and kept her eyes focused to the left."

Margaret tried to run with the idea. "So it could be something on this bulletin board. She could have been looking through the window into the library. Or maybe it has to do with the trophy case."

The bulletin board featured flyers for upcoming school events. There were notices about the science fair, auditions for a school musical, and an upcoming field trip to the Kennedy Center. But nothing looked even the slightest bit out of place or interesting.

"How ridiculous is this?" Margaret said. "Everything's perfect. Even the flyers on the bulletin board are completely straight. It's not a school; it's a movie set."

"The trophy case is worse," I said. "I think they've won every championship in the history of Washington."

We looked at it and shook our heads. There were cups, plaques, awards, and ribbons for all sports from football to cross country to volleyball. Margaret zeroed in on one in particular.

"This is for last year's district soccer tournament," she said with a sour face. "We lost in the semis to Sidwell Friends."

"How long did it take you to get over that?" I asked.

She gave me a raised eyebrow. "What makes you think I'm over it?"

I looked down at the trophies. Not only were there tons of them but each one was perfectly aligned and shiny like new. Which is why I noticed the smear. It was tiny, but it was real.

"What's this?" I asked, pointing at it.

"OMG, is there dirt on the trophy case?" she said with an exaggerated voice. "How did the maids miss it?"

"You're joking, but you're right. Everything else is spotless. And then there's this." I tapped the substance with the tip of my finger. "It's sticky."

"Okay, eeewwww," said Margaret.

I scraped some off and sniffed it.

"If you taste that I'm going to have to get a new bestie."

I jokingly moved it toward my mouth and then smiled. "I'm crazy but I'm not *that* crazy."

Before we could examine it any further, our sleuthing came to a sudden stop. The sound of a bell echoed through the hallway. At first I thought it was end of the class period, but then I realized it was something different.

Somebody had pulled the fire alarm.

7.

Just Like Magic

THE FIRE ALARM WAS STILL RINGING AS WE assembled alongside the soccer field a safe distance from the school. While most students congregated in little groups or checked their phones, Margaret stood practically mesmerized by the dark green turf with the Chatham Cougars logo in the center.

"It's a nice pitch, isn't it?" I asked.

"The nicest," she replied, her eyes glued to the field. "I played on it once before. It's a special blend of recycled plastic that always feels like freshly cut grass. Even in the middle of winter. It holds firm when you make a cut, but doesn't scratch up your leg when you slide. It's pretty much perfect."

I gave her an uneasy look and asked, "Should I be worried that you're actually tempted to transfer here?"

"Never," she said defiantly. "I'm a Deal Viking and in high school I'll be a Wilson Tiger. Just like you."

"Are you sure about that? You could join Queen Victoria and become Chatham royalty."

"You know how I roll," she said. "It's always loyalty before royalty."

I laughed because it was funny but also because it was true. It was something Victoria could never understand. In her world, whatever was most expensive was best and people were valuable only because of what they could do for her. But Margaret was the exact opposite. Her sense of loyalty was absolute, which is why I felt so bad moments later when the fire truck pulled into the parking lot.

"Check it out," she said, excited as she read the number off the side. "Engine Four."

Margaret's loyalty extended to the DC Fire Department, especially Engine House 4. As a newborn she'd been abandoned at the firehouse, and the six firefighters on duty watched over her through the night. She thought of them as her long-lost uncles, and even though only one of them was still there, whenever she saw their truck, or any fire truck for that matter, she always felt a connection.

She also felt a bit empty.

"As soon as we're done with this case, we've got to follow up some more," she said. "We've got to keep looking."

"Sure," I said, trying to force a smile. "Definitely."

And that's why I felt bad. She wanted to keep looking for her birth parents, and what I could never tell her was that I had already found them. Or at least her father. He was a notorious criminal known as Nic the Knife. She'd been left in order to protect her from that life, and when I came face-to-face with him, he warned me that if she knew the truth it would endanger her.

So rather than a loyal friend, I felt like a conspirator.

"Tom Munson's out there somewhere," she said. "I know we can find him."

Tom Munson was the one firefighter from that night who we hadn't been able to track down. He also was the one who'd answered the door and taken the baby. She thought that if we could locate him, she could get some answers.

"Of course we can," I said, trying to sound like I believed it.

She smiled and I felt like the world's worst friend. There was an awkward silence as I tried to figure out what to say next when we saw a black SUV with heavily tinted windows race along the driveway on the opposite side of the field. The vehicle was definitely government issued and very much in a hurry to get off campus.

"Check it out," Margaret said as it passed the security gate and zipped out onto the street. "Think it's the Secret Service taking your girl somewhere?"

"First of all, she's not *my girl*," I said. "But I doubt it's her. She told me she was going to meet me before algebra. Why would she say that if she was going to leave?"

"Maybe she didn't plan to leave," said Margaret. "Maybe it's an emergency exit. We can add that to the green and purple stripes and the sticky goo on the trophy case."

"Not a lot of clues to go on," I admitted.

"So what about the fire alarm?" she asked, turning back to the school. "You think it's Loki's handiwork?"

"Loki or maybe . . . Tanner?"

She gave me a look. "Why do you say that?"

"He looked pretty worried about taking that algebra test next period."

"You really think he'd pull a fire alarm just to get out of taking a test?"

"I don't think it's outside the realm of possibility," I said. "But I admit that I might be prejudiced due to my total distaste for bullies."

She paused for a moment before she said, "You know I was

more than happy to jump in there and put him in his place."

"I know," I replied. "And I appreciate it. But you can't always come to my rescue."

"True," she said. "But if you want to stand up for yourself, you're going to have to actually stand up for yourself. Don't let guys like that push you around. You're Florian Bates, secret consultant to the FBI—that's way cooler than anything he's ever done."

"Yeah, but like you said, it's *secret*," I replied. "Nobody knows about it."

"*I* know about it, and more important, *you* know about it," she said. "Nobody else matters."

It may have seemed cut-and-dried for Margaret, but I've always struggled with bullies. I think it's because on a basic level I don't understand them. The clues I see and the mysteries I solve all involve me identifying logical patterns. But people being mean to other people just because they can get away with it doesn't seem logical at all.

We heard the crackle of voices come over a walkie-talkie that belonged to a nearby assistant principal, so we snaked our way through the social clumps until we were close enough to eavesdrop.

"Have we identified where it was pulled?" asked a voice that sounded like Dr. Putney.

"Performing arts center," came the reply. "Rear hallway."

Margaret gave me a look and whispered, "Isn't that where Lucy went?"

"It's also near the cafeteria, so it would've been easy for Tanner to get there too."

A minute later we saw Putney walking toward the performing arts center with one of the firefighters. Not long after that, the alarm finally stopped ringing and a call came over the walkie-talkie that everything was clear.

As we headed back into school Margaret said, "You're not going to like this but I have a theory."

"What is it?" I asked.

"Lucy is Loki."

I gave her a look. "I figured that's what you were going to say. What's your logic?"

"TOAST," she replied. "Look at all the little things. The server was hacked by someone in orchestra. She's in orchestra. The fire alarm was pulled in the performing arts center. She was in the performing arts center."

"That's not much to go on."

"It's just a theory, but think about this," she said. "Forty-five minutes ago she told you she was going to meet you outside the cafeteria before algebra. But then she left campus in a hurry. What happened in between? You think she had a cello emergency? No. The fire alarm was pulled. That's what happened. And what did Marcus say was the Secret Service's only objective?"

"To protect her," I said.

"That's right," she replied. "Maybe they know she pulled it and they whisked her off campus to keep it from blowing up into something big. Maybe they're protecting her from getting in trouble."

I'll admit that I didn't want it to be Lucy, but I still thought Margaret was making some major leaps in her thinking.

"We're not even sure she was in the SUV," I said. "There are a lot of important kids who go to school here. It could have been any of them."

"Let's just see if she shows up for class," Margaret said knowingly.

"Let's," I replied, trying to sound more confident than I actually was.

Margaret and I sat next to each other in sixth-period algebra, and when Lucy didn't answer roll call, she turned toward me with an exaggerated look of surprise and whispered, "Oh no, I did not see that coming."

A few minutes later when we found out the test had been postponed because of the time lost to the fire alarm, I returned the favor. "What?" I whispered with equal exaggeration. "You mean pulling the fire alarm actually succeeded in stopping the test?"

The teacher gave us a dirty look and we stayed quiet the rest of the period. After school Margaret and I decided to check out the scene of the crime where the fire alarm was pulled. It happened in the performing arts center, and since she'd had her music class there, she led the way.

"Nice building," I said as we entered.

"Really nice," she agreed. "Just like everything else around here."

The PAC, which is what they called the building, had an auditorium, a smaller stage called the black box, and practice rooms for chorus, band, and orchestra.

"The alarm was pulled in the rear hallway," Margaret said. "That's back here."

She opened a door and we entered a long corridor that bent in a semicircle behind the rehearsal rooms, connecting them with the backstage area of the auditorium. It was designed to move people and instruments in for a performance.

The fire alarm was located midway along the hall, tucked inside a little alcove where there was a water fountain and a door marked ELECTRICAL SUPPLY PAC-1. We were startled to see a boy drinking from the fountain. The alcove had hidden him from view as we approached.

He was Asian, about my height, his dark brown eyes framed with wire-rimmed glasses. In addition to his school uniform he wore a Baltimore Orioles baseball cap.

"Hello," he said.

"Hi," we both responded.

There was an awkward moment as all three of us stood there. We wanted to examine the crime scene, but even though he was done drinking, he didn't seem to be in any hurry to go anywhere.

"I'm Yin," he finally said.

"Hi, Yin. My name's Florian."

"Margaret," she said, extending a hand to shake. "Nice to meet you."

"Nice to meet you," he replied.

We all just stood there for a moment more. I looked over and saw that someone had used marker to scrawl "Loki" under the fire alarm. Margaret and I shared a look, but Yin leaned back against the wall and started to look at his phone. He wasn't going anywhere, so eventually we continued on.

"What's he doing?" whispered Margaret.

"I have no idea," I replied.

"Did you read the name under the alarm?"

I nodded. "Loki strikes again!"

When we got back to the main hall Margaret said, "Did Lucy tell you she was going into a practice room?"

"Yes."

"Those are in here." She motioned toward a pair of double doors with a sign that said ORCHESTRA. "Let's take a look."

We entered a massive room with chairs and music stands set up in a semicircle. There were smaller rooms and offices off to the sides. Black instrument cases were neatly stacked on shelves across two walls. Larger instruments such as a bass drum, harp, and piano were arranged in the back. On the far wall were four doors in a row marked PRACTICE ROOMS 1–4.

"Hi, Ms. Allo," Margaret said to the teacher who was straightening the music stands.

"If it isn't our new piano player," she replied.

"This is my friend Florian," Margaret said. "He's the other exchange student from Deal, and I was just showing him around." She turned to me. "Ms. Allo is the music director for the school."

"Welcome to Chatham," she said. "Do you play an instrument?"

"No," I said, slightly embarrassed. "I sang in the chorus at my old school but instruments have always eluded me."

"It's never too late to start," she replied. "We've got beginners' classes."

"Well, the facilities certainly are nice," I told her.

"Thank you. We remodeled last year and are quite happy with how it turned out."

The sound of beautiful cello music came from one of the practice rooms.

"Wow," I said. "Someone's pretty good."

"Actually," she answered, "someone's amazing and has been in there practicing for hours getting ready for a big performance next week."

A smile began to form as I wondered if this was the explanation for Lucy's disappearance. Maybe she'd been in here practicing the whole time.

I stepped closer to listen and for the first time noticed there was another person in the room. A woman sat at a table silently grading papers. She didn't look up at us. She just kept grading.

I was just about to say something to her when the music stopped and the door to the practice room opened. Margaret and I both shared a stunned look when we saw who had been practicing.

It wasn't Lucy.

It was Yin.

Which seemed to defy all logic. How had he been inside that little room practicing for hours when we just saw him in the rear hallway a few minutes earlier?

8.

Yin

IT WAS BETTER THAN ANY MAGIC TRICK I'D ever seen.

From the moment we'd set foot in the orchestra room, we'd heard Yin playing his cello in one of the adjoining practice rooms. But this was impossible because we'd also seen him down the hall just minutes earlier. There was no way he could have entered without us seeing him. And even if there was, he couldn't already have been playing when we arrived. Add to this the fact that Ms. Allo, the music teacher, said he'd been practicing for hours, and you can understand the giant knot in my brain.

Yin understood it too. Which is why before I could ask

him a question, he cut me off and said, "Hello, my name is Yin. It's nice to meet you." (This, despite the fact that we'd just met and introduced ourselves.)

"I know who you are," I said, even more confused. "Don't you re . . ."

That's when I recognized the desperate look in his eyes and noticed that the other teacher in the room was suddenly interested in us. She was also Asian, possibly Yin's mother, and it occurred to me that she might be the one he was trying to deceive.

I changed midsentence and instead of saying, "Don't you re-member," I stammered for a second and turned it into "Don't you re-alize . . . that . . . everybody knows Yin . . . the amazing cellist? It's nice to meet you in person. I'm Florian."

I shot Margaret a look, but she'd already reached the same conclusion. She wasn't going to blow his cover either. At least not yet.

"Hi, Yin. My name's Margaret. You play beautifully."

"Thank you very much," he replied, a look of total relief on his face. "It's nice to meet you both."

The woman started speaking to him in Chinese, so I have no idea what they were saying. But after a brief conversation he turned back to us and said, "Sorry, I have to leave. We're late for an appointment."

Even though the woman seemed to be in a hurry, Yin was careful and methodical as he put away his instrument. First he loosened the strings on the bow and placed it in the case. Next he lifted the cello, pushed in the end pin that stuck out from the bottom, and gently laid it in its case. Finally he pulled out a soft cloth and wiped the surface.

"Rosin dust," he explained when he noticed how intently I was watching. "You should clean it off every time you put the cello away."

"You take good care of it," I said.

He smiled. "It takes good care of me."

He shut the case and snapped the latches. As he carried it over to the storage area, I wandered to the practice room he'd been using and peeked inside. It was small, about three times the size of a closet. There was a piano with a bench against the wall, a chair, a mirror, and a music stand. There was no other door or window.

"How'd you do it, Yin?" I whispered to myself.

A sign-up sheet on a clipboard hung by the door and I saw that three practice rooms had been reserved during lunch, when the fire alarm was pulled. One by Lucy. Another by Yin. And a third by someone whose initials were RIB.

"Thank you for the practice time," Yin said to Ms. Allo as they exited. "See you tomorrow."

"See you both," she responded.

"Good-bye," said the woman I now assumed was his mother.

"Bye," Margaret and I called out to them.

They left in a hurry, but that wasn't necessarily suspicious. Especially if they were late for an appointment.

Once the door closed behind them Margaret turned to the music teacher and said, "Wow! He's amazing."

"A genuine prodigy," she replied. "I've never seen—or heard—anyone like him. Not at such a young age."

"You must be really proud," I said. "How long has he been your student?"

She laughed. "I can't take credit for teaching Yin. I'm just lucky that I get to have him in my class. He arrived just after the start of last school year and has played and studied with the National Symphony Orchestra ever since."

"You're telling me he's in middle school and the NSO?" said Margaret amazed. "Okay, now I'm officially impressed."

She wasn't the only one.

That evening we went online and found dozens of articles praising Yin's amazing musical accomplishments. Each told a variation of his biography: He grew up in the city of Nanjing, China, where he began playing cello at age four and started composing music by the time he was six. And each was sprinkled with high praise such as when the musical director of the NSO declared him a "once-in-a-generation talent" or the Chinese ambassador said his loan to the National Symphony was "a gift from China to the people of America."

But none of the articles mentioned the skill that most caught our attention—his ability to seemingly be in two places at one time.

"We're not crazy, are we?" Margaret asked. "We did see him in the hall right before we walked into the orchestra room?"

"Yes, we did," I said emphatically.

"And we saw him come out of the practice room right after that?"

"Absolutely. So do you know what that makes him?"

"A shape-shifter?"

"No," I said. "It makes him our prime suspect."

I accentuated the statement by taping his picture to the middle of the wall where we were starting our caseboard.

"I still have him second," Margaret said. "I'm not ready to knock Lucy Mays out of the top spot."

We may not have agreed on the order, but I definitely considered Lucy a suspect too. I taped a photo of her next to the one of Yin. I also put up a stick figure drawing I made of

Tanner (with a particularly dopey expression) and a picture of barbecue ribs.

"Okay, how are ribs involved?" asked Margaret.

"The other person who reserved a practice room during lunch has the initials RIB," I replied as I smiled at my own cleverness. "I was being waggish."

"Waggish?"

"It's a British term," I said with a London accent. "It means funny or witty."

"I know what it means," she said. "I just don't know why you're using it. Just like I don't know why you're speaking like that."

"What's the matter?" I said, keeping the accent. "I thought everybody loved the way the Brits talked."

"Okay, who are you and what have you done with my best friend?"

I sighed and returned to my normal voice.

"I was just trying out new material," I said. "You know, trying to stand out a little bit more."

"Material for what? You're a seventh grader, not a stand-up comedian."

"No, but it's hard to compete with musical prodigies and presidential family members," I countered. "Or big jocks who play lacrosse and have long flowing hair."

She took a deep breath and thought for a second before speaking.

"I want to give you some advice," she said. "Don't be that guy."

"What guy?" I asked.

"The funny guy. Or the wild-and-crazy guy. Or the British-accent guy. Be *yourself.* Be Florian. You're going to have to trust me on this. Florian is more than enough. Florian is awesome."

"I was being myself today at lunch when Tanner walked all over me," I said. "You were there. You saw that. It's not fun."

"I know. But do you understand how Yin being in middle school and the National Symphony at the same time is impressive?"

"Of course I do. It's absolutely amazing."

"Yes, but it's no more amazing than you being in middle school and the FBI at the same time. And I know, it's a secret, but it's still amazing."

"Tell that to Tanner and Tori."

"You have a gift just like Yin does. Use it. The first time you met me you used TOAST to read me. Are you saying you can't read Tanner? You can't study him for ten seconds and figure out how to outsmart him? 'Cause if I'm being honest, he doesn't seem all that smart."

"I guess that might work," I said.

"Great," she replied. "So tomorrow you'll use your skills to outwit Tanner?"

"Right."

"Does that mean now we can use them to try to find Loki?"

"Of course."

Over the next hour we built our caseboard. We had the pictures of our suspects in the middle and around the edges put information about each of the incidents.

"Here are the names of the girls whose lockers were vandalized," Margaret said as she put up an index card with five names on it.

"And this is everyone who had access to the orchestra's group page on Chat Chat," I said, taping up a list that Marcus had e-mailed to us.

"I know Chat Chat is off-line," said Margaret. "But it would be helpful if they could let us access it just to read what was on it. There might be a clue there."

"Let's make up a list of requests for Marcus to give to Dr. Putney," I said as I pulled out a notepad and started writing.

We made notations under the pictures to signify connections to each incident. Underneath Yin's photo Margaret wrote "FA" for fire alarm because we'd seen him there and knew that he was in the vicinity and "CC" for Chat Chat because as a member of the orchestra he had access to the group page.

"Put the same notations under the barbecue ribs," I said.

"We don't even know who RIB is," she replied.

"True, but we know he or she was near the alarm when it got pulled," I reasoned. "And if you use the practice room then you're probably in orchestra. So RIB had access to the Chat Chat page."

"Good point," she said as she wrote beneath it.

"There's no connection between Tanner and the lockers or the orchestra," said Margaret. "I'll put an 'FA' down, although we don't really know that he was near the fire alarm."

"Thank you," I said. "I still think he's a candidate."

"But Lucy's the only one who's three for three. We can connect her to the lockers, Chat Chat, and the fire alarm. I'm also going to put a little red sticker on her picture."

"What's the red sticker mean?" I asked.

"Suspicious behavior," she said. "Her sudden departure from campus during the fire alarm."

"Then put one on Yin's too," I retorted. "We know he's hiding something."

She put a sticker on his picture.

The value of the caseboard is that it's a visual representation of your mind. In that way it lets you look inward by looking outward. We both stood there and stared for a moment and then Margaret just blurted out two unexpected words.

"Moncrieff Tate!"

"What?" I asked, beyond confused.

"Victoria's grandfather," she said. "The director of the board of trustees. He was in the video."

"Okay, I should have been more specific," I replied. "I remember who he is. I was asking why you just shouted out his name for no particular reason."

She smiled at me. "I like it when I have these moments when I know something and you don't."

She sat at the computer and searched for Moncrieff Tate. He was a big-time businessman, so there were plenty of pictures. She began moving through them until she found what she was looking for.

"He was wearing this same tie in the video," she said, pointing.

I was still confused as she got up and I took her seat. I looked at the tie for a moment and then it hit me.

"Three stripes, purple, green, purple," I said.

"Just like inside the locker," she replied.

Then it was my turn to have a realization. "And now I remember where *I* saw it," I said as I got my phone and opened my photo gallery. "Check it out."

I handed her the phone and she looked at the picture I took of Becca, the girl who wouldn't look at Lucy in French class.

"The back of a girl's head?" she said.

"I was staring at it all through second period. Look at her hair ribbon."

Margaret grinned when she saw it. "Purple, green, purple." She looked up at me. "What does it mean?"

I shook my head. "I have no idea. But I intend to find out."

We printed both pictures and taped them to the wall.

We sent an e-mail to Marcus (or rather the secret drop box we use to communicate with him) catching him up and giving him our list of requests for Dr. Putney.

"So what's the plan for tomorrow?" Margaret asked.

"I'll keep an eye on Lucy," I said. "But I'm also going to find out everything I can about Yin."

"I'll try to see if I can learn more about Tanner from Tori," she said. "And keep on the lookout for purple and green stripes."

"You should see if you can reserve one of the practice rooms."

"Why?"

"So we can snoop around," I said. "One of them has a piano."

"Sounds like a plan," she said. "And what are you going to do if Tanner gives you a hard time?"

I took a deep breath. "Remind myself that I'm Florian Bates."

"Then I have no doubt you'll crush him," she said. Then she stopped for a moment and looked over at the caseboard we'd made for the search for her parents. "Just like I have no doubt that one day you'll figure out where I came from."

I didn't respond; I just sat there and tried not to give anything away.

9.

Sorry, Bro

OUR SECOND DAY AT CHATHAM WAS FILLED WITH us trying to follow up on our initial leads, learn as much as possible about Lucy and Yin, and discover how someone could get in and out of a practice room without anybody else seeing. It was also filled with an endless stream of schoolwork.

This is the part that Sherlock Holmes never had to deal with. And yes, I know he's fictional, but real-life detectives don't have to deal with it either. I'm pretty sure Margaret and I are the only ones at the FBI who have to worry about solving algebraic equations at the same time we're solving cases.

The fun started in life science with a pop quiz about the differences between mollusks, arthropods, and echinoderms. (You know, because it's so embarrassing when you call one of them by the wrong name.) Then Madame Thibault assigned us a five-minute oral presentation—to be done entirely in French—about one person from French history who most affects our daily lives.

She also gave me the stink eye because I was looking around the room instead of paying attention as she went over the assignment. I was focusing on my FBI assignment at the time. I kept an eye on Becca and noticed she wore the same hair ribbon and still used hand sanitizer way more often than she needed.

Twice I tried (and failed) to strike up a conversation with Lucy. Since her official hosting duties were over, I didn't have the built-in excuse of walking with her between classes. Still, when I saw her in the hallway before science I jokingly said, "Hey, I thought you were going to meet me outside the cafeteria after lunch yesterday. I had to find algebra all on my own."

To which she replied, "Sorry about that." No explanation, just: "Sorry about that."

And on the way from French to gym, I said, "Can you believe that assignment? Five minutes, in French, about a historic figure. Who do you think you're going to talk about?"

To which she shrugged and responded, "I don't know."

We were back to three-word answers. Frustrating. But on a more positive note, since I knew what to look for, I was able to confirm that between classes she definitely was making it a point to check the trophy case in front of the library. The sticky residue from the day before was gone. I was determined to see if it made a return.

While I didn't know what the mark meant, it seemed to indicate that someone was secretly communicating with her by leaving a signal. If she had something to do with Loki, it might mean other people were involved too.

Third period was gym, and when I went into the boys' locker room, I discovered one important fact that had eluded my attention the day before: Tanner and I were in the same PE class. I hadn't noticed earlier because all we did was run on the track and I was trying to catch up to Lucy. But there was no missing him this time.

He made sure of that.

"Is that your name?" he asked as he saw me put on my shirt. "Alice?"

Because I was only a guest, I didn't have any Chatham gym clothes. I just used my normal ones: maroon shorts and a gray T-shirt with the name ALICE DEAL written above a Viking logo. Apparently this was hilarious.

"Hey, guys, check it out," he continued. "His name is Alice."

"Alice *Deal*," I said. "It's not my name; it's the name of my school."

"Whatever you say . . . *Alice*." He laughed. And since he thought it was funny, all of his buddies thought it was hysterical. I was Florian no longer. In the obnoxious world of locker room thugs, I'd become Alice.

Things got even more fun in the gym when I found out we were playing floor hockey, a sport I knew virtually nothing about but which luckily involved lots of physical contact. The coach split us up into teams of five and had us rotate playing.

Tanner was, of course, the best player on the best team. They kept winning, which meant they stayed on the court as new teams came out to challenge them.

"Next victim!" he'd call out at the end of each game as the losing team walked toward the bleachers.

I dreaded the moment when it would be our turn and I would be the "next victim." He'd completely succeeded at getting under my skin and I didn't know what to do about it. Then I remembered what Margaret had told me the night before. She said that I needed to use my strengths to counter his. So I went with TOAST and studied him, looking for any little details that might add up to something big.

The first one I noticed was the way he'd try to fake out his opponent during face-offs. He did a flurry of feints and moves with his hands and stick that were impossible to keep up with. But if you simply ignored them and stared at his feet, his forward foot always pointed in the direction he was going to hit the puck.

The second thing I picked up on was his big scoring move. He'd stand facing away from the goal and when the puck came to him, he'd lean back hard and use his body to clear out space, then he'd spin around and shoot. It worked every time.

"Next victim!" he called out when they won yet again.

We walked onto the court and I think I surprised everybody when I said I wanted to take the face-off. My teammates were certainly happy not to go up against Tanner, and he was even happier to see me come his way.

"Alice!" he bellowed to the laughter of his friends. "So happy you could join us."

The coach shot him a look but didn't say anything. Then, as the coach got ready to drop the puck, Tanner started moving his stick back and forth to distract me, but I ignored it and looked at his feet. I knew he was going to my left so I just went that way when he hit it.

I stole the puck and quickly passed it to a teammate, who shot it into the goal. Just like that we were up one to nothing.

"Nice one," the goal scorer shouted to me as he jogged back into position.

"More like *lucky* one," Tanner sniped under his breath.

I smiled because that's when I knew I had him. Now I was under his skin.

Another face-off. Another steal. Another goal.

The score was two to nothing and the kids in the bleachers were beginning to sit up and take notice.

Tanner was too good an athlete to keep making the same mistake, so that was the last time the face-off trick worked. But a few plays later I saw him with his back to the goal setting up to score. I knew exactly what he planned to do, so I slipped into position behind him.

He leaned his considerably larger (and sweatier) body back against mine and snarled, "All right, Alice, you're about to get schooled."

The puck came to him and he went to slam back and clear me out of the way. But before he could, I stepped to the side. There was no one there for him to lean against so he lost his balance and fell flat on his butt.

While he tumbled, I stole the puck and ran the length of the court and scored. This drew applause from the crowd and high fives from my teammates. It was a glorious sports moment but the exhilaration lasted only about twenty seconds. That's how long it took for the next play to get under way. I wasn't anywhere near the puck when Tanner steamrollered me and I slammed into the floor.

"Foul!" the coach called as he blew on his whistle. "Foul!"

Foul or not, it didn't matter. I was done for the day. Every inch of my body ached and it took me about twenty seconds to catch my breath. When I finally did and opened my eyes, I saw Tanner leaning over me to offer a hand up.

"Sorry, bro," he said with a mischievous grin. "I guess I didn't see you there."

I didn't respond and I didn't take his hand. I got up on my own (slowly) and walked over to the bleachers trying not to limp. I didn't want to give him the satisfaction of knowing how much I hurt.

The pain continued all through fourth-period ancient history, during which we had an in-class writing assignment about the contributions of Roman architecture. (A lucky break for me since I'd lived in Rome and was able to use specific examples.) And I was still aching as I made my way through the cafeteria line.

"Why are you walking like that?" Margaret asked.

I gave her a look. "Because I took your advice during PE." She had no idea what I was talking about, so I said, "I'll explain it later."

Thanks to Lucy's warning, I knew to skip the Neptune Nuggets (the thought that it might be illegal to call them fish sticks would haunt me for some time) and went with the pizza again. I also reminded myself that I should start bringing a lunch.

"Where do you want to sit?" Margaret asked.

"How about there?" I suggested as I nodded toward a table on the far side of the cafeteria where Yin sat alone.

"You think you can make it that far?" she joked.

"I'll do my best," I said with a faint smile. "Just don't rush."

"I've got good news," she told me as we walked. "I reserved a practice room this afternoon. Meet me in front of the performing arts center after school and you can look for any trapdoors or secret entryways while I work on my piano."

"Excellent," I said.

"And I've got a lead on the mysterious RIB."

"Boy or girl?" I asked.

"I don't know," she replied. "But I do know that he or she also has a practice room booked for after school, so we will find out."

"I'm glad one of us has made progress. I feel like I've been running in circles."

We reached Yin's table and Margaret asked, "Are those seats reserved?"

He looked surprised. "You want to sit with me?"

"Of course."

"That's wonderful." He smiled. "Please, join me."

We sat down and he seemed genuinely pleased to have someone to share lunch with. I got the impression that he usually ate alone and I felt kind of bad considering we were there with an ulterior motive. I also noticed that the woman we'd seen him with the day before was sitting at a nearby faculty table. She was definitely watching us.

We told Yin our situation, or at least our cover story, that we were on an exchange program from Deal.

"Like me," he said. "I'm on an exchange from China."

"Where in China?" I asked, even though I knew the answer. I didn't want him to know that we'd researched him.

"Nanjing," he said. "My parents are both professors in the music department at Nanjing University."

"But isn't that your mother there?" I said, motioning toward the faculty table.

He rolled his eyes. "No. That's Mrs. Chiang. She's not my mother. She's my . . . I don't know the exact word . . . sponsor."

He explained that his family was still back in Nanjing

and that he was living with the Chiangs, who worked at the Chinese embassy. The embassy had arranged a deal with Chatham for him to attend and her to teach Mandarin so she could keep an eye on him. She seemed more like a chaperone than a sponsor.

"How do you like Washington?" asked Margaret.

"I think it's great," he said. "Although, between school, the National Symphony, and composing, I don't get much time to explore it. Mostly I see it on Saturday afternoons. The Chiangs always take me someplace on Saturday afternoons."

By this point I felt really bad for him. He was away from his family. Away from his country. And had little time to be a kid. I decided that he needed friends more than we needed to ask him about the practice room. So I didn't bring it up. Instead I tried to get to know him. Not because he was a suspect but because he was worth knowing.

"So you like baseball," I said.

He gave me a curious look. "No. Why would you think that?"

"Yesterday you were wearing a Baltimore Orioles cap."

He laughed. "No, I don't like baseball. I like songbirds. I like anything that's musical."

This made all of us laugh. We continued talking and had a really good time until Tanner made an unwanted appearance.

"How goes it, Alice?" he said, making a point of slapping me square on the back for maximum sting.

I winced in pain.

"Oooh, sorry, I forgot. Still hurting?"

"No, I'm fine," I replied.

"I see you've met Yo-Yo," he added with a nod toward Yin.

I could tell that Yin feared him, which made two of us. Luckily, there were three at the table.

"His name is Yin Yae," said Margaret. "Not Yo-Yo. You should learn it."

"My mistake," he said, sensing that Margaret was not one to mess with. He continued on, but when he left, our happy mood was gone. I looked over and noticed that Mrs. Chiang had paid particularly close attention to Tanner's visit.

"He started calling me Yo-Yo last year," he said. "At first I thought it was a compliment. I thought he was comparing me to Yo-Yo Ma, who is a great Chinese cellist. But then I discovered that he was just making fun of my name. I don't even think he knows who Yo-Yo Ma is."

"Yeah, I'm pretty sure you're right about that," said Margaret.

It was quiet for a moment before I asked, "What are you doing this Saturday?"

"What do you mean?" he said.

"You told us that you take little field trips on Saturday afternoons," I explained. "Where are you going this Saturday?"

He thought for a second. "The zoo."

"Can I meet you there? Would the Chiangs be okay with that?"

He flashed a huge grin. "Of course. That would be great." He turned to Margaret. "Both of you?"

She smiled right back at him. "Are you kidding? I'm all about the zoo. I wouldn't miss it."

"Great! We'll all go to the zoo." He smiled and added a word that broke my heart. "Friends."

After the bell rang, as Margaret and I walked to algebra together, I turned to her and said, "Just so you know, I asked as a friend. Not because he's a suspect."

She looked at me and said, "You think I didn't know that? You're not the only one who can read people, Florian."

We sat down in algebra, and because the fire alarm had postponed it the day before, we had to take the unit test. Tanner sat one row behind me and an aisle to the right. I could see him with my peripheral vision when I turned my head slightly.

Here, away from the jungle laws of the gym and cafeteria, he wasn't talking tough or giving me a hard time. This was not his element. He was obviously still nervous about failing the test and what that might do to his eligibility to play lacrosse—which presented me with a dilemma.

I considered him a suspect who I needed to be able to study, but I also knew that he was a bully who tormented kids like Yin and me. Winning him over might help the case, but it would make me feel lousy. I weighed the options and made a decision that challenged my morals.

I decided to let him cheat off my test.

I didn't do anything overt, just moved my paper to the edge of my desk and slid ever so slightly to my left, giving him a clear view of my answer sheet. I started answering the questions and when I glanced over, I could see him copying every one down.

We'd gone over the unit in depth at Deal and I knew it cold. When I finished and put my pencil down, I was certain I had a perfect score. Seconds later I heard Tanner put his pencil down and let out a huge sigh of relief.

After class I didn't say anything to anybody, not even Margaret. I just got up and headed to English, unsure if I'd made the right decision.

Tanner caught up with me just outside the door to my next class.

"Dude, tell me you aced that test just now," he said.

"Yeah," I answered. "It was easy. I got a hundred percent. I'm certain of it."

He let out a huge sigh. "I was all wrong about you. I was a total jerk and you saved me."

I noticed we'd caught the attention of a few people in the hall, including Lucy.

"What do you mean?" I asked. "How did I save you?"

He let out a hardy laugh. "If you don't know, then you don't know. We'll keep it that way. I still owe you."

"You didn't copy off my test, did you?"

He just flashed a grin and shrugged. "Like I said, if you don't know . . ."

"Because I wasn't taking the same test as you."

That's when the smile disappeared and panic crossed his face.

"What?!"

"Yeah, I was taking the test my teacher sent over from Deal," I explained. "If you copied off my paper, you just got every answer wrong."

He started breathing deeply, unsure if I was joking or not.

I wasn't. That had been my moral dilemma. I didn't make him cheat, but I knew that he would. He was going to get into trouble because of what he did, but in a way I was responsible.

"Oh no," I said. "If you bombed the test, then that's going to knock you off the lacrosse team. And when the teacher realizes all your answers are the same as mine, she's going to know you cheated. That's going to get you in trouble with the honor code."

"Wait a second," he said, piecing it all together. "Did you . . . It's going to ruin everything . . . You did that on purpose . . . didn't you?"

I said the one and only thing that came to my mind. "Sorry, bro. I guess I didn't see you there."

10.

The Practice Room

THE BELL RANG, THE DOORS OPENED, AND students flooded from their classrooms, filling the hallway with the sounds of overlapping conversations, lockers closing, and rubber soles squeaking across the floor. The school day was over, which made everyone happy.

Except for me.

I was the exact opposite of happy as I scurried through the crowds, checking over my shoulder every few seconds to make sure I wasn't being followed (pursued? hunted?) by Tanner. While sitting in seventh-period English I'd begun to appreciate the magnitude of what I'd done to him and realized that if he wanted revenge, I'd be at my most vulnerable during the chaos that followed the afternoon bell.

I spied Margaret in front of the PAC, or performing arts center, and rushed right toward her.

"Hey," she said.

"Hey," I snapped back as I grabbed her by the arm and pulled her inside.

"Okay, someone's in a rush," she answered, trying to keep up. "What's going on? Did you figure something out?"

"Not unless you count solving our next case," I answered.

"You already know what our next case is?"

"It's a murder. My murder, to be precise. Tanner did it. Or rather, he will do it the second he sees me again. I imagine it will be violent, so there's a good chance you won't be able to identify my body."

I found an out-of-the-way corner behind a half wall and a drinking fountain, stopped, and took a deep breath that quickly became a series of very deep breaths.

"I'm thinking there's part of this story that I've missed," she said. "Why don't you tell me what happened?"

I described the escalating nature of my encounters with Tanner throughout the day. I filled her in on what happened in gym class, reminded her of the back-and-forth at lunch, and then told her about letting him copy off my algebra test.

"But we took a different test," she said, confused.

"Exactly," I replied with a smile. "But he didn't know that. And I didn't tell him until after he'd copied all my answers and turned it in."

"Wow!" she said once she put it all together. "I said to stand up for yourself, but . . . Wow!"

"By the way, I blame you," I added as I gave her my angry eyes. "Getting me all riled up. Telling me to use TOAST. You know I can't resist that."

"Blame?" she said. "I don't want *blame*. I want *credit*. I know you're scared and all, but what you did . . . it's . . . beautiful. Like years from now nerds are going to pass that story along in whispers as a beacon of hope."

"I just want to make sure the story doesn't end with the line, 'And he gave everybody a thumbs-up as they loaded him into the ambulance.'"

I could tell she thought I was overreacting, but she knew I was upset so she didn't say it out loud. "Okay, so what do you want to do about it?"

"I don't know. Hide. Get plastic surgery. Enter the witness relocation program. I'm open for suggestions."

"How about we solve the case so we can go back to Deal?" she offered.

"That would be great," I said. "I don't suppose you've had any major breakthroughs."

"Sorry, no, but there was a minor development by the fire alarm. Come on, I'll show you."

She leaned out and made sure Tanner wasn't lurking nearby, then we hurried over to the back hallway. Because it curved behind the rehearsal rooms, you could see only about a third of the way as you walked.

"I came by this morning before music and saw a man installing it," she said.

"Installing what?"

As we neared the little alcove with the fire alarm, she looked up and waved at a security camera attached to the ceiling. "That."

"They've already put in a security camera? That was quick. I guess they figure if Loki returns for an encore, they'll get a picture."

"Yeah," said Margaret. "And I think it's exactly what he wants."

"Why do you say that?" I asked.

"Because I don't think Loki's going to repeat himself. He's having fun coming up with new ways to cause chaos and if the school keeps focusing on stopping the pranks that have already happened—like they did when they closed down Chat Chat or here with the security camera—then they'll always be looking in the wrong direction when he strikes again."

"It scares me sometimes."

"What?" she asked.

"How good you are at thinking like one of the bad guys."

She smiled proudly and I examined the fire alarm. A fresh coat of pale green paint now covered the area where "Loki" had been scrawled the day before. I took a couple of pictures of the fire alarm, the hall, and even the security camera before we headed to the orchestra room. When we got there Ms. Allo was looking over a student's shoulder at a computer. Because their backs were turned toward us, I couldn't see who was helping her, but I could tell she was showing her how to use a computer program.

"Then you click which instrument you want," she explained.

"Okay, click French horn," replied Ms. Allo. "And then show me how to copy those three measures and have them repeat."

"You just click this and drag it over here," the girl said, and demonstrated. "Couldn't be easier."

"Ah-mazing. Absolutely amazing." She noticed us and smiled. "This transcription program is going to change my life. No more hours of endless notation by hand."

As she talked to us, she stood up and revealed the student who was helping her.

"Becca?" I said, caught off guard to see one of our potential suspects. It was the germophobe from French class who refused to look at Lucy and wore the hair ribbon with the purple/green/purple triple stripe.

"Do I know you?" she asked, confused.

"I'm in Madame Thibault's class with you," I said. "At least I have been for the last two days. My name's Florian."

Obviously I hadn't made any impression on her because she just stared at me blankly. This was probably because like everyone else in the class except for Lucy and me, she was a high school student, which meant she didn't really pay much attention to lowly seventh graders.

"Okay, well, hi," she finally said.

"Becca's the student leader of our wind ensemble," said Ms. Allo. "We're working out some new arrangements for the fall concert."

Becca put some papers into a folder and slid them into her backpack. I thought she was getting up to leave, but instead she picked up her instrument case and headed toward the practice rooms.

That's when it dawned on me that Becca Baker was RIB—Rebecca I. Baker. That meant she'd been in one of the practice rooms when the fire alarm was pulled. She was no longer someone who just acted unusual. She was a suspect.

"Wait," I said, trying to stall her so Margaret and I could read her. "Do you know who you're going to do your report on?"

"What report?" she asked, annoyed.

"Five minutes on a French person who impacts your daily life," I said. "Madame Thibault acted like it was a big deal."

"I haven't really thought about it."

Although her social signals indicated she wanted to move along, I couldn't have cared less. I kept pressing the conversation. "I'm thinking of doing mine on Blaise Pascal. He was the French mathematician who invented the computer."

"Actually, he invented the calculator," she said smugly. "You better get that right in your report. Charles Babbage built the first computer, and he's British, not French. Now, if you don't mind, I need to practice my flute."

She walked off, and Margaret and I made some small talk with Ms. Allo before we went into practice room number two. This was the room where Yin performed his amazing disappearing/reappearing act the day before.

"What was that about?" Margaret asked as she pulled out the piano bench and sat down. "I'm doing mine on Blaise Pascal," she added in a goofy voice that apparently was an impression of me.

"It was a test," I said. "She passed. Or failed. It depends on how you look at it."

"What kind of test?"

"Becca's the girl I told you about from French class," I explained. "The one with the hair ribbon and a copy of *Bulfinch's Mythology*. Now it turns out she's also RIB, which means she was here when the fire alarm was pulled."

"Okay."

"That makes her a suspect," I said. "But more important, she's a suspect with something none of the other suspects have demonstrated."

"What's that?"

"Computer skills," I said. "You saw her helping Ms. Allo when we came in."

"That doesn't mean anything," said Margaret. "Teachers are the worst when it comes to computers. Last week I had to show Ms. Hendricks how to save an e-mail."

"True," I replied. "But there was more to it than that. Her backpack has the logo from the Stanford University summer science program."

"And the test was to see if she knew who Pascal and Babbage were?" she said, getting it.

"And she did," I replied. "She knows computers. So as the leader of the wind ensemble she not only had access to the Chat Chat page but also has the technical know-how to crash the system."

"Nice detective work," said Margaret. "See what a little fear of dismemberment can do to motivate you?"

"Very funny," I said.

"Now try to use it to figure out how Yin got in and out of this room," she replied. "But you're on your own because if Ms. Allo doesn't hear any piano music coming out of here, she's going to get curious."

Margaret started playing scales, which I found soothing. I think it's because the gradual progression of notes fits with my sense of logic and pattern. I looked around and one of the first things that occurred to me was that all of the practice rooms were rectangular but the hallway that ran behind them was curved. Geometrically speaking that meant there had to be small pockets of space that were unaccounted for between the practice rooms and the hallway. The question was how to access them.

The walls were covered with large acoustic tiles designed to eliminate echoes. The tiles were big squares of foam wrapped in fabric and held in place by wooden frames. There was also a narrow mirror like you'd see on the back of a door.

"What's the mirror for?" I asked.

"To check your posture while you're playing," she answered.

I got up and checked to see if the mirror or the tiles were

movable, but they didn't seem to be. I took some pictures, sat in the chair, and started thinking.

Margaret, meanwhile, pulled a piece of sheet music from her backpack and put it up on the music rack. She started playing, and after listening for a little bit I said, "That's nice. What is it?"

"It's the song I'm using for my talent show audition," she said. "Which, by the way, is in two days, and I'm completely unprepared for it."

"You're doing a song?" I asked. "Does that mean you're going to sing, too?"

She gave me an apprehensive look. "Maybe."

My eyes lit up. "Will you sing it for me?"

"No," she said, as though it were a ridiculous request.

"Why not?" I said. "If you can sing it in front of the whole school you should be able to sing it in front of me."

"It's just . . . *different*," she replied.

"C'mon. We're besties. You said so yourself. It's not like you can be embarrassed. And even if you were, all you have to do is look at the picture of me crying on the roller coaster and we're all square again."

She thought about it for a bit before finally nodding. She started to play the melody again, but this time she also began to sing:

I haven't got a clue
What I'm doing here with you
I guess it must be true
It's just something that friends do

But all throughout our history
No matter what the mystery
The thing that's always true
Is that it's always me and you

She stopped and gave me a raised eyebrow, perhaps a little self-conscious or unsure as she explained, "I'm figuring it out, so it's very much a work in progress."

"Wait a second," I said. "Figuring it out? You mean, you wrote that?"

"Well, I'm still writing it, but yeah."

"When did you learn how to write a song?" I asked, incredulous. "It's really good."

"Thanks." She looked at me for a moment and asked apprehensively, "You get that I wrote it about us, don't you?"

"What do you mean?"

"The song," she said. "It's about us. 'I haven't got a clue.' 'No matter what the mystery.' It's about our friendship and the mysteries we've solved together."

"You wrote a song about our friendship?" I asked, truly touched.

"Yeah. Why not?"

"Wow. That's the coolest thing ever."

"I'm glad you like it," she said. "I'm thinking of playing it at your funeral after Tanner finally finds you."

"Okay, you're no longer cool. Now you're just mean," I joked. "So what's stumping you? Not about the case; I mean about the song."

"I've never written one before, so it's been a challenge, but in a fun way," she said. "Like right now I haven't figured out a chorus I like, and I'm still trying to decide if there needs to be a bridge before the final verse."

"You realize I have no idea what you're talking about," I said.

"You probably know more than you think," she responded. "You used to sing in the choir at your old school."

"Yeah, but I wasn't any good. There were no auditions. All you had to do was sign up and you were in."

She handed me the music and pointed to different parts as she talked. "The verse is the main lyric, kind of like the poetry part. And the chorus is the part that repeats. I've tried a few different ones, but none of them really work for me. And the bridge is a transition from the chorus into the last verse. That's when everything changes up right before the big finish."

"Kind of like when all the clues come together before you solve a case," I joked.

"Actually it is."

She demonstrated it for me and started playing some notes, but something must have triggered an idea because just like that it was as if I were no longer in the room as she started playing a series of notes over and over with slight changes.

I stopped talking so she could concentrate and I went back to studying the room. Maybe her brainstorm would help give me one.

The fabric that covered the acoustic tiles had something of a kaleidoscope design made up of musical notes, instruments, and profiles of famous composers. The pattern seemed random, but if you let your eye isolate one item at a time, like the trumpet or Beethoven, you could see that it was actually consistent. And once I realized that, I was able to notice that one tile was wrong.

"Check this out," I said, interrupting her work.

"What?" she asked.

"Mozart," I answered as I got up and pointed to the tile along the floor next to the mirror. "On every other one, he's in the top right corner, but here he's in the bottom left and upside down. Do you know what that means?"

She looked at me and replied, "I can honestly say I don't have any idea what you're talking about."

"It means that someone has taken it off and put it back upside down by mistake."

I got down on my hands and knees and reached around the back of the frame and pulled gently. Nothing happened, so I pulled a little harder. Finally it started to budge. Then it popped off and I fell backward. Behind the tile was a door about two feet by two feet that I opened to reveal a crawl space.

I looked back over my shoulder at Margaret, whose eyes had opened wide.

"Now, isn't that interesting?" she said.

11.

Oh! Susanna

THE DOORWAY TO THE CRAWL SPACE WAS SMALL, and I had to turn my shoulders diagonally just to poke in far enough to get a good look.

"What do you see?" asked Margaret.

"Mostly darkness," I answered. "I can make out some shapes and a few slats of light, but that's about it."

It took a little contorting, but I managed to dig my phone out of my pocket and turn on a flashlight app that let me see computer cables, electrical wiring, and the silver caterpillar-like ductwork that carried heating and air-conditioning. After thirty seconds, I pulled myself back into the practice room.

"Think we should go all the way in there?" Margaret asked.

"Not *we*, me," I answered. "You have to start playing again or Ms. Allo will get curious."

Margaret didn't want to miss out on any adventure, but she knew I was right. She resumed playing and I corkscrewed my way through the opening. I was halfway before it dawned on me that it would have been much easier if I had gone feetfirst.

Once I was through, I turned the flashlight app back on, held it up against my forehead like a miner's lamp, and started crawling. As I got farther away from the piano music, I could make out the faint sounds of a flute and realized that I was next to the room where Becca was practicing. There looked to be another small door leading to it, but I couldn't check without popping in on her.

Instead, I continued my slow crawl, careful not to touch something that could electrocute me, and stopped when I reached the slats of light. They were coming through a large vent cover and I listened to make sure no one was on the other side before I pressed my face up to it and looked through. I could easily see the pale green wall of the rear hallway.

I checked the photos I'd taken of the alcove and saw that

the vent was located between the fire alarm and the water fountain. It was tempting to push it open, but the security camera would have videotaped it—not a great way to stay undercover. Since there wasn't enough space to turn around, I had to crawl backward toward the sound of Margaret's piano playing, which took some time.

"Where does it go?" she asked as I squeezed back into the practice room.

"Exactly where you think it does," I answered. "Right to the fire alarm."

"So does that mean Yin is Loki?"

I brushed the dust off my pants and shrugged. "It means he knows about the crawl space and that he might be Loki. But I saw a door to at least one other practice room. So any one of them might have done it."

"So it could have been Yin, Becca, or Lucy."

"That's right," I answered. "Except for one thing."

"What's that?"

"I was able to go without attracting attention because you stayed in here and played the piano," I explained. "But each of them was alone. We even heard Yin playing ourselves."

"Did we?" Margaret flashed a huge smile. "Close your eyes and listen."

"Okay," I said, unsure where this was going.

I sat there on the floor with my back pressed against the foam of the acoustic tile and listened. The music was beautiful and filled the room . . . but it wasn't coming from the piano.

"How'd you do that?" I asked, opening my eyes.

"Playback," she said with a huge grin. "It's really high quality."

She showed me how the room was equipped with a recording system so students could listen to themselves.

"The sound quality's amazing," she said. "Sitting right here next to it, it's obvious the music isn't coming from the piano. But I don't think Ms. Allo or anyone else would be able to tell that from out there."

"That's brilliant," I said. "So you record yourself and then you can play it back and buy yourself plenty of time to crawl around."

"What do we do now?" asked Margaret.

"Play a little bit more while I put everything back the way it was," I said. "Then we need to go out there and wait for Becca. I want to get to know her better."

When we reentered the orchestra room, we were greeted by the screeching of very bad clarinet music as Ms. Allo worked with a beginning student struggling to play a lesson. It was hard to make out the tune, but when he stopped she smiled and tried to sound encouraging. "That's better. Just keep practicing."

Once he'd packed up his instrument and left, Margaret asked her, "Was that 'Oh! Susanna'?"

"Somewhere in there," she answered good-naturedly. "That song is the bane of my existence."

"Why's that?" I asked.

"First of all, here we call it 'My Dear Chatham.' It's the school's alma mater and we have to play it at every event and function. Every. Single. One."

Margaret replied, "But it sounds a lot like . . ."

"Oh no, it's exactly like 'Oh! Susanna,'" she said. "This school goes back to when that song was considered fresh and new. John Rees Chatham himself wrote new lyrics to go along with the music."

"Isn't he the guy who founded the school?" I said.

"He most certainly is," replied the teacher. "Which is why they'll never let me change or update it, no matter how many times I plead. And I plead often."

We all laughed.

"Here you go," she said, handing the music to Margaret. "You're going to have to play it if you're still here when we have our next pep rally."

Margaret looked at the music for a second and then

passed it to me. I studied it while the two of them continued talking. I found it interesting, especially after Margaret had explained a little bit of what she was dealing with trying to write her song. The more I looked, though, the more it was obvious that Margaret's was much better.

My alma mater Chatham School
Ever proud and true, has
Given me
All I can be
Together me and you

Her wisdom was imparted
Each and every day
Remember thee
It will not be
Unless we clear the way

(Chorus)
My dear Chatham
Carry me so strong
Learn with me
Until we
Bravely march along

I reread it a couple times and then I looked up at them and said, "I'm sorry but this is dreadful. The words don't even make sense."

"You noticed that." The teacher laughed. "Luckily, we rarely ever have to sing it. Usually we just play, which is bad enough. It turns out John Chatham was a much better doctor and educator than he was a songwriter."

"Don't forget paleontologist," joked Margaret. "He discovered that fossil on display in the Founder's Room."

"Right," I said, chuckling. "The jawbone of a giant ground sloth."

"Another one of our peculiar symbols," said Ms. Allo. "We're the cougars, not the sloths. Although I will admit that some of my students are very sloth-like in their behavior. But at a school like this, tradition and history play an important role. The headmaster and the board of trustees take it all very seriously, but they also provide me with enough support to run a great music program, so I'm okay with it."

I understood exactly what she meant. The history of the school was everywhere, whether it was the name of a benefactor chiseled above a doorway or a fossil displayed like a championship trophy. There were constant reminders that the school's history went back to the 1860s. And that's when it clicked. Or at least began to click. I wasn't completely sure at first, so I had to do a quick search on my phone. I found an article and by the time I'd read the second paragraph, I turned to Margaret.

"Come on," I said urgently. "We've got to go."

She gave me a confused look. "Are you sure?" She nodded toward the practice room where Becca was still playing the flute.

"Positive," I said, checking my watch. "We're going to run out of time."

I grabbed my backpack and rushed for the door.

"Okay, thanks for everything, Ms. Allo," Margaret said, hurrying to keep up. "I forgot we had to be somewhere."

By the time Margaret caught up to me in the hallway, I was already on the phone with my dad. As a museum security consultant, he'd made friends in high places at the Smithsonian, and I hoped at least one of them owed him a favor. I explained that we were working on the case and asked if he could get someone to help us.

"We're going to the Smithsonian?" Margaret asked, when I got off the phone.

"You bet we are," I said.

"Why?"

"It'll only make sense when I show you," I said. "So I'll do that on the Metro, but we have to hurry because the museum closes in about an hour and we want to check this out today."

I think part of me thought that if I could solve the mystery that day, I'd never have to deal with Tanner. I kept an eye out for him as we sprinted from the school to the Van Ness Metro station. It wasn't until we were sitting on the train, however, that I was able to show Margaret what I'd seen.

"Here," I said, digging into my backpack. "Check this out." I handed her the sheet music to "My Dear Chatham."

She looked at it and hummed along. "Just like 'Oh! Susanna,'" she said. "How is this a clue?"

"It wasn't until you mentioned the fossil in the Founder's Room," I said.

"The jawbone of a ground sloth," she replied. "And once again I ask, how is this a clue?"

"The scientific name of the sloth is inscribed on the plaque. It's *Megatherium*," I reminded her. "Now look at the first letter of every line of the song. Just go straight down the left edge."

> *My alma mater Chatham School*
> *Ever proud and true, has*
> *Given me*
> *All I can be*
> *Together me and you*

Her wisdom was imparted
Each and every day
Remember thee
It will not be
Unless we clear the way

(Chorus)
My dear Chatham
Carry me so strong
Learn with me
Until we
Bravely march along

"What's the Megatherium Club?"

"That's where it gets really good," I said as I read from the article I found on my phone. "The Megatherium Club was a society of scientists and naturalists founded in the 1860s at the Smithsonian Institution."

"The plaque on the fossil said it was on loan from the Smithsonian," she pointed out.

"That's right," I answered. "That's just too many coincidences. There has to be some sort of connection between the school and the club. My dad says he knows someone who might be able to tell us about it. He's trying to reach her now."

With its towers, turrets, and gothic architecture, the red sandstone building known as the Smithsonian Castle looked more like it belonged in old England than modern-day Washington. We arrived fifteen minutes before closing, and the security guards were checking our backpacks when a woman walked up to me.

"Are you Jim Bates's son?" she asked.

"Yes," I said. "Florian. And this is my friend Margaret. Are you Dr. Taylor?"

"Yes," she replied. "It's nice to meet you."

"Thank you so much for helping," I said.

"Your dad has been a tremendous help to us, so I'm more than happy to return the favor," she said. "He tells me you're interested in the Megatherium Club."

"Very much so."

"Well, why don't you put these on and we'll see what we can find," she said, handing us each a visitor's badge on a lanyard. "Follow me."

She led us across the Great Hall and through a door marked MUSEUM PERSONNEL ONLY.

"There was a time when the Castle and the Smithsonian were the same thing," she explained as we walked. "This building held all the artifacts. Joseph Henry, who was the director of the institute, lived upstairs with his family, and many of the scientists who traveled the world looking for specimens to add to the collection lived down the hall in a dormitory."

"That's kind of cool," said Margaret.

"You're not kidding," replied Dr. Taylor. "It was an amazing concentration of intellectual horsepower, and that's what led to the creation of the Megatherium Club."

"How so?" I asked.

"These scientists lived together, worked together, and had fun together," she said as we entered a storage room whose walls were lined with climate-controlled metal-and-glass cabinets. "The Megatherium Club was a combination of all three."

In the middle of the room were gray file cabinets with wide flat drawers. She handed us each a pair of white cotton gloves, so we wouldn't get dirt or fingerprints on any artifacts, and we put them on as she opened one of the drawers. It was filled with neatly organized manila folders. She pulled out one marked "Megatherium Club."

"Let's start here," she said, opening the folder to reveal a stack of papers and photographs. She handed us a browning image of four men posing around a small wooden table. It was printed on thick photo paper, and even with the gloves on, we were careful to touch it only on the edges. The men in the picture wore dark wool suits, one the uniform of a Civil War officer. Each had a mustache and two had beards.

"The founding foursome," she said, pointing to each one as she listed them off. "Robert Kennicott, Henry Ulke, Henry Bryant, and their leader, William Stimpson. He was so influential they sometimes called it the *Stimpsonian*."

"And what did they do?" asked Margaret.

"During the day they helped collect, sort, categorize, identify, build, and study the amazing collection we have today," she replied. "They also lived here in the Castle and in the evenings would sometimes invite prominent thinkers and scholars to give lectures or lead discussions. And then sometimes they had fun."

"And by fun you mean . . . ?"

"They had sack races across the Great Hall. They drank wine out of ancient Etruscan goblets. They serenaded Joseph Henry's three daughters." She chuckled at the thought of it. "He wasn't very happy about that. But most of all he was unhappy because of the pranks."

Margaret and I shared a look at the mention of pranks.

"Whenever a new member joined the group, he was required to pull off a big prank as part of his initiation. The final one was the most infamous," she continued. "One day Harriet Henry, Joseph's wife, opened a closet expecting to find clothes and instead came face-to-face with a mummy."

"You mean like . . ."

"Yes, an ancient Egyptian, taken from a tomb, wrapped in bandages, and wearing Mrs. Henry's favorite hat," she continued with a laugh. "They say her screams could be heard for blocks in every direction."

"What happened?" asked Margaret.

"Secretary Henry disbanded the Megatherium Club that night," she answered.

"When was that?" I asked.

"Eighteen sixty-six."

"That's about the same time John Rees Chatham founded the school," I pointed out.

"Yes, Colonel Chatham," she said, flipping through the file until she pulled out another picture. This one was of two men in uniform. "That's him with Henry Bryant, one of the original founders. They were field surgeons together during the Civil War."

"And Chatham was in the club?" I asked.

"Oh yes," she said. "In fact, there were rumors that he secretly kept it going despite Henry's orders."

We looked at some more pictures and then she retrieved a small box from a nearby cabinet. "Here's a real treasure," she said as she opened it. "It's a membership button. It's the only one known to exist because Henry gathered all the others up and melted them down."

It was a metal button about the size of a quarter. The words "How How" were painted on it and its ribbon had three stripes: purple/green/purple.

"It's just like the locker," said Margaret. "The same colors and the same words."

"What's 'How How'?" I asked

Dr. Taylor smiled, "It was their secret greeting. Why?"

Margaret and I shared a look before I answered, "I think the Megatherium Club may still be alive and strong."

12.

Natural History

THE TIGER WAS SUSPENDED IN MIDAIR, TEETH snarling, claws extended, frozen in that instant before attacking its unsuspecting prey. From our vantage point, the intended victim appeared to be Marcus, but he was oblivious as he faced the opposite direction, his head bobbing ever so slightly to the music playing on his earbuds. If this were a jungle in Southeast Asia, there'd be no way of saving him, but here in the Smithsonian's National Museum of Natural History, he was perfectly safe from the big cat and all the other stuffed animals on display in the Hall of Mammals.

As he typically did when meeting us in the field, Marcus had shed his normal coat and tie, which screamed federal agent, in order to blend in and protect our covert status. He wore a loose-fitting baseball jersey with GRAYS written across the chest and the number twenty on the back. Since both he and Margaret are African-American, I think most of the tourists around us assumed he was her father and we were on a visit to the museum. Certainly no one suspected we were three agents having a clandestine meeting to discuss a case for the FBI.

"You didn't have to come all the way down here," he told us as he took out his headphones and tucked them into the pocket of his jeans. "I would have gladly met you closer to the school."

"We were already in the neighborhood," replied Margaret. "At the Smithsonian Castle."

We'd texted him to meet up while we were still with Dr. Taylor and picked the natural history museum because it stayed open later and was just a few blocks from his office at FBI Headquarters.

"Besides," I added, "there's an exhibit we want to check out."

"Which one?"

"Follow me and I'll show you."

We zigzagged through the crowd, past the giant bull elephant in the rotunda, and entered the Fossil Hall. While most people were instantly drawn to the massive T. rex skeleton, we bypassed it and went straight to the Ice Age exhibit.

"Here it is," I said. *"Megatherium."*

We gazed up at the fossilized skeleton of a giant ground sloth. It stood nearly thirteen feet tall and its arms were posed so that it almost looked as if it were about to have a fistfight.

"Megatherium?" asked Marcus. "Where have I heard that word recently?"

"When we were in the Founder's Room at Chatham," answered Margaret. "The jawbone in the fancy display case?"

"That's right," he said, remembering. "So this sloth has something to do with the case?"

"That's what we're thinking," I replied.

We told him all about the Megatherium Club and our theory that it might still be operating as a secret society at Chatham Country Day. I even pulled out the music to "My Dear Chatham" and showed him how the club's name was hidden in the lyrics.

"Okay, that's interesting," he said. "But what does it have to do with a fire alarm or computer hacking?"

"A key tradition of the club was that in order to become a full member, pledges had to pull off a prank," I explained. "The bigger the better."

"Like the time a guy hid a mummy in a closet and almost gave a woman a heart attack," added Margaret. "That was the prank that got the club disbanded."

"At least that's the official story," I said. "But what if it didn't get disbanded? We know that John Rees Chatham was a member. We know that he founded the school and wrote the song. What if he just moved the club from the Smithsonian to the school and it's still going strong?"

"And now you think some recently added members are trying to outprank each other."

"That would explain a lot," I replied. "The headmaster said pranks used to be common at the school. Maybe those were all the handiwork of Megatheriums. They've been dormant for a while but now they're coming back."

"Why?" he asked.

"We don't know," I answered. "But for the first time since we've started, we have a motive and explanation that at least makes sense."

"Ha," exclaimed Margaret, interrupting us. "I just found another connection."

"Where?" I asked.

She pointed at a plaque on the *Megatherium* display. "It says this exhibit was made possible through a generous gift from none other than . . . Moncrieff Tate."

We shared a look.

"The chairman of the board of trustees at the school?" said Marcus. "Okay, I'm convinced there's a connection."

"And we know he's a member of the club because of the stripes on his tie," I said.

"You just lost me again," said Marcus. "What stripes?"

"There are two symbols of membership that we're aware of," I said. "One is their secret greeting, which is the phrase 'How How.' The other is the use of a purple/green/purple triple stripe."

"Like this." Margaret handed him her phone to show him the picture she'd found of Moncrieff Tate wearing the tie.

"We found the same stripes and phrase painted in Victoria Tate's locker," I said. "Which probably means she's a member too."

"Actually, we don't know that it was Victoria's locker," corrected Margaret. "We just know that it was one of the two that were side by side. It could have been Lucy's."

"True," I said. "But doesn't it make more sense that it would be Victoria? After all, she is Moncrieff's granddaughter."

"There were secret societies like this when I was at Harvard," said Marcus. "They're usually made up of the most elite students. Especially ones who come from powerful families."

"That describes half the school," said Margaret. "But when it comes to powerful families, it's hard to top the daughter of the president."

"You know, that's absolutely right," I admitted. "It could be her. Tomorrow we have to figure out whose locker was whose."

"I can find out from Tori."

"We've been operating off the theory that it's one person pulling off three different pranks," said Marcus. "But it could very well be three different people who are part of the same group. Is there any connection between the Megatherium Club and the name Loki?"

"None that we've been able to find," I said. "But we haven't had much time to look for one."

"Try to find it," he said. "You guys are doing great, but if we can find out why the name Loki was selected, we may be able to pull everything together. Anything else you want to pass along?"

We filled him in on some other details as we left the Fossil Hall and walked upstairs to the *Eternal Life in Ancient Egypt* exhibit because Margaret wanted to check out the mummies. We told him about Yin, Becca, and the discovery of the crawl space in the performing arts center. We also explained that Lucy made a hasty exit right after the fire alarm incident.

"Actually, *during* the incident," corrected Margaret. "The bell was still ringing while her SUV was speeding off of the campus."

There was an interesting dynamic that I couldn't ignore. It seemed like I kept trying to find reasons to clear Lucy, while Margaret kept pointing out clues that suggested she was guilty. I don't know why, but it's part of what works so well with our partnership. We keep each other honest.

We reached the mummies and Margaret shuddered as she said, "Imagine opening your closet and seeing that fall out. I'd scream for days."

"Have you had any luck getting us access to the Chat Chat message board while it's still off-line?" I asked Marcus. "That might help us locate Loki or identify other members of the Megatherium Club."

"Putney keeps stalling me on that one," he replied. "I'm thinking of asking the admiral to twist his arm."

Margaret and I shared a look and a smile.

"That'll get it done," she said.

We said our good-byes and separated from Marcus so no one outside would see us leave together. We exited out the back of the building and crossed Constitution Avenue to get to the Federal Triangle Metro station.

The subway was packed with commuters headed home

for the day so we stood in the back of a car holding on to a pair of straps.

"Why didn't you tell him?" asked Margaret as the train rattled to life and we pulled out of the station.

"Why didn't I tell him what?"

She gave me a look. "You know what I'm talking about."

I sighed. "If I told him that some bully was after me then he might have taken me off the case. And I don't want that to happen. Besides, you think I'm exaggerating."

"I never said that."

"You didn't have to," I said. "I can tell. Just like I can tell you think that Lucy Mays is Loki."

She didn't deny it. "It's not that I think she's guilty," she said. "It's just that evidence keeps pointing that way."

As the subway car rattled through the darkened tunnel, I had to admit that she was right.

13.

The Question Marks

"WHY ARE WE GOING TO THE FOUNDER'S ROOM?"
Margaret asked after I had my mom drive past the front of
the school and drop us off in back.

"I had an idea last night and I want to check it out before
school starts."

"Mmm-hmm," she said skeptically. "And was this idea a
way to avoid Tanner by hiding out in the rear of the school
until the bell rings?"

"No, but if that's a by-product I'm okay with it."

"You can't just hide from him."

"I know that and I don't plan to," I declared.

"Then you want to explain this?" She poked me in the

shoulder. "Either you became extra lumpy last night or you're wearing your gym clothes beneath your school clothes so you don't have to go in the locker room."

Sometimes I forget how observant she is.

"I have to get all the way from French class, which is in the upper school, to the gym," I explained. "That doesn't leave much time to change. I'm just trying to be efficient."

"Very convincing," she said with a roll of her eyes.

We reached the Founder's Room and flipped on the lights. Luckily, no one had started the welcome video, so we didn't have to listen to it over and over while we worked.

"So what's your idea?" asked Margaret.

"Yearbooks," I answered. "We know that Moncrieff Tate was a member of the Megatherium Club, so I want to look for him in these old yearbooks to see if we can figure out who he hung out with back when he was a student. Maybe find some more members."

"Actually," she said, "that's a pretty good idea."

"I told you we weren't just hiding out." We walked over to the bookcases, which were filled with yearbooks going back for decades, and I pulled out a pair of slender volumes. "These are from Moncrieff's junior and senior years. Let's start there."

We looked at the index in the senior one and it directed us to five pictures:

A senior class photo in a cap and gown

An action shot of him playing basketball

A group photo of him as a member
of the varsity club

A group photo of the French club
that identified him as president

A shot of him onstage singing with
an a cappella group

The picture of the a cappella group featured five boys, all with crew cuts and blazers. Margaret read the caption aloud: "The Maxillaires dazzle the crowd with their harmonies."

"The what?" I asked as I took the yearbook from her to double-check. "The name of their group is the Maxillaires?"

"Those groups always have names like that that don't really mean anything," she replied. "My dad sang with one called the Whiffenpoofs."

"Except Maxillaires does mean something," I answered.

"It's French. It means 'the jawbones.' As in . . ." I pointed at the *Megatherium* jawbone in the display case on the next table.

"*You* know that," she said. "But do you think *they* knew it?"

"He was president of the French club," I replied. "He had to know. He picked that name on purpose. Like an inside joke."

"But isn't that risky?" she asked. "Maybe someone in the crowd could figure it out."

I gave her a look. "You do realize that you're an undercover FBI consultant who wants to sing a song about solving mysteries at a middle school talent show?"

She laughed. "Well, if you put it that way . . ."

"Besides, I'm sure most people just thought it was a silly name. It only makes sense if you know all about the secret group, and nobody knows about the group except the members."

She looked up at me and grinned. "And us. We know. And now we know four other members."

"Maybe," I said. "Let's look in this one."

We flipped through the other yearbook and found a picture of a group called the Question Marks. They were dressed like old-fashioned newspaper reporters, wearing trench coats and fedoras, posed as if they were at a crowded press conference shouting out questions. The caption read:

*The Question Marks proved to be a valuable
addition to the school newspaper as they were
always more than ready and willing to ask the hard
questions like, Who? What? When? Where? And most
importantly: How How?*

"How How," I said, eyebrows raised. "That's definitely Megatherium."

"And those are some familiar faces."

There were seven students in the picture, five boys and two girls. Four of the boys were also members of the Maxillaires. Margaret pulled a yellow legal pad out of her backpack and started writing down all of their names.

"I'm not sure how much good that will do for us now," I said. "Considering they were members nearly fifty years ago."

"You know how it is with TOAST," she replied with a sly smile. "Crumbs lead to little pieces. Little pieces lead to big pieces. Big pieces lead to culprits."

We started to look for the other members in different yearbooks, but before we could get very far the bell rang and it was time to go to class.

"I think this is a good lead," she said. "I'm going to come back here during lunch and keep looking."

"Sounds good," I said. "I'll join you."

She gave me a look. "And that's because you want to help or because you want to hide out?"

"Help," I said with mock indignation as I started for the door.

"Good," she replied. "Oh, and make sure to find out if Becca is actually a Megatherium or if she just happens to have a hair ribbon with the wrong stripes."

"I will," I replied.

"And when you see Tanner . . ."

"I'll scream like Harriet Joseph when she found that mummy in her closet."

She gave me a look.

"Just kidding," I said. "I'll be smart."

"Which means being safe."

I nodded.

Luckily, I made it to my first two classes without any sign of him and I began to wonder if I'd been overreacting. So far there was no indication he was looking for me.

Even though Becca regularly ignored Lucy, they were seated next to each other in French. This let me take a seat behind Lucy and study them both at the same time. It took half the period to figure out a way to check if either was a Megatherium. The class was reading, so everything was quiet and I thought about the Question Marks. It gave me the idea to whisper two words just loud enough for both of them to hear:

"How How."

Lucy didn't react, but Becca snapped her head around and looked right at me.

"What did you say?" she asked.

I shrugged like I didn't know what she was talking about and muttered, "Nothing."

"What did you say?" she asked pointedly, this time attracting the attention of the teacher.

"Shhh," scolded Madame Thibault.

I just kept looking at my book and let her stew. At this point I had no doubt she was in the club. But I wasn't sure about Lucy. She didn't react at all and I wondered if that meant she wasn't a member or just that she was much less easily rattled.

The instant the bell rang, I switched my focus to making it to gym class in one piece. My plan required expert timing, so it didn't help that when I rushed the door Becca stepped in front of me and blocked my way.

"What's your name?"

"Florian Bates," I answered. "Why?"

"Just curious," she replied cryptically.

She was being confrontational, so I thought I'd tweak her back just a little bit. "Where'd you get your hair ribbon?"

Her eyes opened wide and before she could say anything I added, "Just curious."

I ducked past her and out into the hallway. Margaret had totally busted me when she guessed that I was wearing my gym clothes underneath my school outfit. I didn't care. There was no way I was going into that locker room. Instead I ran into the bathroom down the hall from French. Because I was still in the upper school building, I knew Tanner wouldn't be there. I stripped off my outer layer in one of the stalls and stuffed the clothes into my backpack.

When I came back out into the hallway, Becca was standing right there waiting for me. This was so my life. If I wanted to see her there'd be no sign of her, but now that I was in a hurry, she kept cropping up. I couldn't be bothered at the moment, so I turned the other way and hurried. People gawked, although I don't know if it was because I was running down the hall in an Alice Deal gym uniform or because Becca was pursuing me.

"Florian!" she called to me. "Florian!"

Finally I stopped and turned to her.

"What?"

"You better be careful," she warned. "If you keep talking about things you shouldn't talk about you're going to make some enemies."

"Fine with me," I said emphatically. "They can get in line behind the ones I've already got."

I spun around, popped open the exit door, and left without looking back. Our class was scheduled for another running day, so I skipped the gym and locker room altogether and went straight to the track, where I started running laps.

All of it was starting to build up inside of me and I burned off my frustration by going out at a quick pace. I'd been undercover at the school for only two and a half days and I'd already made enemies of Tanner and Becca, not to mention Victoria and her minions. By the end of the week, who knows how many people would be chasing me down the hall.

I just ran and thought about the case, which was dangerous because whenever I do that I get tunnel vision and tend to block out everything else. I was snapped out of my own little world when I heard footsteps catching up from behind.

Startled, I turned to look back and almost tripped over myself in the process. I even had to put a hand down on the track to keep from falling.

"It's only me," said Lucy as she continued running. "Nothing to worry about."

"I wasn't worried," I lied, trying to recover as I quickly matched her pace. "You just caught me off guard."

We ran side by side and when we turned the corner I

could see the other kids as they trickled out from the locker room to the track. I scanned their faces looking for trouble.

"He's not here," she said.

"What are you talking about?"

"Tanner," she replied. "He's not here. He's been suspended for three days."

I let out a huge sigh of relief. "Is that true?"

"Violation of the honor code," she said. "He won't be back until Monday."

I closed my eyes for a moment and said a silent prayer as my mood instantly lightened and my pace slowed to something more manageable. Even better, I realized that if Margaret and I could solve the case by the weekend, I'd never have to see him again.

"I tried to tell you after French," she said. "But you left in a hurry."

Yeah, I thought. *A hurry to hide in a bathroom and change clothes.*

"I just wanted to get out here and start running," I told her, although I knew she was onto me.

We jogged for a bit and she said, "Can I ask you an awkward question?"

"Sure. Awkward questions are kind of a specialty of mine."

"Did you do it because of me?"

I turned to look at her as we ran. "Did I do what because of you?"

"Let Tanner cheat off of you knowing he'd flunk the test and get in trouble. Were you trying to impress me?"

"That doesn't even make sense. What does Tanner have to do with you?"

She slowed down for a moment. "Tanner Caldwell? You really don't know?"

"I really don't."

"His dad's Pete Caldwell," she answered as if that should mean something. "The senator from California who ran against my father for president."

"I thought he ran against the governor of Michigan," I said. "Tom Prescott."

"In the general election, yes," she replied. "But in the primaries he ran against Caldwell, who was heavily favored. That's why Tanner hates me so much. He thought his dad was going to be president instead of mine. He's been horrible to me since the first day I set foot on campus."

"I honestly had no idea," I told her. "We lived in Italy during the election and they didn't cover the primaries that much. I only heard about the main campaign."

We ran a little bit more while she thought about it.

"Then if it wasn't for me, why'd you do it?" she asked.

"Because he's a bully," I said. "He picks on kids like me. Kids like Yin."

"You know Yin?" she asked, surprised.

"A little bit," I said. "He's nice. I'm going to the zoo with him on Saturday."

"You're going to the zoo with Yin Yae?" she said, her surprise now disbelief.

"Yeah," I said. "So's Margaret."

She didn't respond and we ran almost half a lap before she spoke again. "You know, Madame Thibault said that we could work in teams for the French project. So would you like to be my partner?"

This caught me completely off guard. "Sure," I replied. "That would be great. Want to meet in the library after school?"

"I can't. I have a cello lesson. But if you'd like, you could come by my house at five. We could work on it there."

"Okay," I answered. "Where do you live?"

It didn't dawn on me how stupid my question was until I'd already said it.

"Pennsylvania Avenue," she said with a chuckle. "It's a big white house with columns."

"Okay, I actually knew that one." I thought about it for a second and asked, "But what do I do? I can't just walk up and knock on the front door."

"You'll need to talk to Malena," she said, pointing at the Secret Service agent watching from near the bleachers. "We'll do it at lunch. She just needs some background information for a security check, but it's all pretty basic. Then all I have to do is leave your name at the guard gate."

"That's it?"

"Yep," she said. "You show up there and they'll ask you why you're visiting. Just say that you're supposed to work on homework with me. But when you do, you have to use my Secret Service code name. That's how they know it's real."

"Cool," I said. "What's your code name?"

"You've got to promise not to tell anyone," she said, more jokingly than serious.

"I promise," I said.

She smiled for a moment before saying it. "Loki."

I froze in my tracks and she laughed as she continued running.

14.

Rock Hounds

MARGARET LOOKED UP AT ME FROM BEHIND A stack of yearbooks and shook her head in total disbelief. "How'd you find that out?"

"She told me herself."

"She told you that her Secret Service code name is Loki?"

"And you should have seen the way she said it," I replied. "She laughed like it was all a big joke."

Margaret closed the book she was looking through and placed it on the pile as she considered this. "So that means there are two possibilities. One: She's Loki and not being very subtle about claiming credit for all the pranks. Or two: Someone wants to point the finger at her."

"It could be either," I said. "But the part I don't get is how come Dr. Putney didn't mention it? I'm sure he knows her code name."

Margaret flashed a proud grin.

"I may have a theory on that. While you've been off doing who knows what, I've been in here working. I started with the Question Marks and the Maxillaires and followed them through the rest of their time at Chatham," she continued, motioning to the yearbooks. "And every year or so, they'd pop in another new group or club with some of the same kids as well as some new ones. "

"Like what?" I asked.

"The Fossil Club," she said as she reached over and showed me one of the books. "Or the Young Smithsonians," she added as she handed me another. "Once you know what you're looking for, then you find a definite thread running through the history of the school. I've got a list of more than thirty-five likely members."

The front page of her legal pad was now full; a column of names ran down the left with notations and dates written along the right.

"Impressive," I said. "But what's your theory? Why do you think Dr. Putney didn't tell us about Lucy's nickname when he first told us about Loki?"

"You know what a rock hound is?"

"Someone who looks for fossils?" I answered.

"Look at this picture of the Chatham Rock Hounds taken nearly thirty years ago," she said, opening one of the yearbooks to a page marked with a pink sticky note. "Check out where they had their group photo taken."

I looked at the picture and smiled. "In front of the *Megatherium* skeleton at the Museum of Natural History."

"That's right," she said. "Now look at the rock hound standing second from the left."

The face looked familiar but I didn't recognize who it was until I read the caption. "David Putney?" I looked up at her. "The headmaster's a Megatherium."

"And so is Lucy," she said. "I found out that it was her locker with the stripes and 'How How' painted on the inside, not Victoria's."

I plopped down into the chair next to her. "So you think he didn't tell us her code name because he didn't want us to suspect that it was her?"

"Exactly."

"Then why involve us in the first place?" I asked. "Why have us investigate when it might lead us to his secret organization?"

"That's a good question," she said. "But if someone is

trying to make it look like Lucy's guilty, then he'd want the problem solved as quickly as possible."

I thought back to French class when I tried to test Becca and Lucy by saying "How How." Becca took the bait instantly and even went so far as to follow me to the bathroom. But Lucy was calm. She didn't react at all. Unless her reaction was something much more calculated.

"Maybe that's why she invited me to the White House?"

Margaret turned to me, surprised. "I'm sorry, what?"

"Lucy invited me to come to the White House later today," I said. "That's why I'm late. I've been giving all my information to the Secret Service."

"Why did she invite you?"

"She said it was because she wanted to work on our French project together," I answered. "But maybe what she really wants is to get me in the most intimidating place on the planet and tell me to stop snooping around the Megatherium Club."

"Wow! That is so cool," she said. "You're actually going to the White House? Not as a tourist but as a guest."

"Well, I don't think we'll be hanging out in the Oval Office, but yeah."

"Well, that's fantastic," she replied. "Use TOAST to find out everything you can about her. Especially try to figure out who might want to make her look bad. If someone is setting her up, it's got to be someone who really hates her."

"She said that Tanner and she are mortal enemies," I told her. "Their fathers ran against each other for president."

"Tanner Caldwell is Pete Caldwell's son?" she asked.

"Yep."

"That explains a lot," she said. "His dad seems like a jerk too. Oh, and I found out she hates Yin."

"Really?" I asked, surprised. "Why would she hate Yin?"

"Because he's better at playing the cello than she is," she said, as though it should be obvious. "When she arrived she was the star musician of the school, which is a big deal because she wants to go to Juilliard and play in an orchestra someday. Then along comes Yin to steal her thunder and all of her solos. Apparently Mrs. Chiang complained to the board of trustees about the way she treats him."

"How did you find this out?"

"Victoria's grandfather is the director of the board," she said. "We've begun to bond and she's opening up more. She's also the one who told me whose locker was whose."

"Lucy did have a funny reaction when I told her that we were going to the zoo with Yin."

It was a lot to take in and we sat quietly for a moment until the door opened and Dr. Putney's assistant entered the room with a prospective student and his parents.

"What are you doing in here?" she asked, surprised to see us. "And why are you making such a mess?"

"Sorry," Margaret said. "We've just been looking through some of the old yearbooks. The senior partner at my mother's law firm went to school here and I was looking to see if I could find a picture of him so I could tell him I'd seen it."

"Well, you're supposed to be at lunch right now," she said, softening. "Clean this up first, though."

"Yes, ma'am," we both said as we quickly cleaned up the table. Margaret slyly slipped the legal pad into her backpack without anyone noticing as I put the yearbooks back on the shelf.

"By the way," Margaret said to the family as we were leaving. "The school is amazing. You should definitely come here."

We slipped out into the hallway. "That was good. Quick thinking."

"It helps that it was true," she said. "Last night I found out my mom's boss was a Chatham alum. I thought that made for a better excuse than admitting what we were actually doing."

"Good call," I agreed. "Let's meet back here after school and look some more."

"Aren't you supposed to go to the White House after school?"

"Not until five," I said. "So we can look for at least an hour."

Through the last few class periods of the day I tried to process what we'd learned. For all the twists and turns, the one that surprised me most was the idea that Lucy hated Yin. She didn't seem the hateful type and he didn't seem hateable. I was also struggling with another clue that didn't make sense. If Becca and Lucy were both in the Megatherium Club, why did Becca go out of her way to completely ignore Lucy? You'd think they'd be friendly to each other.

After school I confirmed things with Lucy and met up with Margaret outside the library. "There's something we forgot," I said.

"Yeah," answered Margaret. "Lunch. I was in the Founder's Room the whole period and now I'm starving."

"Okay, we'll make it quick and head over to Warren Burgers," I said.

"Sounds good."

"But the thing I meant was Becca," I said. "She won't even look at Lucy in class, but they're both Megatheriums. You think they'd be friendly."

"Maybe she's jealous," Margaret offered. "Maybe she didn't want Lucy in the club."

"Maybe," I agreed. "But it still seems a little out of whack."

"All I know is that Lucy's locker is the one with the triple stripe and 'How How' painted in it," she said. "What else could it mean?"

I thought about it for a moment. "Nothing else really?"

We went into the Founder's Room and were surprised by what we found. Or rather what we didn't find.

"Where are the yearbooks?" I asked.

"They're all gone," she replied in disbelief.

The bookcases that once teemed with them were now empty.

"What is going on in here?" I asked.

"That's exactly what I would like to know," said a voice.

We turned to the door and saw Dr. Putney.

"What is going on in here?" he asked, repeating my question. "And why are you two so interested in old yearbooks?"

"As I explained to your assistant . . . ," said Margaret.

"Don't tell me about the senior partner at your mother's law firm," he said. "Tell me what you're really looking for."

"Loki," I said. "Just like we said we would Monday morning in your office."

He eyed me suspiciously. "Well, you won't find Loki in old yearbooks, that's for sure. Loki is a kid out there making me look foolish."

I thought it was an odd way to put it. As though the prankster were doing this to him personally and not the entire school.

"And it seems to me that you're looking for all sorts of things except for Loki," he continued, his voice rising slightly. "I just had a troubling meeting with one of our top students."

"Becca," I said to myself. She must have gone to him and told him that we knew about the Megatherium Club. Add that to what his assistant told him she saw and he figured out what we'd been up to.

"Now let's sit down and straighten this out," he commanded.

"Actually," said Margaret, "I think we'll be leaving now." She moved toward the door and he blocked our way.

"First, hand me your backpack," he demanded.

I wondered if his assistant had noticed the legal pad after all.

"No," she said. "It's my backpack and you have no business with it."

"Actually, a student is required to hand over a backpack when instructed by a member of the staff," he informed us. "It's right there in the student handbook."

"*Actually,*" Margaret said, not bending, "I'm not a student at this school. I'm a consultant with the FBI. And according to the National Security Act of 1947, if you try to forcibly take it from me, you'll be committing a felony."

"The National Security Act," he scoffed. "I think you're overestimating your role with the Bureau."

"Really," she said. "I think you're underestimating the fact that both of my parents are attorneys." She looked up at him and added, "Exceptionally talented attorneys. I can't remember the last time either one of them lost a case."

There was a quiet moment before Margaret spoke again.

"Now if you don't mind, I'm going to go have a hamburger and Florian's been invited to the White House."

He finally relented and stepped back so we could open the door and leave. As we walked down the hall I marveled as Margaret strutted, exuding pure confidence. I could live a hundred years and never come close to finding a friend as impressive as her.

She was a total rock star.

15.

Try Not to Pass Out

MARGARET AND I WOLFED DOWN SOME BURGERS before I went home to begin the unexpectedly difficult task of deciding what to wear. As I changed out of my school clothes it dawned on me that I'd never been to the home of someone in charge of a global superpower. I wasn't exactly sure about the dress code.

No matter what I pulled from the closet, it seemed wrong. A collared shirt and khakis looked overly dressy for an afternoon homework session, but cargo shorts and a T-shirt were way too casual for a building that hosts state dinners.

I tried on six combinations (twelve if you count the tucked versus untucked shirt variations) without any success before I got desperate and searched online for "Lucy Mays and friends."

I was hoping to find a few images of her with other kids to give me some guidelines. Unfortunately, most of the photos were taken at formal events and most of the friends were girls. So they weren't much help on the fashion front. But that doesn't mean the pictures weren't useful.

Two actually seemed relevant to the case. The first was from a White House birthday party, and the second was backstage at the Kennedy Center after a performance of the Washington Youth Symphony. In both Lucy was laughing with none other than Becca Baker. So while they may not have been on speaking terms at the moment, that wasn't always the case.

I would've kept searching, but I was running out of time and assumed that White House protocol considered being late far worse than wearing the wrong color combination. I decided to go with an unbuttoned oxford over a gray T-shirt along with jeans and a pair of black sneakers Margaret called "Chucks." I figured if it seemed too casual when I got there, I could always button up the shirt and tuck it in.

Clothes, however, were just the beginning of my nervousness. I'm not the most socially skilled person on the planet (that's more Margaret's turf), and as I rode the Metro

I began worrying about every little thing from the way I talked to my somewhat forgetful relationship with the rules of etiquette. By the time I'd walked from Farragut North station to the guardhouse I was a total wreck. So much so that I worried it might make me seem suspicious.

"Welcome to the White House," said the guard in a friendly yet firm manner. "May I have your name please?"

"Florian Bates," I answered, trying to project cool. "I'm here to do homework with Luce . . . I mean . . . I'm here to do homework with Loki . . . who I go to school with . . . who invited me." (Not so much when it comes to the cool.)

He smiled at my awkwardness and started looking for my name in a binder.

"Hey, Tommy, I've got this one," a woman's voice interrupted from behind.

I turned to see that it was Malena Sanchez, Lucy's lead Secret Service agent. Despite the fact that she was only my height and had a youthful face (which helped her blend in at school) she always radiated total confidence and intimidation. She wore her black hair pulled back in a short ponytail and was a master of the unflinching stare. I'd never once seen her smile. Until now. Unfortunately it was at the guard and not me.

"Malena," said the guard, happy to see her. "How are you doing?"

"Very well, thank you," she replied warmly. "I just turned in the paperwork on young Mr. Bates here, so he won't be on the sign-in sheet. But you should be able to find him in the computer."

He typed my name onto a keyboard.

"Here we go," he said when he found it. "Florian Bates. Meeting with Loki in the residence." He looked at me and smiled. "That explains why you're getting the escort. Do me a favor and smile at the camera."

"You think the press is going to take my picture because I'm going to the White House?" I asked him, surprised.

"Not the paparazzi," he said, trying not to laugh. "I meant the one on my computer." He pointed at a small camera on the top of his monitor and I flashed an embarrassed grin. Moments later he handed me a visitor's pass, and Agent Sanchez led me up the driveway past a half-dozen television news crews getting ready to go on air.

"Excited?" she asked, reading my mood. "Or nervous?"

"Both," I admitted as I tried to soak it all in. "It's pretty overwhelming."

"Yes, it is," she replied. "And I don't want to rain on your parade, but I met you out here because I want to have a talk before you enter the residence. There are some topics I can't discuss at school with Lucy present."

Just when I thought things couldn't get more intimidating, the unflinching stare made a return.

"First of all, I know that you're working for the FBI," she informed me. "How that's possible, I haven't the foggiest idea, but you need to realize that my sole job is to protect Lucy from any threat." She stopped walking for a moment to emphasize the statement as she reiterated, "*Any* threat."

It took me a few seconds to realize she meant me.

"I'm not a threat," I said. "Not in the least."

"Is that so?" she asked.

"Yes, it is," I replied as I began finding some confidence. "The director of the FBI asked me to figure out who's pulling the pranks at Chatham. That's all I'm going to do. If it turns out that the person is Lucy, then I'll pass that information along and let the people in charge figure out what to do with it. If it's someone else, perhaps someone trying to make Lucy look bad, then I'll find that out as well. And in that way, we're both protecting her. But I'm not going to do anything to Lucy. I'm just looking for the truth. Besides, *she* invited me here."

"Yes, she did," she said. "But only because you lied to her."

"I haven't lied to her," I answered, beginning to feel even more self-assured. (That's the beauty of working on these mysteries: They make me more confident than anything else in my life.) "I really am a student from Deal on an exchange to Chatham. Lucy and I are in the same French class. And I'm here so we can work on a project for that class. I may not have told her everything about myself, but I haven't directly lied to her." Then I looked at the agent and added, "Unlike you."

This caught her attention.

"What's that supposed to mean?" she asked, irritated.

"Today at lunch when Lucy and I were talking about this assignment, you said that you don't speak French."

"Right," she said assertively, "because I *don't*."

"So you didn't take French in school when you were growing up?"

"Sorry to burst your bubble," she replied. "But I took Spanish in high school and Mandarin in college. No French."

"Then explain this: In class there's a boy who sits two rows in front of Lucy; I think his name is Jacob."

"And . . . ," she replied.

"And yesterday in class he was having trouble with his translation. He was supposed to say, '*Je mets mon petit dejeuner sur la table de la cuisine*,' which means 'I put my breakfast on the kitchen table.' But instead of '*petit dejeuner*' he said '*petit derriere*,' which translates as 'I put my little butt on the kitchen table.'"

She snickered at the memory.

"I know. It was funny," I continued. "Everyone laughed, including Jacob. And including you."

"Like you said, it was funny."

"But how did you know that?" I asked. "How could you know it was funny unless you understood what he was saying?"

Her lack of a response told me I was right.

"So now we've established that you do in fact speak French. That means either you lied again just now when you said you didn't study it in high school or college, or you learned it as an adult when you were stationed overseas."

"And what makes you say I was stationed overseas?"

"Your class ring is from the US Naval Academy, which means you were either in the navy or the marines. There are twenty-nine countries for which French is the official language. Other than France and the Democratic Republic of the Congo, most are small. I doubt any of them have a US Navy base."

"Nor does any have a marine base," she added.

"True. But one thing I learned living in London, Paris, and Rome is that the marine corps provides security for all American embassies around the world. I bet you worked security at an embassy in one of those twenty-nine countries. Protection detail just like this. And when you left the military it seemed natural to move into the Secret Service."

This time I was the one who stopped for emphasis.

"Which brings me to the really interesting point," I said. "Why lie about something so insignificant?"

"Exactly," she replied.

"My guess is that you want everyone to think you don't understand so that they'll feel free to speak openly in front of you. Almost tempting them to use French to say anything confidential. It's not because you want to hear gossip. It's just that you're looking for any bit of information that might help you protect Lucy better. Any slight slipup that lets you foresee trouble. That's what we have in common. We specialize in identifying little pieces of information. For you those clues help you keep Lucy safe. For me they help solve mysteries."

"And you think you can solve this one?" she asked.

"I have no doubt."

"Then why haven't you asked me who I think Loki is?" she wondered. "I've been at the school for each of the pranks. I'm observant by training. Shouldn't you ask what I know?"

I shook my head. "No, because we've already established that you're willing to lie, so I couldn't trust what you'd say. But more important, you're too good at your job. That's obvious. And your job is to protect her. Not to help me. Margaret and I will figure it out. We don't need your help for that. You just keep Lucy safe."

By this point we'd reached the entrance to the building.

"Before we go inside there's something I want to tell you out here where no one can hear us," she said. "You can't repeat it. Not to anyone. I would deny it under oath if you did."

"Okay," I said with a gulp.

"During the primaries I was on the protection detail for the Caldwell family. I spent a lot of time with Tanner and really got to know him well. I was more than ready to give my life to save his. That's my job. That's what I do. And the trick you played on him with the algebra test . . ."

She stopped midsentence to take a breath and I worried she was going to come down on me hard.

"What you did to him," she continued, "was maybe the most beautiful thing I've seen in my entire life. We're talking 'rainbows over a rose garden filled with unicorns' beautiful."

She gave me a sly half smile and I laughed.

"Thanks," I said.

"I shared it with some of the other agents on his detail, and let me say, you made their day too."

"Well, your secret's safe with me."

"One last thing," she added. "You know how scary and intimidating this feels coming to the White House?"

I nodded.

"Imagine living here. Imagine if your father were the

president and everything you did—every mistake you made or bad haircut you got or zit that popped up on your nose—imagine it was on display for the world to see and comment about. Imagine what it's like to be Lucy."

"It must be hard," I said.

"In ways that you and I can never realize," she said. "You know, if you search online for 'Lucy Mays hair' you get more than nine hundred thousand hits? Nine hundred thousand comments about a thirteen-year-old's hair. There's no way to take that type of pressure and not act out a little."

I wondered if she was trying to make an argument for why Lucy should be forgiven if she was in fact Loki.

"I'll keep that in mind," I replied.

We walked into the entrance hall and it took my breath away. There were chandeliers, presidential portraits, an antique piano, and more works of art than at most museums. Malena led me past the tourists and a couple of guards and turned down a massive hallway with bright red carpeting and columns along both sides.

"This is the Cross Hall," she said, briefly taking on the role of tour guide. "When the president gives an address to the country, you usually see footage of him walking down this hall toward the podium."

"You're right," I said, recognizing it.

"And speaking of pictures, this is the last place you can take one. So if you'd like a souvenir . . ."

She held out her hand and after a moment of hesitation I handed her my phone. "That'd be great."

"Why don't you stand over there by the painting of President Kennedy?" she suggested. "It's my favorite one in the building."

Unlike most portraits, in which the person is looking directly at the artist, in this one the president was looking down with his arms crossed. It seemed as though the weight of the world were on his shoulders. I stood next to it and Malena snapped the picture.

"My mom's an art preservationist so she'll really appreciate the picture," I said. "Thank you."

"No problem, but none beyond here," she said. "We're going upstairs into the private residence and for a whole lot of reasons we don't allow any photos up there."

We peeked into the State Dining Room, which was being prepped for some big event, and then we went up the stairs.

"The first family lives on the second floor," she explained. "You and Lucy are going to work in the Treaty Room."

"That sounds official," I said hesitantly.

"Every room here is official," she replied. "But the first family uses it as a study."

The stairs led us to a little hallway and I peered into a room that looked like a small beauty parlor. No matter where I looked, every work of art, piece of carpet, or swath of wallpaper was intriguing. I was trying to take it all in and as a result wasn't exactly paying attention to where I was going.

"Watch out!" warned a voice. A friendly hand on my back kept us from running into each other.

I turned to apologize but when I did my mouth suddenly froze and my eyes opened wide. I just stood there for a moment before I finally got the words out.

"I'm so sorry . . . Mr. President."

16.

The Treaty Room

I'D BEEN IN THE WHITE HOUSE FOR LESS THAN FIVE minutes and already completely embarrassed myself by nearly slamming into the president of the United States.

Alexander Mays would have been intimidating even if he weren't the most powerful person in the world. He was big—not just tall but thick with broad shoulders like a football player. He looked down at me and, in that deep familiar voice I'd heard so many times on television, demanded, "Who are you?"

For a few panicked-filled moments I thought he was angry. But then he smiled, and I realized he was just having fun with me.

"Florian Bates," I said so softly I couldn't be certain he'd heard me.

"He's a friend of Lucy's from school," Malena added, coming to my rescue. "They're working on a project together."

"Florian Bates?" he repeated, trying to place the name. "I feel like I've heard that somewhere."

"Maybe Lucy mentioned I was coming over?" I offered sheepishly.

"No, it wasn't Lucy. It was . . ." Suddenly his eyes opened wide with recognition and he smiled. "It was Dave Douglas."

It took me a moment to realize he was talking about Admiral David Denton Douglas, director of the FBI. I knew him only as Admiral or Director Douglas. It never occurred to me that his friends might call him Dave.

"Admiral Douglas mentioned *me*?" I said, stunned. "To *you*?"

Now the president got very excited and grinned as he said, "The National Gallery and the spy ring at the Chinese restaurant. Those were both you, right?"

I nodded, half-embarrassed. "Yes, sir."

He gave me a big handshake. "Well, I'm a fan, Florian. Feel free to run into me any time you want."

"Thank you, sir."

"I'd love to stay and chat, but I have to call the British prime minister."

"Tell him I said hello," I said, trying to be cool and humorous but failing at both.

"Try not to walk into a wall or break any china," he joked as he headed for the stairs. "Some of the stuff up here is pretty expensive."

Once he was gone Malena turned to me and asked, "What was all that about the National Gallery and Chinese spies?"

"Just some cases I worked on," I said, trying to sound humble while my heart was about to explode with pride. "I don't think I'm allowed to tell you much more than that."

She looked at me differently, maybe even a bit impressed, and said, "I can respect that."

We went into the Treaty Room, which the first family used as a study. On the far wall a portrait of Ulysses S. Grant looked down at a long desk with a computer and neat stacks of files and books. Closer to the door was a sitting area with an overstuffed couch and three leather armchairs arranged around a coffee table. Lucy was on the couch working on her laptop. She wore an Orioles cap, jeans, and a T-shirt with the name of a band I didn't know.

"Hey, Florian," she said.

"Hi, Lucy," I replied.

"Want something to drink?" she offered.

"No, I'm good," I answered as I went over to one of the chairs. "Is it okay for me to sit here?" I asked, unsure if it was an antique or something.

"Of course," she said.

I sat down, put my backpack on the table, and unzipped it.

"Want me to show you around before we get started?" she asked.

I really would have loved that. I'm sure every object in every room came with an amazing story. But I thought about what Malena had said about how hard this was for Lucy and realized the best thing I could do was act like we were just in a regular house.

"Maybe later," I said.

When she smiled I could tell that I'd made the right decision. She asked if I had any difficulty with security and I told her that everything was easy. (I don't know if that's always the case or if it was accelerated because of my FBI status.) We made small talk for a moment and then jumped into the assignment.

"So what French person affects your life the most every day?" she asked.

"I don't know," I said. "It dawned on me that Lafayette Square is right across the street and it got me thinking that he could be a good one. Without Lafayette the American Revolution might have failed completely and we wouldn't even have a country now. I also thought about Napoleon and Marie Curie."

"I thought of those three," she said. "But I bet there are at least two presentations on each of them. I want to do someone different. Less obvious."

"Okay," I replied. "You're great at music. Do you have a favorite French composer?"

"I love Debussy," she answered. "But I don't know what we could say about him for five minutes."

"Maybe you could just play the cello for four and a half and then I could talk for the last thirty seconds," I joked.

Unlike when we were at school, the conversation flowed naturally. There were no three-word answers here. Despite the fact that we were where we were, it didn't feel all that different from hanging out in my front room with Margaret. (You know, if my front room had a grandfather clock that once belonged to John Quincy Adams and if Margaret were the suspect in a case I was working on.)

In addition to working on our project, I was supposed to uncover information on three different subjects:

Lucy's membership in the Megatherium Club

An explanation of the tension between her and
   Becca Baker

A list of enemies who might set her up, starting
   with Yin and Tanner

"What do you think of Madame Thibault's class?" I
asked. "It's kind of weird being in there with all those high
school kids."

"I don't mind that so much. Most of the time I'm surrounded by adults, so at least they're kids."

"Are you friends with any of them?" I asked. "Like that
girl Becca, who sits next to you?"

She gave me a sour look. "Definitely not friends with her."

She didn't illuminate beyond that and I wasn't sure how
hard to push for information. I didn't want to scare her off.

"Oh," I said. "I figured because you were both into music
you might be."

"We used to be," she said. "But now she treats me like
I'm garbage. Actually, she treats me like I'm not even there."

"Does that mean you're *frenemies*?" I asked. "Someone
told me that term, but I'm not exactly sure I get it."

"No, we were friends and now we're enemies, but there was no overlap." She looked up with a hurt expression. "And I really don't want to talk about it."

"I'm sorry," I said. "I didn't mean to pry."

"It's okay," she said.

There was a brief lull in the conversation and she asked, "How'd you learn to speak French so well?"

"My family lived in Paris for nearly three years," I said, which led into a brief history of the Bates family. I told her about my parents working in museums and our somewhat nomadic path through Boston, London, Paris, Rome, and now Washington. She seemed genuinely interested.

"What about you?" I asked. "Where did you learn to speak French so well?"

"I grew up in New Orleans," she said. "French is a big deal down there. So are music and food, which just happen to be my two favorite things."

"They're very high on my list as well," I said. "Well, I can't play music, but I enjoy listening to it."

"I love to play," she said. "My dream is to play in a symphony. You know, when you try out for a symphony nobody knows who you are. Not even if you're a man or a woman."

"What do you mean?" I asked.

"You audition behind a screen," she explained. "All the

people who pick are sitting in the audience, but they can't see you. And you don't talk so they can't hear your voice. They only know how well you play."

I saw her expression and wondered how rare it must be for her to ever be anonymous like that.

"You're playing the cello on Monday at the Kennedy Center, right? We're all going on a field trip to listen."

"I am playing *a* cello," she said. "Not *the* cello. That'll be your buddy Yin."

"What do you mean?"

"Well, the whole youth symphony will be performing, but Yin is the featured soloist," she explained. "Of course, he should be, considering he composed the music we're playing."

"Seriously?"

"And it's good," she said with admiration. "He's unlike anyone I've ever met. If he wanted to go to Juilliard he could go right now."

"What's he like to hang out with?" I asked.

"You can tell me after you guys go to the zoo this weekend."

"You don't know?"

She shook her head. "We don't really talk much."

I remembered that Margaret said Mrs. Chiang complained to the board of trustees about the way Lucy treated him and I wanted to dig further, but it seemed too risky.

The conversation hit a lull until a booming voice came from the hall.

"How's the homework going?"

I turned to see that it was the president with a friendly smile on his face.

"We're still trying to figure out who to do our presentation about," said Lucy. She started to introduce us. "Dad, this is Florian—"

"Florian and I are old friends," he said, cutting her off. "We ran into each other in the hallway earlier." He shot me a politician's wink and added, "The British prime minister wanted me to say hello."

"Thanks." I laughed.

"So what's the assignment?"

He was looking right at me, so I answered. "We're supposed to give a five-minute presentation about a French person who impacts our daily lives."

He nodded as he considered this. "Who's in the running?"

"Lafayette, Napoleon, and Marie Curie," said Lucy.

He gave us an unimpressed look and in desperation I threw in, "Maybe Blaise Pascal."

"I've got one for you," he said with a slight clap. "Pierre Charles L'Enfant."

Lucy and I gave each other blank looks.

"Who's that?" we said in unison.

"The architect and civil engineer George Washington appointed to design the city we now call home," he answered. "He affects your life every time you're stuck in traffic, whenever you get lost trying to find your way around Dupont Circle, and especially when you look out and admire views such as that."

He pointed out the window toward the Washington Monument and the Jefferson Memorial.

"I like it," I said. "We could talk about him for sure."

"And if you promise not to tell anyone that I let you handle them," he said conspiratorially, "I believe some of his original plans are downstairs in the library."

He stayed and talked to us for a few minutes and it was obvious that Lucy and he had a good relationship. Then when he went to leave he turned and asked, "Florian, what are you doing for dinner tonight?"

"I think we're having leftovers," I said.

"Would you like to stay here and have dinner with us?"

I tried to keep calm. "I'd have to ask my mom for permission."

He smiled at this. "I'm pretty sure she'll say yes, but why don't you call her and let me ask for you."

My mind went wild trying to imagine how my mother would respond as I dialed and handed my phone to him.

"Hello, Ms. Bates," he said when she answered. "This is Alex Mays."

There was a pause before he said, "Yes, *that* Alex Mays." Another pause. "No, I'm not joking."

He listened for a moment and said, "Yes, ma'am, he's been very well behaved and they've been working hard. I just wanted to see if it would be okay for him to stay for dinner."

She answered, "Of course," loud enough for me to hear it standing a few feet from him.

"I'll have someone from the Secret Service drive him home when we're done."

He gave me back the phone and told me, "Now she's going to remind you to keep your elbows off the table and your napkin on your lap."

I took the phone and that's exactly what she told me, along with other reminders about using my best table manners during dinner.

"We're having Peruvian chicken, which is just delicious," he said once the phone call was over. "With limoncello cake for dessert."

"That sounds great," I said.

Then he looked at me with a twinkle in his eye. "And afterward, I want to show you something special."

17.

Peace and Friendship

LUCY AND I DID SOME RESEARCH ON PIERRE Charles L'Enfant and then went downstairs to the library, where the White House curator showed us a drawing from 1791 that laid out the original plan for the city. Although some of the names had changed (for example the Capitol and Capitol Hill were originally called Congress House and Jenkins Hill) the basic layout looked remarkably like modern-day Washington.

"Is that what I think it is?" I asked, pointing at the lower corner where someone had written "G. Washington."

"President Washington's signature," said the curator, nodding. "And some of these notations over here are his as well. He'd been a surveyor, so he had a great interest in the design of the city."

Even Lucy seemed impressed by this.

We ate dinner in the family dining room, which was small and intimate by White House standards but still bigger than any room in my house. Modern art hung on the walls, and while I didn't recognize any of the artists, I could tell the works were museum valuable.

There were four of us at a round table. The president sat across from me, while Lucy and the first lady sat to each side. Peruvian chicken comes with the leg and thigh still attached to the breast, so it was a constant battle to remind myself not to use my fingers, but instead to cut off small pieces. I was also thrown by the fact that a butler was serving us. I didn't know when I was allowed to reach for something or supposed to ask. At one point I sat there frozen as I tried to figure out what to do.

"I know how you feel," the first lady whispered as she leaned over toward me. "Sometimes I get nervous, and I live here."

This made me laugh and I finally began to relax.

"Florian just moved to Washington from Rome," Lucy said.

"Is that right?" asked her mother. "Are you Italian?"

"Half," I answered. "My mom's Italian and my father's

American. I was born in Boston, but I've lived most of my life in Europe."

"Rome is one of my favorite cities in the world," she replied. "When I was in college, I spent a semester there and loved every second of it."

"Okay, Florian, I'm going to put you on the spot and I want an honest answer," said the president as he flashed me a humorous version of a death stare. "Imagine it's the World Cup and Italy is playing the United States. What team are you rooting for?"

I tried to hold back a smile as I answered, "I'd rather not answer that here in the White House."

"That's what I suspected." He turned to the butler and instructed, "No cake for him."

"Hey! That's not fair," I protested. "Besides, you said we're having limoncello cake, and that's Italian."

"Good point," he said. He turned back to the butler again. "He can have cake. Just make his piece a little bit smaller."

After that it no longer felt like I was at the White House. It was just dinner with a friend and her parents. They asked a lot about my family and me. The president told bad jokes that made me laugh and Lucy roll her eyes. And we discussed the upcoming youth symphony concert.

"I'm really looking forward to the field trip," I said. "I've never been to the Kennedy Center before and I can't wait to hear Lucy play."

"Well, you won't be able to hear *me*," she corrected. "I'm just part of the orchestra."

I couldn't tell if this was modesty talking or if she felt stung by the fact that she didn't have a solo. But I didn't mention Yin and neither did they. After an awkward silence her mother spoke up.

"You'll love the Kennedy Center, Florian," she said. "It's a real treasure."

"Now, if everybody's done," said the president, "why don't we have dessert in the Treaty Room. There's something I want to show Lucy and Florian."

We got up to go but first Lucy's parents made a point of going into the kitchen to compliment the cook on the dinner. The president also continued his joke about making my piece of cake smaller than everyone else's.

The butler served the dessert on the coffee table where Lucy and I had worked earlier.

"There's something I want to show you," the president said after we had a few bites. "Put down your cake for a second and come over here. You too, Lucy."

We walked over toward an antique cabinet in the corner of the room.

"You'll never read about it in school," he said. "But it's an unofficial, somewhat-secret tradition that goes from president to president."

He opened the cabinet to reveal rows of small little drawers—six across and nine high.

"What do they hold?" I asked.

"History," he said. "Going back to Mr. Big—George Washington himself. Each president has left behind a small token to be shared with everyone who follows in the job. Each one is a cross between a memento and a good luck charm."

He opened a drawer on the third row and pulled out a gold pocket watch. "This belonged to Abraham Lincoln."

"Really?" I said.

"Really," he answered. "And Lyndon Johnson had it in his pocket when he signed the Civil Rights Act because he thought he was continuing the work that Lincoln had begun more than a century earlier."

I didn't reach for it. I just looked closely and marveled at it.

"You can hold it, Florian," he said. "Just be careful."

I took it for only a few seconds, worried that I might somehow break it or tarnish it.

"It's amazing," I said.

"Isn't it?" said Lucy as I handed it to her. "I love this cabinet."

Her father reached for the first drawer and pulled out a small compass. "This belonged to George Washington. He carried it with him during the Revolutionary War and President Lincoln carried it at times during the Civil War. He said he liked it because the arrow always pointed north, toward the Union side of the battle."

He handed the compass to me and I was mesmerized.

"This is so cool," I said.

"I think so too," he said. "And lately I've been focused on the third drawer."

"What's in it?" I asked.

"Yeah," said Lucy. "You've never shown me that one."

"Why don't you open it and see," her father said.

She opened the drawer slowly, careful not to disturb whatever was inside, but it was empty.

"There's nothing here," I said.

"That's right," he replied. "There should be a special coin that Thomas Jefferson had minted for the Lewis and Clark expedition. It's a peace medal and has his picture on the front and the words 'Peace and Friendship' on the back."

"Where is it?" I asked.

"That's a mystery," he said. "Because Jefferson is so popular, it was a favorite memento of many presidents. In 1904 Teddy Roosevelt carried it with him when he went to the world's fair in St. Louis, which celebrated the Louisiana Purchase, one of Jefferson's greatest achievements. But it was Franklin Roosevelt who found the most inspiration in it. He kept it on his desk when he gave his fireside chats."

"What were the fireside chats?" I asked.

"They were speeches he made directly to the American people. They weren't flowery with a lot of poetic language, just plain talk about the problems the country faced. He did thirty of them and they were carried on the radio all over the country. They really helped the nation get through the Great Depression and World War Two. He liked to keep the medal turned so that he could see 'Peace and Friendship' while he talked. He wanted to remind himself what was most important."

He returned the compass and pocket watch to their proper drawers and closed the cabinet. As we walked back to the sitting area, he picked up a file from his desk and placed it on the coffee table. He opened it to reveal a stack of pictures.

"Here it is in this picture," he said, picking up a photograph of President Roosevelt delivering one of his fireside chats. He handed it to me and I looked at it with Lucy.

In the photo President Roosevelt was behind a desk crowded with microphones featuring the names of different networks like NBC and CBS. He was reading his speech from a binder and right next to it you could see the small medal.

"Right there," I said, pointing it out to Lucy.

"That's the last time he saw it," said President Mays. "He forgot to take it and when he went to look for it later it was gone."

"Someone probably picked it up as a souvenir," suggested Lucy.

"Maybe," said her father. "But everyone who was there was questioned and they all denied taking it. He even offered a reward and a promise of immunity."

I looked up at the president and realized this was the reason he'd invited me to stay for dinner. Admiral Douglas had told him about me and he wanted to know if I could figure out what happened to the peace medal. The problem was that he also knew that I was covert and undercover, so he couldn't ask me directly to solve it. All he could do was bait the hook.

"What room is this?" I asked, referring to the picture.

"The Diplomatic Reception Room," said the president. "Down on the ground floor."

"Do you have any other pictures of it from that time?"

Now he knew he had me. "Here's a whole file of them," he said, handing me the folder.

I started looking through them while he continued talking.

"Every president since FDR has tried to find that coin. They've scoured that room. They say that one night John Kennedy and his brother Robert spent hours crawling around on the floor looking for it."

"What about you, Dad?" asked Lucy.

"I've looked more often than I'd like to admit," he said. "You know how much I love Jefferson."

"If no one's seen it since 1940," said Mrs. Mays, "I think you might have to just accept that it's gone."

While she was saying this, I was comparing two of the pictures and blurted out, "Maybe you don't."

The president grinned. "Why's that, Florian?"

I double-checked the pictures to make sure I was right. Then I looked up and kind of sheepishly said, "I think I might know what happened."

18.

Mind the Gap

LUCKILY, THE DIPLOMATIC RECEPTION ROOM WAS being used the next day for an event, so it'd already been blocked off. This meant there were no visitors or staff walking through on their way to the South Lawn. Still, President Mays instructed the Secret Service to momentarily "secure the perimeter of the room" so no one could peek in on us.

"What are you doing?" Lucy asked me as we hurried down the stairs trying to keep up with her dad. He was excited and taking the steps two at a time.

"I think I know where the peace medal is," I told her.

"How's that even possible?"

I didn't have an answer for that. At least not one I could

fully explain in a couple flights of stairs without blowing my cover.

"It just is."

We reached the ground floor and the president poked his head into the curator's office asking him to join us. "John, why don't you join us in the Reception Room. We're working on a little project and could use your expertise."

"What type of project?" he asked.

"Just indulge me for a moment."

The room was directly across the hall and Secret Service agents were already standing at each door. I had no idea how they got there so quickly but it sure was impressive. Once we were all inside, President Mays shut the door and said, "All right, Florian, take it away."

I'm more confident in my mystery solving than any other aspect of my life, but at that moment I was worried about what would happen if I'd misread a clue. I hadn't foreseen all the people who were suddenly involved. I hadn't realized how many eyes would be on me. It hadn't dawned on me how incredibly embarrassing it would be if I was wrong. But there was no going back, so I just forged ahead.

I looked at the picture of FDR giving his fireside chat and then I looked at the room. They seemed drastically different. "How has the room changed since 1940?" I asked the curator.

"In 1960 it was redecorated as a drawing room in the Federal style," he informed us. "That's when the color scheme was changed, and soon after that Mrs. Kennedy selected the wallpaper. The regency chandelier was added in 1971 and the rug in the 1983."

"Okay, wow," I said, impressed. "You really know your stuff."

"Yes, I do," he answered with a fair amount of pride.

"Were the dimensions or basic layout of the room changed?"

"No," he replied. "They are still the same as they've been since 1902."

"That's good," I said as I walked to the center of the room and stood directly beneath the chandelier so I could orient myself. The room was a large oval about thirty-five feet long and thirty feet across. A portrait of George Washington hung over the fireplace, the wallpaper featured a panorama of hand-painted scenes of American life, and the rug had emblems of all fifty states along the border.

"Where in this room was President Roosevelt sitting?" I asked, handing him the picture of FDR.

He looked at the photo for a moment and then walked to a spot about ten feet away. "Approximately here," he said.

I joined him, took the picture, and laid it down on the floor to mark the location.

"And are these two spots the same?" I asked, showing him two photographs of the room, one before and one after the changes.

"Yes. That's the wall between the vestibule and the entrance to the hall," he said. "May I ask what we're doing?"

"Trying to find the Jefferson peace medal," said the president.

This stunned the curator. "The room has been gone over countless times since then," he said to the president. "It's not still here. It can't possibly be."

The fact that he seemed to be an expert in every detail of the room and the certainty with which he said that the medal couldn't have been there didn't help my confidence. Still, I ignored him and walked to the area shown in the two photos. Every eye was following me closely and I said a quick silent prayer that I was not about to screw things up.

I compared the current wall to the one in the older picture and was relieved to see what I was looking for. So far so good.

"Mr. President," I said, bypassing the curator for this request. "I need a Phillips head screwdriver. Preferably one with a magnetic tip that holds the screws in place."

"Mr. President!" gasped the curator. "As I said, this room has been . . ."

The president held up his hand to quiet him and stared at me. He was trying to read my confidence level and could tell that at this point I didn't have any doubts.

"Somebody get him a Phillips head screwdriver."

"With a magnetic tip," I added.

"With a magnetic tip," he instructed.

Despite the curator's reluctance, there was no way he was going to refuse the president. "One moment," he said with a sigh as he quickly exited the room.

"Oh," I added right as he reached the door. "And a flashlight."

He stopped and thought about saying something but didn't. He just left and I stood there with everyone staring at me. This was the most awkward part of all. Maybe the most awkward moment in my entire life. (Which is saying something.)

Most of the people looked confused. Lucy and her mother seemed concerned. But the president and Malena Sanchez, who was one of the Secret Service agents in the room, had a different expression. They looked . . . excited.

They believed in me.

Still, I couldn't bear to just stand there like that, so I picked up one of the photographs and pretended to study it.

It felt like it took forever for the curator to return.

"A flashlight and a Phillips head screwdriver," he said as he handed them to me. "Magnetic."

"Thank you."

I turned toward the wall and got down on my knees right in front of a vent. It was white, like the wall, with an ornate design. I started removing one of the screws and the president came over to help.

He held the cover while I undid the screws and everybody else watched. The potential for embarrassment had reached epic levels. By the time I was on the last screw, both Lucy and her mother had come over to us as well.

"Careful," gasped the curator, unable to help himself, as we pulled the cover from the wall. The president smiled and laid it gently on the floor.

"Lucy, can you hold this here and point it down?" I said, putting the flashlight into the newly formed gap in the wall.

Once she took it I pressed my face into the gap. It was just deep enough for me to get one eye and most of my nose inside. After looking for about twenty-five seconds I saw the glimmer of a reflection and breathed a sigh of relief. I couldn't be sure what it was, but at least I'd found something. I tried to grab it but it was just beyond my fingertips. Instead I used the screwdriver to reach for it and let the magnetic tip pick it up.

"Gotcha," I said when I heard the plink of metal attaching to metal.

I carefully pulled my arm from the gap in the wall, making sure not to hit the edges and knock it off. There was a collective gasp when the screwdriver came out and everybody could see that something was stuck to it.

"Mr. President," I said, offering it to him.

He pulled it from the tip and wiped away decades' worth of dust with his thumb. He broke into a huge grin when he saw Jefferson's face on the front and flipped it over and read aloud.

"'Peace and Friendship.'"

The first lady squealed. The curator looked like he was going to pass out. And the Secret Service gave me a round of applause led by Malena Sanchez. I'm sure I was still blushing ten minutes later when we were back upstairs in the Treaty Room and I was explaining how it came together.

"Look at this picture," I said, referring to the first one the president had shown me of FDR delivering his address. "There's the peace medal."

I pointed at it and laid it down on the coffee table.

"Now look at this picture," I said.

"The medal's gone," said Lucy.

"That's what I thought," I said. "But if you look closer

you'll see that it isn't gone. It's moved. Look right there."

I pointed to the base of the NBC microphone on the desk in front of President Roosevelt. It was much bigger than the others and was right next to where the medal had been in the previous photo.

"Do you see that little line next to the microphone?"

"Yes," she said. "What is it?"

"It's the peace medal," I said. "The microphone is magnetic and it was pushed up next to the medal, which stuck to it."

Her eyes opened wide and the president took the photo from her and held it up to get a closer look.

"Amazing," he said. "I see it and I still don't believe it."

"How did it get from the desk to the vent?" asked the first lady.

I pulled out another picture that showed a table where all the microphones were placed after the speech.

"They put the microphones over here when they cleaned everything up."

"And once they unplugged the microphone it was no longer magnetic," said the president, getting it.

"That's right," I replied. "And notice that the NBC one is on the edge of the table, pushed right up against the vent."

"So it falls off and plunks into the wall."

"The only part I didn't know was how much the room had changed," I said. "Once I realized that the vent had a new cover but was in the same place, I figured the odds were good that the medal was in there."

The president shook his head in disbelief.

"Florian, how can I repay you?" he asked.

"You already have," I said.

"How so?"

"You've given me a memory that I'll treasure forever." I looked right at him. "Although, if you'd be so kind, I would be honored to finish the job and put it back where it belongs."

"My pleasure," he said.

I walked over to the antique cabinet and opened it.

"Number three, right?"

"That's right," he said.

I carefully pulled open the drawer and placed the peace medal back where FDR had taken it from so many years before.

19.

As Honestly As I Can

I DON'T KNOW WHAT THE STANDARD PROTOCOL is when riding in a Secret Service SUV, but rather than sit in the back, I climbed into the passenger seat next to Malena Sanchez. I'd already had a butler serve me dinner. I didn't want a chauffeur to drive me home.

"Okay if I sit up here?" I asked before clicking myself in.

"Make yourself comfortable," she said.

We pulled onto Pennsylvania Avenue and I checked my phone. It was flooded with messages from Margaret and my mother wanting to know how everything went, what the president was like, and whether I'd discovered anything that would help solve the case. (Well, only Margaret wanted to know the last one.) Since the answers would've taken too long to text, I just replied that I was on my way home and would have much to tell.

Agent Sanchez waited until I was done before she spoke up. "What you did tonight was impressive."

"Which part?" I asked. "Finding the Jefferson peace medal . . . or figuring out that you learned French in the marines?"

She gave a begrudging smile. "Both, I guess."

"Thank you."

We reached a stoplight and she turned to me.

"Do you really think you can figure out who Loki is?"

There was something about the way she asked it that made me think she didn't know the answer. Although she may have just been trying to misdirect me.

"I do," I said.

"You know what? I believe you."

The light turned green and we started moving again.

"In fact, because I believe you, I'm going to give you a one-time offer," she continued. "Think of it as a reward for your performance tonight."

"What's the offer?" I asked.

"I will answer one question, but only one question, as honestly as I can."

"What does 'as honestly as you can' mean?"

"It means I'll answer the question truthfully unless I think it would somehow jeopardize Lucy's safety," she said. "Then I'll just say that I can't answer it."

I considered this for a moment. "If you can't answer, do I get to ask another one?"

"Nope," she told me. "So choose wisely."

We were less than five minutes from my house so there wasn't much time, but I wanted to be careful and pick just the right question. I didn't think I could just get away with a direct "Who's Loki?" If she didn't know, then the question would be wasted. I had to come up with something that would give me information whether she answered it or not.

"Okay, I've got it."

"Give it to me."

"Why did Lucy leave school when the fire alarm was pulled?"

I asked this for a couple reasons. First of all, it was a big part of why Margaret thought she was guilty. A good explanation might change her mind. But even more important, I thought that if Malena refused to answer, then it would indicate that Lucy was at least somehow involved.

"That's your question?"

"Yep," I said smugly.

"Too bad," she said.

"Why? Because you can't answer it?"

"No. Because a boy as smart as you should've been able to figure it out."

My smugness began to fade.

"What happens when a fire alarm goes off?" she asked.

"Everyone in the building goes outside."

"And what do they do when they get out there?"

"Stand around and wait for the all clear to come back in."

"That's right," she said. "Now what's my job?"

"To protect Lucy."

When I heard myself say it out loud I realized that the answer was obvious. I shook my head and added, "Which is impossible to do while she's just standing around waiting outside."

"You got it," she said. "She'd be too vulnerable. Standard operating procedure is to evacuate a protectee from any such situation. No matter where we are, when a fire alarm is pulled, I put Lucy in the car and get out. That's in the Secret Service handbook, so it's not going to tell you anything about Loki."

She was absolutely right. I should have been able to figure that out without asking. I exhaled a dissatisfied breath at the wasted opportunity.

"Don't let it get you down," she said. "You still impressed me tonight."

"What should I have asked?"

She thought about it for a moment and said, "You should have asked why Lucy and Becca stopped being friends."

My eyes opened wide. "Oh, that is good. Why did they stop being friends?"

"Too late. You already used your question. Besides, you're home and I think those people are eager to hear about your night."

I looked up to the house and saw Margaret, Mom, and Dad all anxiously looking out the front window.

"Thanks for the ride," I said.

"My pleasure."

I went inside and recapped the entire visit for the three of them. They were excited (and maybe even a little jealous). A bonus came in the middle of it all when the White House photographer texted me a picture he took of the president and me with the Jefferson peace medal.

"That's going up in my office tomorrow!" exclaimed Mom. "And whenever anyone asks, 'Isn't that your son with the president?' I'll just act like it's no big deal and say, 'Oh yeah, I guess it is.'"

Margaret and I also went over what I'd learned for the case:

1. I'd made no headway with regard to her membership in the Megatherium Club.

2. Lucy's emergency exit during the fire alarm wasn't at all suspicious.

3. Lucy had a noticeable reaction whenever I mentioned Yin. I couldn't be certain that she considered him an enemy, but she definitely was jealous of his status with the orchestra.

4. The most important relationship seemed to be the one between Lucy and Becca. They'd been good friends and now they were enemies. As Agent Sanchez suggested, the reason why might be the key to everything.

"I don't know," Margaret joked once I'd run through it all. "It seems to me like you may have spent more time using your TOAST skills to impress the president than you did advancing our case."

"What'd you get done?" I asked.

"I almost finished my song," she said sheepishly.

"So in other words, I got more done than you."

"I don't know," she joked. "The song's pretty good."

That night I lay in bed running through the previous twenty-four hours in my head. It really was an amazing experience. I'd touched pieces of history that connected to George Washington, Thomas Jefferson, and Abraham Lincoln. But even more eye-opening, I'd seen the first family in a way I never could've imagined.

In some ways the three of them seemed a lot like my parents and me, even though their life was completely different. I thought about how hard it must be for Lucy to have normal kid experiences. And I wondered what the answer was to the question Malena said I should've asked: Why had Lucy and Becca stopped being friends?

I was still working on that the next morning in French class when the intercom buzzed.

"Madame Thibault?" called the voice. "Please have Florian Bates report to the headmaster's office immediately."

Normally when someone is suddenly called to the office the class goes, "Ooooh," as if that person is in big trouble. But this time it was more like "Who?" as though none of them had any idea who Florian Bates was. There was, however, one exception.

Becca turned and gave me an "I told you so" look. "I warned you," she said under her breath. "You shouldn't talk about things you don't understand."

I'd been so distracted by my White House adventure that I hadn't thought much about how badly the previous day had ended at school. Becca had gone to the headmaster and told him I was nibbling around the edges of the Megatherium Club. The last time I saw Dr. Putney, he was trying to get the contents of Margaret's backpack and she was invoking the National Security Act of 1947.

It felt like I was being called in for round two of that fight. I ran into Margaret in the hallway outside the library.

"Any idea what's going on?" I asked.

"I imagine it's the follow-up to yesterday's conversation," she answered.

"That's what I figured too. Do you have that list of names with you?"

"Yes," she said, patting the backpack. "But I also have a copy on my computer at home."

Dr. Putney's assistant was standing at the door. "He's waiting for you," she sneered as she used her fingers to signal us to hurry up.

It turns out the headmaster wasn't the only one waiting.

Putney was sitting at a conference table next to Moncrieff Tate, chairman of the school's board of trustees. Marcus sat across from them.

"Have a seat," Putney instructed us, motioning toward the

two chairs next to Marcus. "We were just talking with Agent Rivers about how you've wandered off course and we wanted to come together so we could refocus your . . . *inquiry.*"

Even though Tate was silent, it seemed like he was in charge. At least on that side of the table. I knew Marcus had our backs.

"Actually," Marcus said, "Dr. Putney characterized it that way. But I'm curious. Do you two think you've wandered off course?"

"No," said Margaret defiantly.

"Florian?"

"I don't think we're off course at all. We have several strong leads and just need to see how it all comes together."

Margaret threw a little gas on the fire by adding, "We might be further along if Dr. Putney had told us about the Megatherium Club right off the bat."

"You see, this is what I was talking about," Putney protested. "Rather than trying to identify Loki, they're spinning some off-the-wall conspiracy theory about a secret society."

"It's not a theory," said Margaret. "If you don't believe me, you can just ask the rest of the Maxillaires or the Question Marks." The mention of these two groups got a rise out of Moncrieff, which is exactly why she did it. "You know, for a secret society, you're not so good at keeping secrets."

"Young lady," Tate said, trying to control his anger, "I don't think you realize whom you're dealing with."

"Actually, I think you've got that backward," said a voice from the doorway.

We looked up to see the ever-imposing presence of Admiral David Denton Douglas, director of the FBI.

"I don't think *you* know whom you're dealing with, Moncrieff," he continued.

"Nice timing, sir," Marcus said as the admiral took a seat next to Margaret and gave her a wink.

"Director Douglas," Putney said, scrambling to stay on top of the situation. "What are you doing here?"

"That's what I'd like to know," he replied. "I should be in my office running the FBI. It's a pretty big job, you know. But I'm here because it seems as though you and I had a miscommunication."

"What sort of miscommunication?" asked the headmaster.

"You called me asking for a favor, and because I have a soft spot for the school, I agreed. That's when I asked Agent Rivers, Florian, and Margaret to do *me* a favor and solve your problem. You see, the favor they're doing is for me, not you. Do you understand the subtle but significant difference there?"

"Y-y-yes, of course I do," said Putney.

"I don't think you do," replied the admiral. "Yesterday you tried to intimidate these two young people because they discovered some ridiculous secret club you've got and now your panties are all in a bunch." He turned to Margaret and me. "How long did it take you two to figure it all out?"

"About an hour," she said.

The admiral laughed when he heard that. "Well, Moncrieff, I can see why you're so embarrassed. Thank God I'm the one protecting national secrets and not you."

"Admiral, this organization has nothing to do with the pranks that have been going on at the school," asserted Putney.

"Does that mean you know who the guilty party is?" he asked.

"Well, no," he admitted.

"Then I guess you don't know if it involves the organization or not," the admiral said with a satisfied grin. "Now, Florian, Margaret, ask your questions. I'd like to hear the answers myself."

I looked across the table and was amazed by how different they appeared. Oh, to be able to silence bullies just by walking into a room.

"Where can we get a list of the members of the Megatherium Club?" I asked.

"You can't," answered Putney.

"Now, seriously," interjected the admiral.

"You can't because no such list exists," he explained. "There are at any one time twenty-one members of the club and their identities are known only to each other. We find out who they are after graduation when they become legacies like Moncrieff and me."

Marcus couldn't believe it. "Are you saying that you have a group on this campus, completely unsupervised, identities unknown, that can get away with whatever it wants?"

"I wouldn't characterize it that way," he replied. "They don't get away with whatever they want. But they are a secret group and that secrecy is an essential part of their connection. It helps build deep friendships that continue long after leaving Chatham."

"But they're not all friends," said Margaret. "Lucy Mays and Becca Baker are enemies. Why?"

Tate and Putney shared a troubled look, and when they did, a possible reason came to me.

"Wait a second," I said, turning to Margaret. "Why do we think Lucy's a Megatherium?"

"Because the symbols of the club are in her locker," she said. "The triple stripe and 'How How.'"

"Right," I said. "But when Lucy was selected to be a member of the honor society, how did they let her know?"

"They put an announcement on her locker," answered Margaret, trying to follow my train of thinking.

"What if that's all it was?" I said. "What if the symbols in her locker were some sort of cryptic invitation to join the Megatherium Club?"

Margaret thought about this for a moment. "That could be. It's a secret society. It's not like you can just fill out an application. Someone has to ask you."

"And they can't put the message on the door to your locker where everyone could see," I added. "That would ruin the secret."

"But that still makes her a member," reasoned Margaret.

This is when I smiled. "Unless she turned them down."

They didn't say anything, but both men on the opposite side of the table squirmed a little bit.

"What do you mean?" asked Marcus.

"What if the Megatherium Club invited Lucy to join them because they wanted those lifelong bonds to extend into the White House, but she had the nerve to turn them down?" I said. "They'd get their feelings hurt and they might want to make her look bad by setting her up as the prankster."

The silence was long, before the headmaster admitted, "We don't know that for certain."

"But you're worried that's what it is," said Marcus. "That's why you wanted help. You're worried the Megatheriums are going to go too far and embarrass the first daughter. And in the process embarrass the school and your silly secret society. And since you don't know who they are, you wanted us to figure it out for you."

Neither one of the two men across the table said anything for a moment until Putney finally admitted, "That was a concern."

"Hmmm," said Admiral Douglas. "You might've mentioned that when you asked for my help."

20.

Trust the River

IT'S AMAZING HOW MUCH THE TONE OF OUR meeting changed once we'd gotten Dr. Putney and Moncrieff Tate to admit that the Megatherium Club existed. While they still maintained they didn't know who the current members were, they began to help us understand how the club worked.

"There are supposed to be twenty-one members," explained Putney. "One from seventh grade, two from eighth, three from ninth, and so on up to six from the senior class. Each year those six seniors graduate and the following year six new members are invited to fill their spots. One from each grade."

"Why do you say 'supposed to be twenty-one'?" asked Marcus.

"Because Lucy didn't become a member, right?" I said. "That threw off their number."

"Yes," said the headmaster. "To my knowledge Lucy was the first person to ever turn down the invitation to join. Since there was no precedent, the student in charge of membership approached me for advice. I consulted with other legacies and advised her that they should wait and pick an extra person from that class next year."

Margaret took notes of what he said, but I kept my focus on Tate. He was already in a bad mood because we were there, but now he seemed particularly agitated by what Putney was telling us. I had a pretty good idea why.

"If there's only one invitation for each class," I pointed out, "that means they picked Lucy instead of Victoria."

"Yes," Moncrieff said curtly. "They ignored generations of tradition because they were blinded by the bright lights of the White House. And look what good it did them. Egg on their face."

Margaret and I shared a look. If Victoria was as angry as her grandfather, then she suddenly shot up the list of possible suspects. This gave her the motive we couldn't come up with before. Not only did Lucy get the invitation

Victoria felt she deserved but Lucy rejected it, adding insult to injury.

"Was Becca Baker the student in charge of membership?" I asked.

"Yes," he said reluctantly.

Malena was absolutely right when she said the key question was why Lucy and Becca were no longer friends. Now we had a strong motive for her, too. If she was in charge of membership and Lucy had been a friend, then she might have been particularly upset by the rejection.

Admiral Douglas looked at me and asked, "Are there any other questions you have for them?"

"Two, sir," I said. "What can you tell us about Mrs. Chiang's complaint to the board of trustees regarding Lucy Mays?"

Rather than answer, Putney turned to Tate, who served as the board's chairman.

"Nothing," he said.

"Nothing as in there was no complaint?" asked Marcus. "Or nothing as in you won't tell us?"

"Nothing as in I *cannot* tell you," Tate replied. He looked at Admiral Douglas. "There must be confidentiality with regard to student discipline. That's the law, David. Even you're not above it."

For a moment it looked like he was going to score a point against the admiral, but then Margaret jumped in.

"You feel strongly about student confidentiality?" she asked.

"Absolutely," he said with all the righteousness he could muster.

"Then why did you tell your granddaughter about the hearing and Mrs. Chiang's complaints? She gossips about it to everyone. Is *she* above the law? Or do you only feel strongly about confidentiality when you don't like the person asking you questions?"

There was another long silence until Admiral Douglas said, "Are you going to answer her, Moncrieff? Or just sit there with that look on your face?"

At this moment I almost felt bad for him. *Almost.*

"Mrs. Chiang contended that Lucy was jealous of Yin and tried to intimidate him," Tate said slowly. "We take bullying very seriously, so we looked into it. Ms. Allo, the music director, assured us that she had seen no evidence of this. In fact, she claimed to have never seen Lucy and Yin say anything to each other beyond hello."

"And now our final question," I said. "How can we access Chat Chat?"

"It's closed down," said the headmaster.

"It still exists," I replied. "You've just taken it off-line and we need to look through it."

"There's a computer lab in the library," he said. "You can come after school and I'll have one of them set up so that it can access the site."

"Let's go with after lunch," Marcus said.

The headmaster gave him a look.

"After school doesn't work, because Margaret has an audition for the talent show at Deal Middle," he continued. "And why don't you make it three computers, so we can work faster?"

"Fine," said Putney. "I'll have them ready after lunch. Is that all?"

"Yes," Margaret and I said in unison.

"Excellent," added the admiral. "Treat these three like you'd treat me." He stood up to leave and added, "Because if you don't, I'll come back and I won't be so friendly next time."

Over the next couple of periods I kept thinking through all that we had learned and by lunch I had two names firmly atop my suspect list: Becca and Victoria. As far as I was concerned the information we found out about the Megatheriums gave them the best motives of all. I wanted to see if Margaret had come to the same conclusion but when I got to the cafeteria I couldn't find her.

Where r u? I texted.

In the PAC, she responded.

I didn't know why she'd be there instead of at lunch, so I wolfed down my peanut butter and jelly sandwich and headed for the performing arts center. I found her in the band room sitting at a table by the practice rooms.

"What's up?" I asked.

"I still have to finish my song before my audition," she said. "So I wanted to see if I could get on a piano."

"Then why are you out here?"

She nodded toward practice room two, and for the first time I noticed that cello music was coming from within. "It's the only room with a piano."

"Is that Yin?" I asked.

She nodded.

"Couldn't he practice in one of those?" I asked, pointing at a pair of empty practice rooms.

"He could, but I don't want to interrupt him when he's playing," she said. Then she lowered her voice and added. "Besides, he might not actually be there."

"Good point."

I walked over to the door and listened. It didn't sound like a recording, but I couldn't tell for sure. After about thirty seconds, the music came to a stop, and when it didn't start up again instantly, I rapped on the door.

"What are you doing?" asked Margaret.

"I'm going to ask him if you can swap rooms."

She gave me a look and I shrugged. He didn't answer so I knocked again and after a few moments the door opened.

"Yes?" Yin said, confused as to why someone would interrupt him.

"I'm really sorry," I said. "But is there any way—"

"Florian!" he said when he realized it was me. "What's wrong?"

"Nothing," Margaret said, interrupting me. "We're sorry. Go back to playing. It was beautiful."

"No," I said. "We just wanted to see if Margaret and you could change practice rooms. This is the only one with a piano."

He looked at her and smiled. "Of course."

"You really don't have to," she said, embarrassed.

"No, I mean it," he said. "I'm happy to change."

"We wouldn't have interrupted," I said, "except she's writing a song and it needs to be finished by the end of school."

Margaret gave me a dirty look, but for the life of me I didn't know why.

"You're writing music?" he said gleefully.

"Not really," Margaret replied. "Not like you do, at least. It's just a silly song for the talent show at my school."

"I don't think it's silly," I said. "I think it's great."

"Well, you know absolutely nothing about music," Margaret pointed out.

"Can I hear it?" asked Yin.

Margaret actually looked pained by the question. "You know what, this was all a mistake. Just go back to practicing."

"One second," I said to Yin.

I walked over to her and whispered, "I stood up to a bully because of you and now he wants to kill me. It's time for you to be a little brave."

She wasn't happy about it and she didn't say anything, but she walked into the practice room and sat at the piano. I stood next to Yin and closed the door behind us.

"I'm not going to sing," she announced. "Just play."

"That's fine," I said. "Just play it."

She pulled the music out of her backpack and put it up on the rack. She started to play, tentatively at first, but then she just played. It was really good and I wasn't the only one who thought so. I could see by Yin's reaction that he liked it too.

"That's excellent," he said when she stopped. "Why didn't you keep playing?"

"Because I don't know what should go next," she replied. "This is the part that keeps stumping me. I think there should be a bridge to connect to the final verse, but I can't figure out what it should be."

"I had the same problem with one of my new compositions," he said. "The bridge is the hardest part."

"How'd you solve it?"

"You need to trust the river," he told her.

She gave him a confused look. "I'm sorry, what?"

"Can I sit down with you?"

"Of course," she said.

She slid over on the bench and made room for him.

"Back home we live near a river that my father and I like to kayak on," he said. "When I'm writing music I always think of what he told me when he was teaching me how to paddle a kayak. He'd say, 'Trust the river,' because he didn't want me to fight the current. It's better if you let the river take you where it's going and just make small adjustments."

"I'm sorry," said Margaret. "But I still don't understand."

"Play the melody," he said. "And just the melody over and over."

Margaret started playing it.

"That's the river," he said. "Look at your fingers; they're flowing across the keys like water." He started playing it too. "Now let the current take you where it wants to go."

Margaret started to understand what he meant and she

tried to find the right notes on the keyboard. My musical knowledge is so limited, I had no idea what they were talking about, but it was still amazing to watch.

"Like this?" she said.

"Yes," he said with a smile. "Now trust the river and see where it goes."

She tried again and this time just committed fully to the idea. She played the melody and then just kept playing for a moment. Then she stopped, totally surprised by what she'd heard.

"Where did that come from?" she asked.

"From you," he responded. "That was all you. It was perfect. That's your bridge."

She played it again and I could tell that she had now solved the problem she'd been struggling with.

"That's amazing!" she said. "I just . . ."

"Trusted the river," he said.

She nodded. "Yin, thank you so much. You don't know how much I've been struggling with this."

This is when it dawned on me that although Yin seemed a little nervous and withdrawn everywhere else on the campus, here he was right at home. In the world of music and instruments, he was a different person. It was almost as if we were meeting him for the first time.

I just stood there silently while the two of them worked out the rest of the song. It was great to see, and for a little while at least, the mystery took a backseat. The bell rang and we walked with Yin back toward the library, where we were supposed to meet up with Marcus so we could look at Chat Chat.

"So you like to go kayaking?" I said. "I don't think I would have guessed that."

"I guess I am a man of international mystery," he said with a laugh.

"Maybe we should do that sometime," added Margaret. "But this weekend we're still on for the zoo, right?"

"I can't wait," he said. "It should be fun. Oh, and I can hear all about the audition for the talent show."

"Sure," Margaret replied, slightly embarrassed.

"See you all later," he said as he turned to go to his locker.

It wasn't until he opened it that I noticed it was right next to the one that had belonged to Lucy Mays.

21.

Friend Circles

"WHAT'S THE MATTER?" MARCUS ASKED WHEN HE saw our expressions as we walked into the computer lab.

"We just found out Yin's locker is right next to Lucy's," said Margaret.

"And?" he said, unsure why that was important.

"That puts him at the scene of the first prank," I said.

"Which gives him a connection to all three," added Margaret.

"So that's good," he said. "That means he's a viable suspect."

"No, it's not good," said Margaret. "Because I don't want him to be guilty. He's nice. Really nice. He just helped me finish writing my song."

"I don't want it to be him either," I replied. "But we have to follow the clues, which means we have to consider him a suspect."

The lab had twenty computers arranged on four long tables. We were set up side by side, which let us look at each other's monitors while we were digging around Chat Chat. For something that had started off as a class project, it was amazing. It had a nice design and was easy to use. It's no wonder it was so popular.

Chat Chat was set up so that each student had their own page and could join different circles. Circles could be classes, clubs, or simply groups of friends. Each student also had a bulletin board to post notes and pictures. We went through our list of potential suspects one by one, starting with Becca, because she was the only one we knew for certain was a Megatherium.

"She's in circles for all of her classes, the orchestra, and a coding club," I said, looking at her page. "Nothing seems suspicious."

"What's on her bulletin board?" asked Margaret. "Pictures with friends? If so, could they be other Megatheriums?"

"It doesn't look like it," I replied. "There's a picture from her summer science camp at Stanford and a few with the Washington Youth Symphony. But that's it. She seems to use it for information and not socializing."

I clicked through her different circles, and then something caught my eye. "Is this significant?" I asked Margaret.

She leaned over from her computer to look at mine. "What?"

"Whenever she posts a message in the orchestra circle, rather than using her name she uses this." I pointed at a message telling everyone about a change for an upcoming performance. At the bottom was a music staff with five notes. "Is it from a specific song or something?"

Margaret looked at it and ran through the notes in her head. After a few seconds she smiled.

"What?" I asked.

"It's her name," she said. "The notes are B-E-C-C-A."

"Clever," I said. "She's mean, but she's smart."

"Smart enough to pull all these pranks without leaving any clues?" asked Marcus.

"No one's that smart," I said. "They always leave a few crumbs."

Next we looked into Victoria. Her bulletin board was filled with pictures that looked like they were taken for a fashion magazine.

"What circles is she in?" asked Margaret.

"None except for the one with her friends," I said. "No classes or clubs. She's the opposite of Becca; she only uses it for socializing."

"Anything in the pictures to connect her to Lucy or the Megatheriums?" asked Marcus.

"No pictures, but listen to this note she posted on her bulletin board about a month ago," said Margaret. "'Instead of forgiving you, I think I'll just go straight to making you regret your mistake.'"

"Not very subtle, is she?" I said.

"No, she's not," answered Margaret. "It's got to be directed at the Megatheriums."

"You could be right," said Marcus. "But even if it is, it would be hard to prove."

"Let's assume that it is," I said. "That was a month ago and the pranks started last week. Why wait?"

"She's got to plan them," said Margaret. "Get her people in on it."

"You think she had help?" asked Marcus.

"This group would do anything for her," Margaret said, pointing to a picture of her lunch bunch on what looked like a trip to the beach.

"Make sure to check each of their pages," said Marcus. "If any of them are involved, maybe one of them slipped up and left us something to find."

"Look at how much fun they're having," I said. "And compare that to Yin's pictures. He's alone in all of them."

I flipped through an online album and in every picture Yin was wearing his Baltimore Orioles cap and standing by himself posed next to some object or in front of some building.

"It's kind of sad," said Margaret.

"He said that the Chiangs take him someplace every Saturday. It looks like he takes a picture at each one and posts it."

"Don't let your emotions affect how you consider the evidence," Marcus said. "Just because you like him and don't like Victoria doesn't change the facts of the case."

We both nodded and started going through Yin's pictures looking for anything that might connect him to Loki or the pranks. The first was one of him at the Smithsonian's Air and Space Museum standing next to the capsule that carried the Apollo 11 astronauts back from the moon. In the next he posed in front of several rows of bronze sculptures. Each sculpture was of a girl standing at attention but with no head. There were just thirty headless bodies.

"Where's that?" Margaret asked.

"I think it's the Sculpture Garden," I replied. "It's right next to the museum where my mom works."

"It's a sculpture called *Puellae*," said Marcus. "It's by a Polish artist named Magdalena Abakanowicz."

We both gave him a stunned look.

"How on earth do you know that?" asked Margaret.

"Do you remember the part where I'm a special agent with the Art Crime team and have art history degrees from Harvard and Georgetown? I had to actually study to get those."

Margaret and I shared an impressed look.

"Anything else you want to tell us about it?" I asked.

Marcus shrugged and added, "*Puellae* is Latin for 'girls.'"

"It should be Latin for 'creepy sculptures,'" said Margaret. "Sometimes I don't get modern art."

"With some artists, that's the point," said Marcus.

"This one's different from the rest," I said, looking at the next one. He was in a kayak, and unlike in the other shots, he had a genuine smile. It reminded me of when we were in the practice room, because I felt like we were getting a glimpse of the real Yin.

"You can tell he loves it," I said.

"Loves what?" asked Marcus.

"Kayaking," I said, turning the screen toward him. "He told us he loved to go out on a river back home with his dad."

"You think that picture was taken in China?" asked Margaret.

"Not unless Maryland is part of China," I said.

Now I was the one who got the strange looks.

"And you know that because the water looks particularly Marylandish?" asked Marcus.

"No," I said as I double clicked the photo to enlarge it. "But if you check out this water tower in the background, you'll see a picture of a giant crab and a Maryland flag on top."

They looked at the image and both nodded. The crab business was big in Maryland and pictures of crabs were on everything.

"Okay, that's a good eye," said Marcus.

"You're not the only one with skills," I joked.

"There's nothing suspicious on any of Yin's circles or on his bulletin board," said Margaret. "Do you still think he's a suspect?"

"As much as I don't want it to be the case, he has to be," I said. "His locker is next to Lucy's, so he could have easily done the superglue. He's the star of the orchestra, so he could have hacked into Chat Chat from their page. And we know that he used the crawl space to get back by the fire alarm. That's three for three."

"What about motive?" asked Marcus.

"You heard what Moncrieff Tate said," I replied. "The Chiangs think Lucy's jealous and tries to intimidate him."

"But Ms. Allo said she'd never seen any indication of that," Margaret pointed out.

"Am I the only one who thought that sounded weird?" I asked.

"In what way?" asked Margaret.

"She said they'd hardly ever even spoken to each other," I replied. "Even if they're not friends, you'd think that based on the fact that they're the two best musicians in school and both play the same instrument, they'd almost have to talk to each other more than that."

"Unless they're purposefully avoiding each other," said Marcus. "Which fits with the theory that she's jealous of him and wants nothing to do with him."

"She's also the only other person we can connect to all three pranks," I said. "That means we have to look into her, too."

"Really?" said Margaret. "I don't want her to be the one either."

"I thought you had her as suspect number one," I said.

"That was before I knew she told the Megatheriums to kiss off," she replied. "I'm starting to like her more and more."

"Well, her Chat Chat page is almost nonexistent," said Marcus. "There's virtually no activity on it. She's in circles for her classes and the orchestra but doesn't seem active, and the only pictures on her bulletin board are ones that other people have posted and tagged her in."

"That makes sense," I said.

"Why?" asked Margaret.

"She wants to blend into the crowd," I answered. "There are already thousands and thousands of pictures of her online. The last thing she wants is to post one that attracts any commentary from anyone else."

We kept looking until the afternoon bell rang. That's when Marcus gave Margaret and me a ride back to Alice Deal Middle School for the talent show auditions. I took a seat in the auditorium, while she headed backstage.

Three singers, a dance team, and an aspiring magician all tried out before it was her turn. There were three teachers sitting in the second row and when they called out, "Next," Margaret pushed a stand-up piano out to the middle of the stage.

"Margaret Campbell, seventh grade," she said. "I'll be performing a song."

"Which one?" asked Ms. Sipe, the drama teacher.

"'I Haven't Got a Clue,'" answered Margaret.

"You don't know what you're going to sing?" she asked.

It took Margaret a second to understand the confusion.

"No." She laughed. "'I Haven't Got a Clue' is the name of the song."

"I'm not familiar with that one."

"It's an original composition," Margaret announced. "This is its world premiere."

All three teachers smiled at this.

She started playing and seemed a little nervous at first. I don't think she did it as well as when we were in the practice room, but she was still good, and when she finished there was genuine applause.

"Very nice," said an eighth-grade English teacher.

"Thank you," said Margaret.

"You wrote that?" asked Ms. Sipe.

"Yes, ma'am. I'm sorry, I stumbled in a few places there."

"That's okay," she replied. "I like it very much, but I think I have a suggestion that might help."

"I'd love to hear it," said Margaret.

"I think it's a duet."

The other two nodded their agreement.

"What do you mean?"

"The song is about friendship," she explained. "But it's sung by one person. If it was a duet, then the friendship would come alive in the performance as well as within the lyrics."

"Do you know anyone who might be able to sing it with you?" asked another teacher.

Margaret smiled, turned to the audience, and looked right at me.

"I think I have an idea."

22.

Tai Shan

THE NEXT MORNING WHEN WE GOT TO SCHOOL we went straight to Yin's locker. It was right next to the empty ones that once belonged to Lucy and Victoria. While everyone else got ready for class, we tried to picture how the first prank could have unfolded.

"They're all distracted getting books and talking to friends," Margaret said. "So even with people around, he could've easily stood here and squirted glue into both of those without attracting any attention."

"Then he closes his locker and heads that way," I say, motioning toward the other three that were ruined. "They're all in a straight line. It would have taken ten, maybe fifteen seconds at the most."

We considered this for a moment and then she turned to me and gave me a slightly worried look. "Are we thinking it's him?"

I shrugged, but before I could answer, a voice startled us from behind.

"Is something wrong?"

We turned to see that it was Mrs. Chiang, who had a suspicious if not outright accusatory look. I had worked out something to say in case we bumped into Yin, but I hadn't expected her. Luckily, Margaret was (as always) quick on her feet.

"We're waiting for Yin," she said. "We're supposed to meet him tomorrow at the zoo and wanted to arrange a time."

"Oh yes, he mentioned that," she said, seemingly accepting this explanation. "Yin's not here today. He has a dress rehearsal at the Kennedy Center. But we can meet you tomorrow at noon. At the front entrance."

"Sounds great," said Margaret. "See you there."

We started walking away but she lingered at the locker for a moment, maybe trying to piece together what we might have been doing. Margaret and I stopped near the entrance to the library.

"I'll be honest," she said. "That woman scares me."

"Maybe that's why Yin doesn't have any friends," I joked. "Because she scares them all away."

"You're kidding, but there may be some truth to that."

"Let's check the trophy case to see if the smudge is back," I said.

I took a step, but Margaret clutched my arm and stopped me. "Not now," she said. "I think she may be watching us."

Sure enough, I looked up and saw that Mrs. Chiang was standing in the hallway next to the door to her class as if she were welcoming her students for the day. But she was looking right at us.

We locked eyes and she gave us a smile. It was not at all warm or friendly. Still, we smiled back and waved.

"Okay," I said as we walked away. "She kind of scares me, too."

"If she stands out there like that between classes, then she should have seen who messed with the lockers," Margaret said.

I nodded and replied, "Maybe she did and doesn't want to tell."

I didn't say it out loud, but Yin was moving up my suspect list. Becca and Lucy were also at the rehearsal, which meant that the only prime suspect at Chatham was Victoria, and she might as well have been absent. I think her grandfather must have warned her about us because suddenly she and her friends treated us like we were completely radioactive. No fake smiles to me. No pleas for Margaret to transfer schools. No room for either one of us at lunch.

Despite days of steady progress and the feeling that we were on the verge of a breakthrough, the week was ending with a thud. Even though I don't believe in the concept of bad luck, it seemed fitting that it was Friday the thirteenth.

"You know what the worst part about today is?" I asked as we sat down at a cafeteria table by ourselves.

"This food?" she answered, plopping her tray on the table.

"Okay, that *is* pretty bad," I agreed when I saw her tray of mystery meat swimming in gravy with carrot slices. "But I was talking about the fact that today's the last day of Tanner's suspension. I really thought we'd solve the case before he came back to school. I didn't think I'd have to face him again."

"You'll be fine," she assured me. "He's not going to do anything to you."

"I wish I felt as certain about that as you," I said. "Although, if you've noticed, the pranks have stopped while he's been away from campus."

"So you think he might be the one behind it all?"

"Wouldn't you rather it be him than Yin?" I said.

We sat quietly for a moment before she asked, "So have you given it any thought yet?"

"What?" I mumbled as I swallowed a bite of my turkey sandwich. "How badly he's going to beat me up?"

"No," she answered. "Have you thought about singing with me in the talent show?"

"You were serious about that?"

"Of course I was. Ms. Sipe said it should be a duet, and since the song's about you and me, it seems like a natural fit for us to perform it."

"Except for one important detail," I pointed out. "I can't sing. I'm total rubbish."

"You were in the chorus at your old school," she said. "And your mom told me you had a beautiful voice."

"Of course she said that. She's my mom. She also hung my crayon drawings on the wall like they were masterpieces. You can't really trust her analysis of my artistic endeavors."

"Well, it wouldn't feel right to sing it with anybody else," she said with a sigh. "Forget about it. I just won't do it."

"Don't do that," I pleaded.

"What?"

"Don't make me feel guilty."

"I'm not trying to make you feel guilty," she said. "Although, if you *do* feel guilty, that might be your conscience telling you something. I think there's a term for that."

"A guilty conscience?"

"That's it," she said. "I wonder what the cure is for that."

"I seriously am a terrible singer," I protested.

"Apparently your mother, and now your conscience, disagree." She gave me one of her patented looks and I knew it was pointless to resist.

"Fine," I said. "I'll *think* about it." (I stressed the word "think" to minimize my level of commitment.)

"Really?" she asked. "And you're not just saying that? You'll really consider doing it?"

"Yes. I will very seriously consider making a fool of myself in front of the entire school by singing a duet with you in the talent show."

She beamed. "I'll teach you the song this afternoon."

"Sounds wonderful," I said. "Now, is there anything else my conscience and I can do for you?"

"If you feel guilty about my lunch, I wouldn't mind half of your sandwich."

I handed it to her and she smiled.

"Thank you, Florian," she said. "This means a lot to me."

"Yeah, well, it's just turkey and cheese."

"I wasn't talking about the sandwich."

I looked up from my meal and smiled. "I know."

After school we went into one of the practice rooms so she could play the song for me a few times. I wasn't ready to belt it out in that environment quite yet, so I just got the tune down and started memorizing the words when I got home. I gave my first full-throated attempt the next morning while I took my shower.

It wasn't pretty, but it could have been worse. I practiced it a few more times before she came over and we left for the zoo. We were standing by one of the lion statues at the entrance when I turned to her and asked, "So how are we going to do this? Alternate parts or sing harmony?"

It took her a second to get what I was saying. "Does that mean you're going to do the talent show?"

"Yes," I said. "I'm going to make a total fool of myself because you're my best friend."

Her grin alone made it worthwhile.

"I think the best approach would be for one of us to sing the first verse, the other to sing the second verse, and then both of us sing the third one together," she offered.

"And what do I do while you're sitting at the piano playing? Do I get a chair or something?"

"I thought maybe you could perform some sort of interpretive dance."

"Okay, I'm out!"

"I'm joking," she replied. "You can either sit next to me on the bench or stand by the piano. Wherever you feel most comfortable."

"Well, I'd feel most comfortable in the audience watching someone else sing," I said. "But we can work with one of those."

She gave me a hug and said, "This is going to be great, Florian. I mean it. You're going to thank me afterward."

A few minutes later Yin arrived with Mr. and Mrs. Chiang. She was much friendlier here than I'd ever seen her at school, and greeted us like old friends. It was hard to believe she was the same woman who'd given us the evil eye the day before. Her husband was a little stiff, although he seemed happy we were there too. Yin told us he worked in the embassy's press office.

"So these are Yin's friends who I hear so much about?" he said as he shook our hands.

"Nice to meet you," Margaret said.

"I'm Florian," I added.

"So what do you want to see?" Margaret asked Yin.

"Everything," he said. "I love the zoo."

First we walked along the Asia Trail. The Chiangs stayed back to give us some space but kept close enough to hear what we were talking about. I couldn't tell if they were overly cautious or outright suspicious of Margaret and me. I wondered if Mrs. Chiang had told her husband she'd caught us snooping around Yin's locker.

"How was the audition?" Yin asked as we watched a sloth bear pull apart an orange with his long curved claws.

"I don't know," she said. "I think I did okay."

"She was terrific," I said.

"So you made it?" he asked, excited.

"I've got a callback next week," she explained. "But I think there's a good chance." Then she leaned toward him and whispered, "Even better, Florian's agreed to sing with me."

Yin beamed. "I didn't know you could sing."

"That's because I can't," I answered. "But apparently you don't necessarily need talent to be in the talent show."

We reached the clouded leopard exhibit and Yin said, "I don't see them. Maybe they're inside."

It took a moment, but I spotted one of them lying in the corner and blending in against the rocks. "There's one," I said, pointing.

"And there's the other," said Margaret. "You can just see a leg and tail poking out from behind that tree."

"You two are good at that," said Yin. "If I get lost in a jungle, I hope you're with me. I forget, what's the English word again for hiding like that?"

"Camouflage," I said.

"That's it," he said. "Wouldn't it be great if we could all camouflage like that?"

I've lived in countries where I have to speak a second language, so I know that phrases don't always match up like you intend. But what he said seemed odd to me. I wondered why he wanted to be able to camouflage. Was he tired of always being under the watchful eye of the Chiangs? Did he feel like people were always looking at him because of his musical talents? It reminded me of when Lucy Mays talked about the anonymity of auditioning for an orchestra behind a screen. They may not have been friends, but it seemed like they both had that in common.

"Let's go see the pandas," Yin said as he tugged a little on his Baltimore Orioles cap. "They're the pride of the embassy."

The giant pandas at the National Zoo actually belong to the Chinese government. They are on loan to the people of America as an offering of friendship and are by far the most popular attraction at the zoo. The panda house has indoor and outdoor viewing areas as well as an around-the-clock panda cam you can watch online. We stood on the outside deck watching one climb a tree for a while and then got in line to go inside.

"Let me take a picture of you two," Margaret said while we waited.

I leaned next to Yin and we both flashed smiles while she snapped a shot with her phone.

"Mr. Chiang, will you take one of the three of us?" she asked. But when she turned, we realized that the Chiangs were still on the deck watching the panda in the tree.

"I guess they want to stay out here," I said.

This surprised Yin and he called to them, "Is this okay? Can we go inside?"

"Yes, yes, have fun," said Mr. Chiang. "We'll wait here."

"It's good that you're with me," he said with a conspiratorial whisper. "Normally they don't let me out of their sight."

While we waited in line we talked about Yin's travels around Washington.

"So every Saturday you go someplace around town?" Margaret said.

"Yes," he said. "Sometimes it's a museum. Other times it's a park. And once a month we go to Maryland, where they own a . . . what's the word, like a house but smaller . . . ?"

"A cottage?" said Margaret.

"That's it," he replied. "They have a cottage on Chesapeake Bay."

"What do you do there?" I asked.

"I like to go out in a kayak and think about music," he said. "I also like the doughnuts."

"Doughnuts?"

"There's a bakery on the corner near the house that's amazing."

Five minutes later we were inside the panda house. It was dark and there were so many people by the glass, we couldn't see the pandas at first. We waited our turn and when we got to the front we were just opposite a cub playing with a ball.

"He's so cute," said Margaret as she took a picture.

"Why don't I take one of you and Yin?" I suggested.

"That'd be great," she said.

"And you'll send it to me?" asked Yin.

"Of course," she replied.

She handed me the phone and Margaret threw a friendly arm around Yin. He took off his baseball cap and ran his fingers through his hair before the two of them smiled and posed so that the cub was in the picture too.

I snapped two quick shots and a man next to me asked, "You want one of all three of you?"

"That'd be great," I said.

He was young and Asian-American, his black hair short and spiky, and his clothes were fairly hipster. He looked like a college student. I handed him the phone and posed next to Yin and Margaret.

"Closer," he signaled, motioning with his hands for us to scrunch together more. "Perfect."

He took a couple of pictures, but when Margaret reached to get her phone, he pulled it back.

"You remind me of this panda, Yin," he said.

It took a second for me to realize that he'd called Yin by name.

"How do you know who he is?" I asked, suddenly suspicious.

"Yin Yae is a gift to the people of America," he said, reciting one of the quotes I had read about him. "He's like the panda, on display for everyone to enjoy, but still very much owned by the Chinese government."

"Give me back my phone," demanded Margaret.

"It doesn't have to be that way," he said, speaking directly to Yin. "You don't have to end up like Tai Shan. You can stay. You can become a symbol for freedom."

Yin angrily responded in Chinese, motioning to us while he did.

"Are they really your friends, Yin?"

Reflexively, we both stepped between them. "Yes, we are," I said. "Now give us back the phone or we'll call the police."

He studied us for a moment and then held the phone out. Margaret snatched it from him and when he started to walk away she called out, "Wait."

He stopped and turned. "What?"

"Say cheese." She snapped a picture of him.

He angrily stepped toward her but she just started dialing.

"I'm calling 911," she said.

He walked away and melted into the crowd of tourists. When we turned back to Yin, he was trembling.

"Don't worry, Yin," said Margaret. "We never would have let him hurt you."

23.

The Daily Dragon

IT HAPPENED SO QUICKLY I WASN'T QUITE SURE what to make of it all. First we were posing for a picture. Then a stranger was getting in Yin's face. And before we knew it the man was gone. Even what he said seemed confusing. It sounded kind of like advice but felt a lot more like a threat.

It certainly rattled Yin.

He was still shaken when we sat on a bench against the back wall of the panda exhibit. Margaret and I were on either side of him, keeping a lookout in case the man returned.

"Are you okay?" I asked.

"Yes, just surprised," he said. "And a little embarrassed."

"He should be embarrassed, not you," said Margaret. "What was that even about?"

"For some people I am a symbol of my government," he said. "They don't like the government, so they don't like me."

"That's ridiculous," she told him. "You're a thirteen-year-old musical prodigy, not a politician."

"Yes, but they see me as a Chinese prodigy, and that's all that matters to them."

"Who's Tai Shan?" I asked. "That man mentioned something about you not having to be like him. Is he a musician too?"

"No. Tai Shan is a panda," he said with a little laugh. "He was born here at the zoo and was very popular but the government demanded he be returned to China. People begged for him to stay, but they refused and he's there now."

"In what way could you be like that?" asked Margaret.

"I am here by permission of my government," he explained. "I have to go wherever they want me to. I have no choice."

I was again reminded that Yin's life was more complex than I could have imagined.

"Come on," I said, signaling toward the entrance, against the flow of people. "Let's go out this way, in case he's waiting by the exit."

"Good idea," said Margaret.

As we got up to leave Yin suddenly panicked. "Wait! Where's my cap?"

At some point during the confusion he'd dropped his Baltimore Orioles hat.

"I need my cap," he insisted.

"There it is," Margaret said in a calm voice. She pointed back to where we'd posed for the picture and it was there on the floor pushed up against the window. She squeezed her way through the crowd and picked it up.

"Here you go," she said as she brushed it off and handed it to him. "Good as new."

"Thank you," he replied, clutching the bill tightly. "This means a lot to me."

When we got back outside we told the Chiangs about our encounter with the man.

"Florian and Margaret were very brave," Yin told them. "They stepped between us and made him leave."

"Thank you so much," Mrs. Chiang said, putting a friendly hand on my shoulder.

"Of course," I replied.

"Here's his picture," said Margaret, showing them the photo she'd taken on her phone.

Mr. Chiang's lips tightened and turned white. "I recognize

him. I don't know his name, but he's a reporter with the *Daily Dragon*."

Mrs. Chiang scoffed and gave a sour look.

"What's the *Daily Dragon*?" asked Margaret.

"An online newspaper," he replied. "They're very critical of our government and embassy. They're always looking for ways to embarrass us. That's one of the reasons we're so protective of Yin."

"We shouldn't have let you go in without us there," added his wife.

"No, it was okay," said Yin.

"Can you send me that picture?" Mr. Chiang asked Margaret.

"Here," she said, handing him the phone. "Just put in your number."

For about a minute the three of them spoke only Chinese. When they were done, Yin turned to us. "Thank you two so much for meeting me here today. Despite what happened at the end, I had a very good time. But I think we need to go back home."

"That's a good idea," I answered. "We can do this again. Next Saturday maybe."

Yin smiled weakly. "That would be nice."

"You two are good friends to Yin," said Mrs. Chiang. "He is lucky to know you."

"Yes," agreed her husband.

"Thanks," we replied.

After they left, Margaret and I wandered around for about twenty minutes looking to see if there was any sign of the reporter. Then we sent a message to Marcus about it and he told us to wait for him in front of the zoo on Connecticut Avenue.

Although he normally drove his hybrid, this time he arrived in the passenger seat of a big SUV with two bicycles in a rack on the roof. Margaret and I both had the same reaction when we saw who was driving.

"Kayla!" we said, thrilled to see her.

Kayla was an FBI agent and had been my instructor at the Quantico training center. She was part kindergarten teacher, part ninja warrior, all awesome. She was always smiling and bubbly yet could disarm a bad guy with a lightning-quick mixture of martial arts and gymnastics. And while they'd never actually admitted it, Margaret and I were convinced that Marcus and Kayla had started dating. Their arrival together was another clue in that direction.

"Hey, guys," she said with her perpetual cheerfulness.

"I hope we didn't interrupt something," said Margaret.

"Just a little bike ride along the Fletcher Loop," she said.

"What counts as little?" I asked.

"Thirty-seven miles," Marcus said, looking like he was about to pass out.

"Yeah, it's probably good that you called," she said. "I don't know how much farther he could have gone."

"I can ride as far as you," he said to her, sounding like he was trying to convince himself this was true.

"It's cute that you believe that," she said as Margaret and I laughed.

"Just get in the backseat."

We hopped in and Kayla drove us to the Hoover Building, which is FBI Headquarters. Since it was a Saturday, the fifth floor was mostly quiet as we walked over to Marcus's office. Although he was the leader of our Special Projects Team, his primary job was still as a special agent in the Art Crime division.

He slumped down on the couch and started rubbing his calves. Margaret and I shot a quick look at Kayla and she just smiled.

In the car we'd given them a basic rundown of what happened, but now Marcus wanted us to go through it blow by blow.

"Start with your arrival at the zoo," he said. "Did you see the reporter earlier?"

"No," I replied. "He just walked up behind me and offered to take the picture."

"How'd he know that Yin was going to be there?" wondered Kayla.

"That's exactly what I'd like to know," said Marcus.

"I don't know how he could've," I said.

"Maybe it's just a coincidence," suggested Margaret.

Marcus gave her a look. "You know what I think about coincidences," he said. "They're always a possibility, but almost never what really happens. You say you got a picture of him?"

"Yes," said Margaret. She pulled it up on her phone and handed it to him. He stood up gingerly and sort of limp-walked over to the desk.

"No commentary," he said as we all tried to suppress the urge to laugh.

"None needed," replied Kayla. "Your brisk pace provides all the necessary commentary."

"What are you going to do?" I asked as he logged in to his computer. "Run his picture through facial recognition software?" (I loved the high-tech equipment he got to use at the Hoover Building and was always excited to see it in action.)

"I could do that," he said. "But, you know, it's probably a lot easier if we just check the *Daily Dragon* website and look at the staff page. If he's one of their reporters, I'm sure they've got a picture of him."

"I guess that would work too," I said unenthusiastically.

It took him only about thirty seconds before he found what he was looking for. "Henry Lu," he said, reading the caption from a picture. "This look like the guy?"

He turned the monitor so we could see it.

"That's him," I said.

"Definitely," said Margaret.

"Good to know," he replied. "I'll share the info with some of our guys and we'll figure out a way to communicate it to the Chinese embassy without ruining your cover."

"I don't think you have to worry about that," I said. "Mr. Chiang works at the embassy and I'm sure he's giving them all the information."

"Good," he said. "I'll still follow up."

"What should we do about it?" I asked.

He gave me a look. "Nothing. You're still on the Chatham case. This is information that we'll pass along, but it's not anything you should worry about."

He could tell I was disappointed.

"I mean it, Florian," he said firmly.

"Okay," I replied. "I understand."

"Speaking of the Chatham case," he continued. "Why don't you update me on the status? Any closer to identifying our prankster?"

"We're still where we were the other day," I said. "Yesterday was a bust but we should be able to figure out a lot on the field trip Monday."

"That is, if Florian doesn't have to spend the whole day hiding from Tanner Caldwell," said Margaret.

I gave her a look, but it was nothing like the one that Marcus gave me.

"Who's Tanner Caldwell?" he asked.

"You have a big mouth sometimes," I said to her.

"Who's Tanner Caldwell?" he repeated a little more forcefully.

I told him all about my run-ins with Tanner, mentioned the fact that he was Senator Caldwell's son, and recounted the story about him copying off my test and getting suspended. He wasn't happy that I hadn't told him, although his disappointment was counterbalanced by how I got my revenge.

Once we were done, Kayla gave us a ride home and Margaret and I went into the Underground to study the caseboard. We had five people we considered potential suspects:

Becca, Victoria, Tanner, Lucy, and Yin. We also thought there was a good chance it was a member—or members—of the Megatherium Club who we didn't even know. But after about twenty minutes of running through them all, I found myself over at the computer looking up someone else.

"What are you looking for?" asked Margaret.

"Henry Lu," I said.

"As in the guy that Marcus very specifically told us not to investigate?" she replied.

"I'm not investigating him," I said. "I'm just curious why he would treat Yin like that. And since Yin's a suspect, it's relevant to our case."

She gave me a look but I just ignored it.

Instead I looked through an archive of his articles. He'd written several about Yin, including a large one called "Prodigy or Propaganda?" that was particularly unfair. But his most common topic was a group called the West Lake Five.

"Who are they?" asked Margaret.

"Five journalists who were imprisoned for writing negative articles about corruption in the Chinese government."

"So in other words absolutely nothing to do with Yin or our case."

"The Theory of All *Small* Things," I said. "You never know where you'll find some TOAST."

She laughed. "That's my cue to leave. I'll see you tomorrow."

"Sounds good," I said.

"Speaking of sounds good," she replied. "We need to practice our song for the talent show some."

"We can squeeze a little in tomorrow," I said.

She headed up the stairs to leave and I started reading. It was going to be a long night.

24.

Field Trip

"UGH," I SAID, SHAKING MY HEAD IN DISBELIEF. "This is a total nightmare."

"You're looking at it all wrong," Margaret replied, trying to put a positive spin on the situation. "Just embrace it. What was it you told me that time? The things that make us different are the things that make us great?"

"Yeah, well, if that's true, then my clothes are making me absolutely amazing right now."

Since we were going to the symphony, and in my experience you're supposed to dress up for that, I came to school in a navy blue blazer and herringbone tie. Both Italian. Both stylish. Both completely inappropriate considering all the

other seventh and eighth graders were wearing identical out-
fits of khaki pants with a school polo shirt. Even Margaret,
who like me didn't have a Chatham uniform, came pretty
close to matching with khakis and a maroon blouse.

"How'd you know what color to wear?" I asked.

"It's all over the school," she said. "Logos, jerseys, the
giant maroon sign on the stadium saying, 'You're now entering Cougar Country.'"

"Pretty big clues," I admitted. "You'd think someone who
fancied himself a detective might have picked up on them."

"You're just not used to American sense of style," she said.
"We're pretty casual on this side of the Atlantic. But don't
worry about it, people probably won't notice that much."

This of course was a lie, because almost everybody did a
double take as we walked to the bus loop. There were four
buses in total, and since we were assigned to them alphabet-
ically, Margaret and I were on the one in front.

Unfortunately, so was Tanner, who was now back from
his suspension and ready to renew his role as my personal
tormentor. He came up behind me while we were waiting to
get on board.

"It's good that you're dressed for a funeral," he whispered
in my ear. "Because you're going to be the guest of honor at
one real soon."

I turned to him and tried not to have my voice quiver when I responded, "What do you want, Tanner?"

"You know what I want," he said. "Just a chance to teach you a little lesson."

I could tell that Margaret was about to jump in, but before she did, another voice interrupted. It was deep and authoritative.

"Is there a problem?"

I couldn't believe my eyes. It was Marcus, only he was dressed like everybody else in khakis and a Chatham polo.

"Who are you?" asked Tanner.

"Substitute teacher," he answered. "They asked me to chaperone. Told me to look out for some punk who's about to get kicked off the lacrosse team for good. Any idea who that might be?"

Suddenly, Tanner didn't seem quite as tough as he did before.

"So I ask again," Marcus continued. "Is there a problem here?"

"No," he replied.

"Good," said Marcus. "Keep it that way."

He turned to me and, maintaining the cover that he was a substitute, acted as if we'd never met. "What's your name?"

"Florian Bates."

"I like the coat and tie, Florian," he replied. "You wear it well."

He gave me a wink and I smiled back. "Thanks."

Margaret and I found a seat together in the middle of the bus. I got the evil eye and an "accidental" bump from Tanner as he headed for the back, but that was as bad as it got. Marcus sat in the front next to Ms. Curtis, our algebra teacher. I noticed his seat gave him a clear angle on the mirror so he could keep an eye on things without being obvious.

"Forget about Tanner," whispered Margaret. "Work the case. If someone wants to prank Lucy, doing it in front of a crowd at the Kennedy Center would maximize her embarrassment."

I nodded and tried to focus.

We rode the bus for about thirty minutes and I tried to organize the last week in my head. The mystery kept taking surprising turns. First it was about pranks. Then we discovered a secret society. And now there was even a secondary case involving international politics. Add to that my issues with Tanner and it's no wonder my thinking was a mess.

"That looks exactly how my brain feels," I said when we reached the traffic jam of school buses in front of the Kennedy Center. There were dozens of them from across the district and Northern Virginia. "Total congestion."

"Just take the clues one bus at a time," she replied. "They're all there. You just have to get them to line up."

Unlike the crazy quilt of vehicles in front of it, the Kennedy Center was sleek and modern, a massive marble building with a flat overhanging roof held up by slim gold pillars.

"Make sure you remember which bus is yours," a teacher reminded us as we exited. "It'll be parked right here when the concert's over."

Because of the concert schedule we had to eat first, even though it was only ten thirty. Schools were assigned lunch zones and I noticed that Chatham got one of the best spots on the giant terrace overlooking the river. This may have been coincidence, but it seemed like the kids at Chatham always ended up with the best of things.

Margaret and I stood by the railing looking out at the Potomac while I ate my salami sandwich and we discussed the case.

"Imagine we're playing Capital Crimes," she said.

"This is not going to be another story about how you almost beat me the other day, is it?"

"No, it's just an exercise," she said. "Although I did almost beat you."

I gave her a look.

"Just imagine we're playing and it's your turn," she said.

"You've got to give it your best guess. Who do you think is guilty?"

I ran through the suspects in my head. "Becca."

She nodded. "Why?"

"She has the best motive," I explained. "She asked Lucy to join the Megatherium Club and was embarrassed when she got rejected. She also has the computer skills necessary to crash the server."

"And she was in the practice room, so she could have easily crawled through the passageway to pull the fire alarm."

"About that," I said. "I don't think she would have done that."

"Why not?"

"It's really dusty and dirty in there," I said. "And she's a germophobe. She uses hand sanitizer nonstop. I just don't see her crawling through that."

"Okay," said Margaret. "What about Victoria? She had motive because she got passed over for the Megatheriums. And her locker was right next to Lucy's."

"True," I answered. "But she didn't have access to the orchestra's page on Chat Chat and she was in the cafeteria when the fire alarm was pulled. Besides, if we're going off the people with a locker next to Lucy, Yin is a stronger candidate."

We turned back away from the river and looked toward the terrace full of students. It stretched as long as a couple football fields and a cool breeze came up off the water.

"What are we missing?" I asked. "What pulls it all together?"

I saw Tanner standing about twenty-five feet from us. He was with Victoria and her friends. I wondered if it could have been all of them working together. They broke rules for everything from dress code to cheating. I'm sure they thought they could get away with whatever they wanted. I absently munched on a chip as I ran through it in my head.

And that's when I noticed someone walking inside the long hallway that stretched along the terrace.

"Where's Marcus?" I asked urgently.

"Over there, keeping his eye on Tanner," she replied, pointing toward him.

I hurried over.

"What's going on?" she asked, trying to catch up with me.

"I need to speak with you," I said when I reached him.

"What's wrong?" he asked.

"Just follow me. I need to be sure."

I kept a quick pace striding through the different school groups and trying to keep track of the man in the hall. The entire wall was made up of giant windows and glass doors so even though he was inside, I could see him clearly. Marcus and Margaret were right behind me.

Finally I stopped when we were close to him. He was alone, looking around as if he wanted to make sure no one saw him.

"Okay, can you tell me what's up?"

I motioned inside the building and asked, "Why is Henry Lu here?"

25.

Red, White, and Blue
(*Hóng Bái Lán*)

IT WAS A TRICKY SITUATION BECAUSE WE COULDN'T just go up to Henry Lu and demand to know what he was doing there. After all, we were undercover as two exchange students and a substitute teacher. We didn't have any authority. Still, Marcus got word to the security staff and they followed up on it. Lu told them he'd gotten a press pass to cover the concert so he could write about it in the *Daily Dragon*. A call to the Kennedy Center press office confirmed this.

"I still think he might be up to something," I said to Marcus. "He's written at least seven articles about Yin, and they're all negative."

"Seven?" said Marcus. "That's a pretty specific number.

You do remember the part where I told you not to investigate him. You're only supposed to be looking into the pranks at Chatham, not Henry Lu."

"I wasn't investigating . . . *him*," I replied. "I was just reading about Yin to see if there was anything I could learn that might help with the case I am working on."

Marcus gave me a dubious look but he let it pass.

"I'll worry about Lu," he said. "You stick with the pranks at Chatham."

"Right," I said.

"I mean it, Florian."

"So do I," I replied. "I'll stick with the pranks."

After we finished lunch we all filed into the concert hall. It was stunningly beautiful. The brochure I picked up in the hallway said it held nearly twenty-five hundred people, and the lower level was packed. There were three balconies that ringed the edge of the auditorium and a special presidential box for the first family that appeared to be empty. Although I wondered if Lucy's mom had come down to listen to the concert but was staying out of sight until it began.

Because Yin was one of our classmates and he was the star of the show, Chatham got prime seating. We filed into rows ten and eleven. It took me a couple minutes to find Henry Lu sitting five rows in front of us along the aisle.

"Look," I said, pointing him out to Margaret. "I wonder what he's up to."

Before I could say something else, someone flicked me hard in the back of the head.

"Where's your guardian angel, Alice?"

I turned to see that Tanner was sitting directly behind me. He went to flick me again, this time in the face, but I reached up and grabbed his finger. I gave it a firm squeeze and started twisting it, a little trick Kayla had taught me at Quantico. It seemed to get his attention.

"I don't need a guardian angel to outsmart you," I said as forcefully as I could, all the while continuing to twist his finger. "There's no doubt you could beat me up if you wanted to. But I've got some bad news. I'll heal quickly, but ten years from now you're still going to be dumb as an ox."

Margaret just started laughing and Tanner grimaced in pain as I continued twisting his middle finger.

"Let go," he said through gritted teeth.

"Do we understand each other?" I asked him.

"Let . . . go."

"I asked you a question, and I made it simple so you could follow. Do we understand each other?"

"Yes," he gasped.

"Wonderful," I replied as I released his finger and he

recoiled back in his seat. "Now stop bugging me. I'm here to enjoy the concert."

For the first time I noticed that some of the kids around him were watching our little exchange and now he was the one they were snickering about.

"Nice," Margaret said under her breath as I turned back around. She gave me a little fist bump down low where no one else could see it. It felt good but I wondered if I'd just stirred up the hornet's nest. I could just imagine him kicking me in the back of the head halfway through the concert.

Even though they were behind the curtain, we could hear the orchestra tuning their instruments.

"I love this part," said Margaret, savoring it. "It's like you can hear a storm coming."

That's when I noticed an empty seat. "Wait a second. Where'd he go?"

"Who?" answered Margaret.

"Henry Lu," I said. "He's gone."

"Think he moved up to a better seat?" she asked.

"He was in the fifth row," I replied. "What could be better than that?"

I scanned the room and didn't see him anywhere. I didn't see Marcus, either. I wanted to get word to him so I sent him a quick text that said Lu had gone. Before I could come up with anything else, the tuning stopped, the lights dimmed, and the curtain rose.

The audience clapped when they saw the musicians. Lucy was sitting in the front row with the rest of the cello section, and Becca was a couple rows back and on the other side with the flutes.

"Where's Yin?" I asked, a little panicked.

"He's the soloist, so they'll give him a separate introduction," whispered Margaret.

"Oh," I said. "That's cool."

The conductor walked out to his podium. He was tall and lanky, his longish gray hair slightly unkempt. He turned to the audience and smiled warmly.

"Welcome, my name is Roger Samuel," he said. "My two favorite things are music and young people. It has been my good fortune to spend most of my adult life working with both. And in all that time, I've never met anyone quite like the young man I am about to introduce to you. Whether he's playing the cello or composing a concerto, he makes the world more beautiful with his music. It's my honor and privilege to present to you today's composer and soloist, Yin Yae."

Yin strode out toward center stage carrying his cello

and there was a nice round of applause, especially from the Chatham section of the auditorium.

"Thank you," he said from the podium. "I know you came to hear us play and not to hear me talk, but I want to take a moment to thank everyone with the orchestra for this opportunity. We are going to play three compositions today. Their names are 'Red,' 'White,' and 'Blue.' Or as we say in Mandarin, '*Hóng*,' '*Bái*,' and '*Lán*.' They were inspired by my time in this lovely country. I hope you enjoy them."

There was more applause as Yin moved to his soloist's position in front of the violins. The conductor stood up at the podium, checked to make sure everyone was ready, and then lifted his baton.

The music was amazing. The fact that it was performed by students my age and a little older was impressive. The fact that it had all been composed by Yin was extraordinary. Now I understood what everybody meant when they said he was unlike anyone they'd met before. I loved watching his expression while he played. His concentration was impossible to miss. The same went for Lucy and Becca. Seeing them like this gave me an entirely different perception of who they were.

"What do you think?" I whispered to Margaret.

"Spellbinding," she said, and it was not an exaggeration.

It was so good it pushed the mystery out of my mind. I

just lost myself in the music. I didn't think about the pranks or Henry Lu. I didn't worry about Tanner or the Megatherium Club. I just listened.

I know that Margaret saw a similarity between what I did with mysteries and what Yin did with music, but to me there was none. I saw things that other people didn't, and I recognized that that had a certain value. But Yin created something that would otherwise not exist. And that was unique. Like the conductor said, he made the world more beautiful than it would have been without him.

Applause filled the concert hall when they finished the first composition, which ended with a very dramatic run of string music and timpani drums. I could even hear Tanner clapping behind me.

"Wow," said Margaret. "Just wow."

Yin stood up and took a bow and there was more applause. I was so happy for him. He motioned to the conductor, who handed him the microphone.

"That was 'Red,'" he told us. "We are going to take a brief intermission and when we come back we will play 'White' and 'Blue.' Thank you so much for your generous reaction."

He handed the microphone back to the conductor and strode off the stage.

With the performance temporarily on hold, I reverted

to mystery mode. I checked and saw that Henry Lu's seat was still empty. He'd left before the first note was played and never returned. I couldn't figure out what he was up to. Why bother coming down if he wasn't even going to listen to the music? Everyone headed out to the hallway for intermission and I looked for Marcus without any luck.

The fear was that the next prank would happen during the performance so Margaret and I wanted to keep an eye on Victoria and Tanner. Victoria's group still gave us the cold shoulder, but as far as we could tell they were all there in a cluster talking. Tanner, meanwhile, had disappeared into the crowd. The part of me that didn't want to deal with him was pleased by this development. The detective part was not.

"Okay, Yin's performance was number one for the day," Margaret said when we were off by ourselves. "But your smackdown of Tanner was a close second. I'm so proud of you."

I grinned. "It was pretty good, wasn't it? I just couldn't have you come to my rescue again."

My phone buzzed and I looked down to see a message from Marcus.

"What is it?"

"Marcus wants us to meet him down by the stage."

"Why?" she asked.

I shrugged. "I don't know. He just said to meet him there."

We went back into the auditorium and headed toward the stage. There were students everywhere and a low roar of talking filled the room. We saw Marcus down in front on the left-hand side.

"Excuse us," I said as we tried to work our way through a crowd of middle schoolers.

As we got closer I could read his expression. He had that laser-focus look that surfaced when it was time for action.

"Something's wrong," Margaret said when she saw it too.

"Yes, it is," I replied.

I was less polite as we pushed through the last groups until we broke free. Finally we reached him and he led us to a door to the backstage area.

"What's the matter?" I asked.

"Just wait," he said.

He closed the door behind us and made sure we were alone. We were in a small hallway with two doors and an elevator.

"What's wrong?" I asked more forcefully.

"Yin," he said. "He's vanished."

26.

The Unfinished Symphony

UNLIKE THE CONCERT HALL, THE BACKSTAGE AREA was anything but elegant. Instead of marble hallways and plush carpet, there were cinder-block walls and concrete floors. Metal cabinets, wooden lockers, and large black travel cases on wheels filled most rooms. And as we followed Marcus we had to snake our way through the "piano garage," where three grand pianos were arranged like interlocking puzzle pieces.

Finally we reached a dressing room with Yin's name written on a piece of tape stuck to the door. Marcus knocked quickly but didn't wait for a response before entering.

"Excuse me, but you'll need to keep out of here," said a voice from within.

It was the conductor, and before Marcus could respond, a woman spoke up.

"No, he's supposed to be here," she said.

I stepped into the room and saw that it was Malena Sanchez from Lucy's Secret Service team. Also in the room were Lucy and Mrs. Chiang. Both looked upset. Margaret shut the door behind us once we were all in.

"This is Special Agent Marcus Rivers of the FBI," continued Malena. "I've asked him to take over the scene. The FBI's much better equipped for this than the Secret Service."

Once everyone was satisfied with Marcus being in the room, they turned their attention to Margaret and me. Malena almost blew our cover when she said, "And these two are—"

"Friends of Yin's," interrupted Marcus. "They were with him this past weekend when he had a threatening encounter with a man who was in attendance today. Margaret is my niece and told me about it. I've asked them to come so they might be able to shed some light on what is obviously a fluid situation."

"He was here today?" Mrs. Chiang asked us. "The man from the *Daily Dragon*?"

"Yes, ma'am," I said. "He was seated in the fifth row, but he got up and left before the concert even began."

"Maybe he came backstage to hurt Yin," she suggested.

"Let's not get ahead of ourselves," cautioned Marcus. "The man's name is Henry Lu and he had press credentials to cover the concert. I saw him answer a phone call and get up to leave. For all we know he was called away on a different story. We will definitely pursue that lead, but right now let's go over what we know for certain."

"Tell him what happened," Malena said to Mr. Samuel, the conductor.

"Five minutes into intermission I came back to congratulate Yin on his performance so far," he said. "He wasn't here, which seemed unusual, but I wasn't worried until I came back a few minutes later and he was still missing. Then I noticed this."

He pointed to a folder containing Yin's sheet music. A blue sticky note was on the outside. Written on it was:

HELP

KEY

BRIDGE

Margaret and I shared a nervous look.

"So you thought that someone might have taken him, but in the process he managed to leave us a clue?"

"I didn't know what to think," he said. "I just went to Agent Sanchez and alerted her."

"That was smart," said Marcus. "Other than that, are there any signs of a struggle, anything out of the ordinary?"

"No. Everything else is exactly where it's supposed to be."

"We need to get to the bridge," said Mrs. Chiang. "We need someone at the Key Bridge looking for him."

"It's already taken care of," said Marcus. "The instant Agent Sanchez contacted me, I alerted the FBI. She mentioned the note so I had a team sent to the bridge and another is headed here to help. They should arrive at any moment."

"Good," she said, reassured.

"Who else knows he's missing?" asked Marcus.

"Just the people in this room," answered Malena.

"And whoever took him," added Mrs. Chiang.

"Right," Marcus said coolly. "I understand you're upset, but again I want to caution you on assuming the worst."

Marcus thought for a moment and turned to the conductor.

"How long have you been in intermission?"

"Seventeen minutes," he said, checking his watch. "It was only scheduled for fifteen so I'm sure the musicians are getting curious."

"We want to minimize how many people know. So I

think the first thing to do is get the orchestra back onstage performing. Otherwise we have fifteen hundred middle school students getting restless and asking questions."

"We can't go onstage," Lucy interrupted. "Not without Yin. He's the soloist."

"No one else can play his part?" asked Marcus.

"You could, Lucy," said the conductor. "You're more than capable."

"I don't know," she said, nervous.

"I do," he replied confidently.

"Do that," said Marcus. "Get back onstage, announce that Yin is feeling sick but that Lucy is going to step in for him."

"Okay," said the conductor.

Things were moving quickly, but Marcus had a calming effect on everybody.

"I need to alert the embassy," said Mrs. Chiang.

Marcus thought about this for a moment and realized he couldn't stop her. "Of course you do. But I would ask two things. First of all, try to keep what you tell them to the facts that we know are certain. The truth is bad enough; there's no need to escalate it. Second, ask them to work with our office before making any announcements."

"My husband works in the press office," she said. "I'll explain the situation to him."

"Thank you," he said as he pulled a business card out of his wallet. "This is the press liaison director for the FBI. Tell your husband he can call her directly whenever he wants."

She went off to a corner to make the call, and Lucy started talking through the music with the conductor. This left a brief window for Malena to come over to us and speak in hushed tones.

"I don't want to tell you how to do your job, but I think you have to consider the possibility that he left on his own."

"Why do you say that?" I asked.

"There's no sign of a struggle," she answered. "And that hallway out there's pretty crowded. It'd be hard not to notice him being dragged out of here."

"My thinking exactly," said Marcus.

"But there's another thing," she said. She looked back over her shoulder to make sure no one could hear her. "Remember when I told you I took Mandarin in college?" she asked me.

I smiled at the memory. "Yes."

"It's a complex language that relies on accent, emphasis, and specific characters for precision," she said. "When Yin translated the titles of the three compositions . . ."

"'Red,' 'White,' and 'Blue,'" said Margaret.

"Right," answered Malena. "He used very literal trans-lations. I mean, the titles on the sheet music and the program are the Mandarin words for 'red,' 'white,' and 'blue.' But what he actually said sounded more like the words for 'terror,' 'sadness,' and 'difficult.'"

"What does that mean?" asked Marcus.

"I don't know," she said. "I just know that's what he said."

"We better get back out there," the conductor announced. "It's already been twenty minutes."

"That's my cue," Malena said to us. "I go where she goes."

"Thanks for the help," Marcus replied. "We've got this."

"I need to take the sheet music," Lucy said. "Yin's copy is the only one with the solo on it."

"Can you leave the folder?" asked Marcus.

"Of course," she said.

"Okay," he said. "Let me get it for you."

He flipped open the folder with a pencil, careful not to disturb any potential fingerprints. He looked to make sure there were no other clues and then picked up the music and handed it to her.

"Here you go."

Ever since we'd entered the room, it seemed as if Lucy were avoiding eye contact with me. I don't know if she was suspicious about why I was involved or if it was just that she was upset about what had happened. Still, as she left the room, I tried to give her an encouraging smile.

She walked right by me without reacting,

Mrs. Chiang left too so that she could continue her conversation in private. That left Margaret and me alone in the room with Marcus. He locked the door to ensure no one came in on us.

"Okay, we've got to think fast," he said. "If word of this gets out, it's an instant media circus and that helps no one."

"I still think it's significant that Henry Lu disappeared before the concert even started," I said. "Maybe Mrs. Chiang was right and he came backstage to lie in wait for Yin."

"I'm suspicious of it too," he said. "But I don't want the Chinese embassy to sound the alarm so I downplayed it. I already have two agents looking for Henry Lu. They're good and they will find him."

"Excellent," said Margaret.

"Okay, look at this," I said, pointing at the blue sticky note. "The swirl at the top of the *P* in 'HELP' and the bottom of the *Y* in 'KEY' go over the edge of the paper."

They both examined the note.

"It's a small square. He was probably frantic. So he went over the edge," said Margaret. "There's nothing suspicious about that."

"No, I don't think it's suspicious," I replied. "But in both places the ink should have left a mark on the folder."

Marcus smiled when he saw where I was headed. "That means he wrote the note somewhere else and then stuck it here."

"Or that maybe someone else like Henry Lu wrote the note," I suggested. "And is trying to send us in the wrong direction."

"You know who else it could be?" said Margaret. "Loki."

Marcus and I both gave her a look.

"You think Loki's moved from pulling fire alarms to kidnapping?" he asked.

"No," she said. "But when I was at Girl Scout camp one summer, some girls pulled a prank where they put something in a girl's food that made her have to go to the bathroom. When she did, they locked her in and left her there for three hours."

"And you didn't help her?" I asked. Then I saw her expression and realized a different explanation. "Oh wait, you were the girl."

"It's not important to pinpoint the victim," she said. "I just think Loki might have done something like that to Yin. He could be locked in a bathroom somewhere."

Marcus let out a frustrated grunt. "You're absolutely right," he said. "That's the case we're dealing with. He could be locked in a bathroom as a prank, kidnapped as a political prisoner, or somewhere in between. There are just too many options."

"What should we do first?" I asked.

"We have to stay here until the team arrives to lock down the room," he said. "And we have to be careful not to touch anything. So look around, carefully, for any possible clues. It's time to employ the Theory of All Small Things to maximum effect."

The problem was there just weren't that many places to look. The room was nice for a dressing room, but it wasn't exactly big. I opened a closet and it was empty.

"Where are his clothes?" I asked

"What do you mean?" asked Marcus.

"Don't you think he'd have clothes to change into after the concert? Something other than the tuxedo?"

"I don't know," said Margaret. "I've been in orchestras where most of the people come already dressed."

"I'd think he'd at least have his Orioles cap," I said.

"Good point."

"The one he had on in the pictures we saw," said Marcus.

"He wears it everywhere," I said. "At Chatham the students have to wear a uniform, and the second the final bell rings, he reaches into his backpack, pulls it out, and puts it on. It's almost like a security blanket."

"And it's not in the closet?"

"Nope," I said.

"Maybe it's in the cello case," he suggested.

Marcus took out his car keys and used them to flick open the latches on the case so he wouldn't ruin any fingerprints. Then he carefully opened it.

"Is it in there?" Margaret asked.

"No," he said. "Just the cello."

"Marcus," someone said, knocking on the door. "It's Kayla."

He unlocked the door and opened it. She was there with four agents. Marcus gave them a quick rundown of the situation, but before he could do much more, one of the agents spoke up.

"We appreciate your help," he said. "We'll take it from here."

Just like that, the other agent started barking orders. He instructed one agent to seal off the room we were in and told another to find a space they could make a command post. It was all happening quickly.

I couldn't read Marcus. I don't think he was ready to hand things over to someone else but he didn't make the slightest protest. I was still trying to read his reaction when the agent pointed at Margaret and me.

"Who are they?"

"Friends of the victim," Marcus replied. "They witnessed an incident that may be linked."

"Have we taken their statement?"

"Yes," he told them.

The agent looked directly at us and said, "Thank you for your help. You'll have to leave now."

And just like that we were off the case.

27.

A Different Type of Expert

MARGARET AND I WERE WITH KAYLA IN A cavernous backstage room. The walls were covered with giant posters of past Kennedy Center events, and a basketball hoop was attached to an overhanging balcony. Since the orchestra had resumed playing, we couldn't really get back to our seats without attracting attention. So we just stood there trying to make sense of the sudden turn of events.

"What just happened?" asked Margaret.

"A CARD team has taken over the investigation," explained Kayla. "That stands for Child Abduction Rapid Deployment team. As soon as the Bureau determines a minor's been kidnapped, they're given total control of the situation. This is their area of expertise."

"Maybe," I said. "But I still think we can help. We've already found a couple clues and we're familiar with Yin and the situation."

"And I'm sure Marcus will share those clues with the team," she reassured me. "But your covert status makes it impossible for you to be directly involved. I know you want to help, but don't worry. These agents are good at this. The very best."

"What about Marcus?" asked Margaret. "Is he going to be part of their team?"

"They'll keep him around until they're fully up to speed," she said. "Then they'll ask him to leave too."

"He won't like that."

"No, he won't," she agreed. "But he'll do it because he understands the procedures."

Margaret and I both nodded reluctantly.

"Now, I've got to go see how I can help. Are you two okay?"

"Yes," I said.

"Thanks," added Margaret.

Kayla headed back toward Yin's dressing room, but we just stayed there for a moment.

"I feel like my head's spinning," I said. "Forty-five minutes ago we were watching Yin onstage and now he's vanished."

"Are you worried about him?" Margaret asked.

"Of course I am."

"Do you have faith that those guys are going to find him?"

I paused before answering. "You heard her. They're experts. The best."

"That wasn't the question, Florian. I asked if you had faith that they're going to find him."

I thought about it for a second and reluctantly shook my head. "Not really," I admitted. "They already have a plan in mind and they're just going to go with that. I'm worried they're going to miss the little things. I'm worried they'll miss the TOAST."

"So am I," she said. "Tell me, did they have a CARD team looking for you when you were kidnapped by Nic the Knife?"

"Yes."

"And were they the ones who found you?"

"No," I replied. "Marcus found me."

"That's because he had the skills *and* also cared about you," she said. "Just like we care about Yin."

I gave her a look. "Are you saying you want *us* to look for him?"

"No, I *am* looking for him," she replied. "I'm saying that if you want to help, you can come along."

"Margaret, we've got to be smart."

"I know," she said. "But in my entire life I've never felt more useless than when you were missing and I was just sitting at your house waiting for information. It was awful."

"There was nothing you could've done," I reminded her. "By the time you knew anything was wrong I was already tied up in the back of a van somewhere in Northern Virginia."

"Right, but that's not the case this time," she said. "This just happened. Yin's still nearby. This time I can help."

There was no further discussion. She just started walking briskly and I followed her down a hallway that ran directly behind the stage. The music was loud and momentarily my thoughts shifted from Yin to Lucy. She had just been thrust into a nearly impossible situation playing intricate solos that she hadn't practiced in front of a large audience.

"Listen," I said, signaling Margaret to stop. "You're the one who knows classical music. How does she sound?"

We stood silently for a moment as Lucy played a solo, and when she was done, Margaret gave me a big smile. "Good. Really good."

We exited through a door that led to the Hall of Nations. It was long and narrow with plush red carpet, polished marble walls, and the flags of nearly two hundred countries hanging above us. It's also where we saw Dr. Putney nervously pacing back and forth in the middle of a phone call.

"Well, he was technically under the supervision of the symphony, not the school," we overheard him saying. "So that liability is not on us. The Kennedy Center is supposed to take care of all security. When the news breaks, make sure he's identified as a member of the Washington Youth Symphony and not as a Chatham student."

Margaret shook her head and whispered to me, "He's more concerned with who gets the blame than he is with finding Yin."

"Not a surprise," I said. "But you still haven't told me what we're doing."

"I will in a second," she said.

Again, she left no room for debate as she approached Dr. Putney. When he got off the phone he turned and saw us.

"What are you two doing out here?" he asked. "You should be in the concert hall right now."

"Actually, we're helping the FBI look for Yin," said Margaret.

It was a total lie but there was nothing I could really do about it at this point, so I just nodded as confidently as I could.

"You know about him?" he said.

"Yes, and we have to follow a lead," she responded. "But we didn't want to leave the building without telling you. We know you're concerned with student safety and didn't want you to panic if we didn't show up at our bus."

"Right," he said. "That's good."

"Will you tell Ms. Curtis?" she replied. "We can't tell her what's up without spoiling our cover, but she's the main chaperone on our bus."

"I'll take care of it," he said.

"Great," she said.

She headed straight for the door and I was right behind her.

"Make sure you find him," he said with genuine concern. I hoped that concern was for Yin's safety and not the school's reputation.

We exited the building onto the entrance plaza, which was still filled with school buses.

"Where are we going?" I demanded once we reached a spot where no one else could hear us.

"The Metro," she replied. "Foggy Bottom is the nearest station."

"You know what I mean," I said firmly. "We were taken off the case and we just lied to get out here. Things are going from bad to worse." I stopped on the top step and stood my ground. "I'm not going any farther until you tell me your plan."

"You're not going to like it," she said.

"I kind of got that idea the first few times you wouldn't answer."

She walked back toward me and let out a sigh. "We're going to see a different type of expert."

"What does that even mean?"

"The CARD team is made up of agents who are experts at finding someone who's been kidnapped," she said.

"Right."

"I thought we might try to talk to someone whose expertise is actually kidnapping people."

It took me a second to piece together her plan. "Do you mean Nic the Knife?"

She smiled. "See? It makes total sense."

"That doesn't make any sense," I said, incredulous. "I was kidnapped and thrown in the back of a van. Nic the Knife's a notorious mob boss. And, oh yeah, he happens to be the US representative of the EEL crime syndicate."

"Yes, yes, and yes," she answered. "And as you just pointed out, all those terrible things make him an expert in this subject. Besides, he owes you. You've never really told me everything that went down when you were in that barn with him, but you kept him from getting into too much trouble. He helped with the missing Monet, so maybe he'll help with this." She started back down the stairs. "Now let's hurry up."

This was, in my estimation, the worst idea in the history of mankind. That's just on the surface of it. It was even worse than that when you consider the part that I couldn't tell her: that Nic the Knife was in fact her birth father. That's what I discovered when I was sitting there with my hands tied behind my back in that barn. That's what I swore to him she'd never find out.

"We can't do this," I said as I chased after her. "This is a very bad idea."

She stopped, and even though she was a step below me since she's taller, we were eye to eye.

"Yin has vanished. We're his friends. Maybe his only two friends on this entire continent. And we're good at solving mysteries. It's the only lucky break he's caught. His only friends also happen to be secret consultants for the FBI. We need to help find him and no one in there is going to let us. So this is the next best way."

"No," I said. "We're going back inside. I'm calling it off."

"I wasn't asking permission," she said. "*I'm* going to visit Nic the Knife. I'd like you to go with me, but I'll go with or without you."

(Okay, so I was wrong. Her going without me was the worst idea in the history of the world.)

"I'll come, I'll come," I said, caving. "I guess the bright side is that if I get shot or end up in the hospital, I won't have to sing in the talent show."

"That hurts," she said. "But I'm going to let it slide. Now let's go find us a criminal mastermind."

28.

Nic the Knife

IT TOOK ABOUT THIRTY MINUTES FOR US TO RIDE the Metro and get to Nic's office. I spent the entire time trying to figure out the first words I would say when he saw us. Despite his career choice, I knew he truly loved Margaret and was determined she be protected from his world of crime. Because of this, he told me, it was vital she never learn that he was her father. My worry was that our unexpected arrival might make him think she knew more than she really did.

The headquarters of Nevrescu Construction were located on the third floor of a nondescript office building in Southwest. The decoration in the reception area was limited to a few plants, some pictures of building projects, and a couple of framed articles about the scholarship foundation he'd created.

"We'd like to speak to Nicolae Nevrescu," I said to the dark-haired receptionist whose nameplate read Ioana. "My name is Florian Bates and this is Margaret Campbell."

"What's this concerning?" she asked, eyeing us with curiosity rather than suspicion. (Of course the fact that I was dressed up for the symphony made me seem even that much more out of place.)

"It's a personal matter," answered Margaret.

"Just tell him that Florian Bates and Margaret Campbell are here," I said. "I think he'll want to see us."

No doubt there were many unusual visitors who came to see her boss, so the receptionist didn't question us any more than that. Instead she just directed us to have a seat while she checked with him.

Within seconds of us sitting down on the couch, the door to an office opened and Nic stalked out into the waiting area. He wore a dark pin-striped suit that had been tailored to make his broad shoulders and powerful arms that much more intimidating. He looked at us, his expression at half-scowl, and checked to see if anyone else was in the waiting area.

"Before you say anything, let me explain," I said, going through the lines I'd rehearsed in my head.

He nodded so I kept on going.

"This is my friend Margaret Campbell. We're in the middle of an urgent situation, and she thought you might have certain insight that would help us. I told her it was not a good idea to interrupt you at work. But she was determined and said she was going to come with or without me. Since she doesn't know *anything* about you," I said, stressing the word, "I thought it would be best if I came along."

He relaxed a little and asked, "So you're looking for my expertise in some matter?"

"Yes," she said.

"Does this have something to do with building construction?"

"Actually, it's a different area of professional experience," I said as delicately as I could.

"It's about a kidnapping," Margaret blurted out.

His eyes opened wide and he scanned the room again to make sure no one else was there.

"I don't know what you think, but . . ."

"A friend of ours was kidnapped," she said. "We're really worried about him. We want to help and to do that we need your help."

In that moment Nicolae Nevrescu was no longer Nic the Knife. He was a father, and even though she didn't realize their connection, his daughter had come to him for help. He looked at Margaret and melted.

"I don't know how I can help," he said calmly. "But come into my office and we will see if there is a way."

She smiled at him and he beamed.

"I'm really sorry," I whispered to him as we entered his office. "I tried to stop her."

There were three chairs around a small coffee table and I took the one in the middle so they were on opposite sides looking at each other.

"Margaret, that's your name, right?" he said.

"Yes," she replied. "Margaret Campbell."

"I'm not sure what you've heard about me, but I don't see how I can help you in this situation," he said, carefully choosing his words. "I promise you I have nothing to do with whatever happened to your friend."

"No, it's not that," she said. "We don't think you're involved. We just can't figure out what happened and thought you might be able to help us analyze the situation."

"I run a construction company," he replied. "I don't know anything about kidnapping."

Margaret gave him a look, and then she realized something. "We're not recording you, if that's what you're worried about," she said. "But if it helps, we can talk in hypotheticals.

Perhaps you like to read mysteries or watch crime shows on television and along the way you've picked up some insight into criminal behavior."

He nodded. "Okay. Let's do that. Tell me about this situation."

"Right," she said. "Imagine a boy during the intermission of a concert. He's a prodigy and the soloist. But when it's time to go back onstage there's no sign of him. He's completely vanished from his dressing room."

"Are there any signs of a struggle?"

"No," we both answered.

"Were there any witnesses?"

"No."

He thought about this for a moment. "But it was in a crowded area. Backstage at a concert?"

"Right," I said.

"Has there been a ransom demand?"

"No, there hasn't," said Margaret.

"Then why do you think it was a kidnapping?" he said.

Margaret and I shared a look for a moment. "Well, there was a note asking for help left at the scene."

He nodded.

"Okay, you need to look at this a different way," he said. "If you don't have any indication how he was taken, you have to ask yourself why someone would take him in the first place. Is there a great deal of money for a ransom? Does taking him apply pressure to someone important? From what I have read and seen on television, these are the telling factors in such situations. If there were a ransom you should ignore everything except for the ransom and how it relates directly to the victim. Once you can figure out the reason, then it's case closed."

I looked up at him with a huge smile.

"What did you just say?"

He wasn't sure which part I was referring to. "Case closed," he said. "You've got it solved."

"You're absolutely right," I said.

"I am?" he said, even more surprised.

"His case was closed," I said to Margaret. "His cello had been wiped down and put away in its case."

"Of course it was," said Margaret. "He's totally OCD about his cello. He always does that."

"When he's finished," I said. "He puts his cello away like that when he's done. But it was intermission. He would only have done that . . ."

"If he knew he wasn't going back out to perform," she said, completing my thought.

"Do you know what that means?" I asked.

"He wasn't kidnapped," said Margaret.

"That's right," I said. "I've got to reach Marcus."

I hurriedly began sending a text to Marcus, and while I was, Nic and Margaret had a brief conversation.

"Thank you," said Margaret. "I knew you could help."

"It was my pleasure," he replied.

My text read, **Huge TOAST. Big breakthrough. Need to talk.**

Margaret gave Nic a funny look. "You're not what I expected you to be like."

He smiled. "That's probably a good thing, I think." Then he added, "I saw you play soccer in the city championship, by the way."

"That's right," she said, smiling at the memory. "Florian told me you had a niece playing on the other team. Sorry we had to beat them."

He had a satisfied look as he thought back to that game. "No, you deserved to win. You were magnificent. I'm sure your parents are awfully proud of you. I know I would be."

I realized it was as close as he would ever get to telling her what he thought of her.

My phone buzzed and I looked down at a text that was all caps. **WHERE ARE YOU?**

"We gotta go," I said. "I think we may be in a bit of trouble."

"Good-bye," Margaret said as we got up and headed for the door.

"Good-bye, Margaret," Nic said. "It was very nice to meet you."

29.

God Save the Queen

MARGARET'S MEETING WITH NIC THE KNIFE WENT a whole lot better than ours did with Marcus. He was furious that we'd left the Kennedy Center. Even more upset that we were working on the case after being told not to. And he almost went full volcano when he found out whom we'd gone to for advice.

But he also thought I was right about the cello case.

The problem was, like us, he was no longer part of the investigation. So the three of us just sat there in front of Nic's office building. We were in Kayla's SUV (which Marcus had borrowed because his car was still at school), trying to make sense of it all.

"Okay, if you're right and he wasn't kidnapped, that means he ran away," said Marcus. "Which also means he could be in real danger."

"We're missing something," said Margaret. "The pieces still don't make sense."

"It's got to be the Key Bridge," I said. "That was the only real clue in his dressing room. And we still don't know what it means. Once we figure that out, then everything else should come together."

"Okay, let's think about the bridge," said Marcus. "It's close to the Kennedy Center, just a few minutes' walk. So Yin sneaks out of the concert and walks to the bridge. What happens then? Does he meet a friend?"

"He doesn't have any friends," I said. "Unless it's a secret from everyone."

"Including the Chiangs," added Margaret. "Because they watch everything he does."

"So if he's not meeting a friend, what's he doing? Walking across the bridge to Virginia? As far as runaway plans go that's not particularly good."

"Right?" I said. "Because if you really wanted to get away in a hurry, you wouldn't walk. You'd take the Metro, which is in the opposite direction."

"But the Metro has security cameras everywhere," said

Marcus. "Every station. Every car. You'd be easy to find. The CARD team was looking at video from the Metro within minutes of getting the case. We know for sure he didn't go that way."

"Walking won't get you anywhere and the Metro will get you caught," I said. "How else are you going to get away?"

Margaret happily began slapping the dashboard. "The river!" she said with a huge smile. "There's a little boathouse under the bridge. My parents and I went there one time and you know what we did? We rented kayaks."

"Brilliant!" I said. "That's absolutely brilliant."

Marcus started driving, and as we rode we filled him in on Yin's love of kayaking. Going to the boathouse and getting a kayak was at least a viable way of running away. But we couldn't drive straight there to check it out because the CARD team had control of the case and had staked out the bridge.

This is why Marcus had the idea to borrow a boat from the harbor patrol, which is where this story began. In case there are parts you don't remember, I'll retell some of the highlights.

We went to the harbor patrol and Marcus tried to convince the sergeant on duty to loan us a boat. Marcus didn't have much luck because the police and the FBI don't get along particularly well. That's when I helped by figuring out the cop had a son named Frankie and a daughter in the Girl Scouts. I reminded him that if they were in danger, he'd want everyone to help find them.

We got the keys and took off down the Potomac in a Zodiac boat. This was less than perfect for me considering I get seasick just looking at the water. By the time we reached the Key Bridge, I was ready to barf over the side.

In fact, I was just about to do that very thing when two sightseeing cruises passed us. The boats were named after George Washington and Thomas Jefferson and since they were giving a cruise through the capital of the United States, I thought it was strange that they were playing the British national anthem.

I asked Margaret and Marcus and they didn't know what I was talking about. She even started to sing the song.

> *My country, 'tis of thee,*
> *Sweet land of liberty,*
> *Of thee I sing*

"No, no, no," I told her. "Those aren't the lyrics. The song is 'God Save the Queen.'" I grew up in Europe, and lived in England for three years, so I was pretty confident I knew what I was talking about. I started to sing the version that I knew:

> *God save our gracious Queen,*
> *Long live our noble Queen,*
> *God save the Queen.*

That's when Marcus figured out the problem. Both of us were right. Both songs had the same tune but different lyrics. And since we only heard the music, we each assumed it was the version we knew best. The same thing had happened when Margaret heard "My Dear Chatham" and thought that it was "Oh! Susanna."

I don't know if it was the dizziness, my stomach, the case, the clues, the music, or all of it. But in that moment I felt a surge moving up through my body. I couldn't tell if I was going to get sick, if my head was going to explode, or if I was going to solve the mystery right then and there. It just bubbled up through me. And then . . .

"I need to get off the boat," I said urgently.

"What's the matter?" Marcus asked. "Are you going to get sick?"

"No," I answered; my nausea had been instantly cured by

my realization. "I told you I'd follow the clues wherever they lead, and that's where they lead."

"How?" said Margaret.

"It's complicated," I replied. "But the first thing you have to understand is that 'God Save the Queen' changes everything."

"Where do you need to go?" asked Marcus.

"Back to the Kennedy Center," I answered. "The room with all the pianos."

"Why are we going there?" asked Margaret.

"Because you play the piano and I need you to play one of Yin's compositions."

Marcus saw the look in my eyes and needed no more convincing. He headed back for the marina before I even started to explain my theory. (I had to explain it all pretty loudly to be heard over the engine, but the amazing thing was this time the boat didn't make me feel sick at all.)

"How does 'God Save the Queen' change things?" asked Margaret.

"Because it reminded me that we make assumptions based on our experiences. You heard the music and thought it was 'My Country, 'Tis of the Thee,' because that's what you know it as. I thought it was 'God Save the Queen' because that's my frame of reference."

"Right," she said. "What does that have to do with Yin?"

"When we all read 'Help Key Bridge,' we thought of the bridges that cross the Potomac, because that's our frame of reference. But it isn't Yin's. When he uses the word 'bridge,' he thinks of . . ."

"Music," said Margaret.

"That's right," I said. "There's a musical bridge in one of the pieces. He mentioned it the other day when you two were talking about composing. He said he'd just rewritten it. It's not the Key Bridge as in the Francis Scott Key Bridge. The bridge literally is a key. A coded message."

By the time we got back to the Kennedy Center, the concert was over and all the students and musicians had gone home. We had to be careful because we were off the case, but there was nowhere else we could go to get copies of Yin's music.

"You here to return my car?" asked Kayla when she saw us.

"Sort of," said Marcus. "I also need to borrow it again. But first Florian and Margaret need to get some music."

"You are not working on this case, are you?" she asked. "Marcus, you can't take that kind of risk."

"They just want to see some music," he said. "Nothing to do with any kidnapping."

And in a way that was true, because there hadn't been a kidnapping. Although I wasn't sure that's how Marcus's boss would react if this went wrong.

Marcus and Kayla stood watch outside the dressing room door while Margaret and I found a binder of sheet music and took it into the piano garage. There were three pianos side by side and when she pulled back the cover from one she couldn't believe her eyes.

"I guess they just have Steinway grand pianos lying around here," she said, shaking her head in amazement.

"Is this a particularly nice type of piano?" I asked, totally ignorant.

"It probably costs about a hundred thousand dollars."

"Okay." I laughed. "I'd say that's pretty nice. Try not to break it."

She sat down, put the music up on the rack, and turned to me. "I'm still not sure what we're looking for."

"Neither am I," I admitted. "I just think there's some kind of message hidden in the bridge. Kind of like the way Becca signed her Chat Chat posts with notes instead of letters."

"The thing is, classical music doesn't typically have a bridge," she said. "It's more common in popular song-writing."

"But he mentioned one the other day in the practice room," I reminded her. "So it has to be in there."

"You're right. Let's find it."

She skipped the first piece, the one we'd listened to earlier, because it was a traditional concerto.

"So if it's not in 'Red,'" I said, "it's got to be in either 'White' or 'Blue.'"

"Which one do you think?"

"Try 'Blue' first," I suggested.

"Why?"

"Because he wrote the note on a blue sticky note," I replied. "Maybe he picked the color for a reason."

She opened the binder to the third piece of music and started scanning it, stopping every now or then to play a few notes. My entire knowledge of musical composition was limited to what Margaret had told me about her song and the little bit I saw when she and Yin worked on it, so I was useless. In addition to the pianos the room had a row of gray metal filing cabinets, a dry-erase board for people to leave messages for each other, and a poster from the musicians' union taped to the door.

"This might be it," Margaret said. She played the same eight notes over and over, tentative at first, until she felt comfortable.

"Yes," she said. "It's definitely the bridge."

I walked over to the dry-erase board and grabbed a marker. "What are the notes?"

"B, E, B-flat, E, A, D, E, D."

I wrote them down as she said them and when she was done she played them one more time.

"Bebeaded?" I said, reading them. "Is that a word? Something to do with a necklace maybe?"

"I don't think so," she answered.

I tried it out in a sentence. "The princess was bebeaded with a necklace of gold, silver, and pearls."

She gave me a look. "Okay, we're in the middle of a crisis, so I'm going to let it slide. But I don't love the fact that you went straight to princess. A lot of women wear necklaces, like scientists, CEOs, Supreme Court justices. Also, your knowledge of jewelry is apparently nonexistent. A silver, gold, and pearl necklace would be hideous."

"That's you letting it slide?" I said.

She laughed. "Okay, I guess I didn't let it slide completely. But I'm confident 'bebeaded' is not a word."

"Are you sure you got the notes right?" I asked.

"Positive," she said with a touch of attitude.

"I know, I know," I said apologetically. "I'm just trying to figure it out. Maybe it's a sentence: Be Bead Ed."

"But the second letter isn't B. It's B-flat."

I added "flat" to the mix and tried to pronounce it. "Beb-flateaded?" I looked up at her and said, "That makes even less sense."

She flashed a smile.

"No, that makes total sense to me," said Margaret.

"It does?"

She got up from the piano and came over to me. "Some people notate B-flat as H," she said. "Bach used to use it to spell his name in some of his compositions. I think it's a German thing."

She used her thumb to erase "B-flat" and wrote an "H" instead.

"There's your word," she said. "Beheaded."

"Wow," I said, unsure what to make of it. "That's kind of a gruesome unexpected turn. Why *beheaded*?"

The door opened to reveal Marcus and Kayla. She signaled us to hurry up and leave, and Marcus was turned talking to some unseen agent.

"Good luck with everything," he said. "Let me know if there's any way we can be any help."

While he kept stalling, Margaret silently put the cover back on the piano and we slipped out the other door. Amazingly we managed to get out of the building without anyone seeing us. None of us said a word until we made it to the parking lot and Kayla's SUV.

"Any luck?" Marcus asked hopefully.

"Oh yeah," I said. "We know what it is."

"Well, tell us," he said. "What is it?"

"The Latin word for 'creepy sculptures.'"

30.

Puellae

THE NATIONAL SCULPTURE GARDEN IS A PARK located next to the museum where my mother works. It's a little bigger than two city blocks and contains more than twenty large-scale works of outdoor art. We were there to see *Puellae*, the sculpture of the thirty headless girls that we'd seen posted on Yin's Chat Chat bulletin board. He'd come here on one of his Saturday adventures with the Chiangs and now I was convinced he'd selected it as a rendezvous point for his getaway.

"Beheaded," I said as we walked up to them. "This is the message that was hidden in the notes of the music. He wanted someone to meet him here."

The bronze girls were posed on the lawn in several rows, shielded from pedestrians by a series of long stone benches that lined the walkway. I scanned the faces of the people in the park hoping to see Yin but there was no sign of him.

"How can we even know if he made it?" asked Marcus.

"We could pull security footage of the park," Kayla suggested.

"Or check out the traffic cameras," I said.

"Yeah, but that's kind of hard to do considering we're not supposed to be on this case," he replied. "We'd never get a warrant."

"We don't need one," said Margaret. "He was definitely here."

"How can you be so certain?" I asked.

She walked over to where two of the benches met and reached for something that had fallen on the little patch of dirt between them. "Look familiar?" she said as she pulled it out.

"Yin's baseball cap."

The three of us converged on her to give it a closer look. "Happy Birthday, Yin" was written along the inside border.

"Okay, this worries me," said Margaret.

"Why?" I asked.

"Because it's not like Yin to leave it behind. If it's here, that means something's wrong."

"You don't know that," I said. "He's on the run. He came here to meet someone. Maybe they rushed off and he didn't realize he'd lost it. Like when we were at the zoo."

"And you saw how freaked-out he got when he thought it was gone," she reminded me. "Even if he's on the run, I think he would've come back for it. This worries me a lot."

I took a deep breath and thought it over. "You may be right."

"Forget about the hat for a moment and think about the friend," said Marcus. "Who'd he come here to meet?"

"I don't know," I said. "I didn't think he had any friends."

"He must have at least one, because he hid the message in the music," said Marcus. "The only reason to hide it is if someone else can find it."

Margaret flashed an "aha" smile.

"But that wasn't his only message," she said. "He also left the sticky note with 'Help Key Bridge' written on it. That was left for the same friend."

"You're absolutely right," I said. "And unlike the music, which was heard by fifteen hundred people, only a few could've seen that note."

"Who found it?" asked Kayla.

"The conductor," said Marcus. "And then he got Malena Sanchez."

"You know, Malena has been on the edges of this mystery every step of the way," I said.

Marcus gave me an incredulous look. "You think a Secret Service agent is involved in an elaborate runaway plan of a thirteen-year-old Chinese national?"

"No," I replied. "It's just that she's always close by to where everything is happening. It's an observation, not an accusation."

"It's because she's always close by Lucy," said Margaret. "That's her job."

I thought about that for a moment and beamed. "You're absolutely right. It's her job to be there at all times." I turned to Marcus and excitedly asked, "Do you know how to reach her?"

"Malena? Yes. Why?"

"I think she has the answer we're looking for."

He was a little hesitant, but he pulled out his phone and called her. He gave me a skeptical look while he waited for the call to connect.

"Malena, this is Marcus Rivers," he said when she answered. "Do you have a second? Florian wants to ask you a question. He thinks it's important."

He listened to her response and then handed me the phone.

"Here you go."

"Hi," I said. "I'm trying to figure out something about Yin and I need to ask you a question. I want to know if you'll make the same deal with me."

"What deal is that?" Malena asked.

"The one you made in the car the other day when you said I could ask just one question and you'd answer honestly if you could."

"If I remember correctly, you didn't ask a particularly good question."

"No, I didn't," I admitted. "But I think this one's much better."

It was quiet on the phone for a moment. "Okay, let's hear it."

I ran it through my head, making sure that my phrasing was such that no matter what she said, it would tell me what I needed to know.

"After the concert today, did Lucy Mays ask you to take her to the Sculpture Garden?"

There was a long pause during which I could hear only her deep breaths. Finally she spoke up. "Give the phone to Agent Rivers."

"Wait! That's not fair. What's the answer?"

"Give the phone to Agent Rivers," she repeated emphatically.

I handed it to him and watched as he listened. I couldn't figure out the conversation because she was doing all of the talking. Marcus nodded along as if he were getting instructions and when she was finished he simply said, "Roger that."

He looked at us with an expression that was hard to describe.

"Are we in trouble?" Margaret asked warily.

"No," he said, bewildered. "We have been asked to go to the White House. Immediately."

He turned to me and gave a little crooked grin and added, "Agent Sanchez wanted me to tell you something. She even repeated it to make sure I got it right."

"What?" I asked.

"She said, 'That, Florian, is an excellent question.'"

31.

The Blue Room

FOR THE SECOND TIME IN LESS THAN A WEEK, I
had the privilege of visiting the White House, although this
visit was more work-related than the first. It was funny to see
how Margaret, Marcus, and Kayla reacted as Malena Sanchez
led us to the Blue Room on the first floor of the residence.

"Wait here while I get Lucy," she said.

The moment Agent Sanchez left, Margaret turned to the
rest of us. "This is amazing!"

"Agreed," said Kayla.

"Have you ever been here before?" I asked Marcus.

"Just on the tour when I was in middle school."

The room was oval and got its name from the curtains, rug,

and fabric on all of the chairs. Each was the color of a bright summer sky. Three windows looked toward the Washington Monument, and on a wall were the official White House portraits of James Madison, John Adams, and Thomas Jefferson. It was beyond impressive. And intimidating.

"I heard Florian Bates was in the building," boomed a voice from behind us.

We turned and were shocked to see who it was.

"Oh my God, Florian," whispered Kayla. "You know the president."

"Yes, he does," said President Mays with campaign enthusiasm. "Now, who do we have here?"

It took me a second to realize that he was looking at me to handle the introductions. "Mr. President, this is Special Agent Marcus Rivers of the FBI."

They shared a firm handshake and Marcus said, "It's a pleasure to meet you, sir."

"Likewise," replied the president. "Thank you so much for your dedication and service to our country."

"And this is Special Agent Kayla Cross."

"It's an honor, Mr. President," she said.

"No, the honor's all mine, Agent Cross."

He reached Margaret and it was the first time I think I'd ever seen her speechless.

"And you must be Margaret," he said before I could even introduce them. "Admiral Douglas has told me about you. I'm a huge fan."

I thought she was going to faint right then and there.

"Yes, sir," she managed to say slightly above a whisper. "I've heard a lot about you, too."

This made everyone laugh. Sensing her embarrassment, the president turned it on me. "Well, Florian, I see you really know how to dress up for the White House."

It was only then that it dawned on me that I was still in the outfit I'd picked out for the symphony. Although it had looked a lot sharper before I spent a day chasing clues all around Washington and racing up and down the Potomac in a Zodiac.

"Yes, sir," I said. "I always try to make a bold statement."

"Please, everyone have a seat," he said warmly.

We moved to a group of chairs and a couch arranged around an antique coffee table.

"Florian, in a moment my daughter's going to come down here and you're going to have to be honest with her about who you are and why you've been at Chatham Country Day."

"Yes, sir," I replied.

"She's not going to like it."

"No, sir."

"She'll be mad at Agent Sanchez and me, too, because we knew the truth and didn't tell her," he continued. "But I'm her dad, and Agent Sanchez's job is literally to step in front of a bullet to save her life. So we'll be forgiven pretty quickly."

"But I won't be," I said.

"No, I don't suppose you will," he said. "That's why I wanted to give you a little help."

"You're going to talk to her for me?" I asked hopefully.

"Not on your life," he joked. "My job's already hard enough. But I thought I might give you a secret weapon."

He reached over and pressed something into the palm of my hand. It felt like a quarter, and when I looked down I saw that it was the Jefferson peace medal I'd found for him.

"Why don't you hold it while you talk to her," he said. "FDR used it to battle the Depression and World War Two, and those are only slightly less difficult to manage than Lucy when she's angry."

I read from the back of the medal. "Peace and Friendship."

"Try to maintain those if you can."

"Thank you."

Moments later Malena came into the room with Lucy. She looked surprised to see us all waiting for her.

"What's going on?" she asked accusingly.

"Florian needs to talk to you," said the president. "It's important."

"Who are these other people?" She turned to Marcus and Margaret. "You were the agent in Yin's dressing room today. And you're the other exchange student from Alice Deal."

"They both work at the FBI," I said. "With me."

She looked confused. "What does that mean? How can you work at the FBI?"

"I'm what's known as a covert asset."

"You mean a spy?" she said, her voice rising. "You were spying on me?"

"No, I'm more a detective than a spy," I tried to explain.

"Oh, that's *so* much better," she said.

"But I wasn't investigating you, at least not directly. My assignment was to identify Loki."

She gave us a skeptical look. "You're here because of some stupid pranks?"

"No, that's why we came to Chatham," I said. "We're *here* because of Yin."

For the first time there was another emotion on her face. In addition to the anger that was directed at me, she showed a flash of concern. "What about him?"

"Ask her what you asked me?" suggested Malena.

I took a breath and squeezed the peace medal in my hand. The next few questions would determine if I was on the right track or not. "Did you ask Agent Sanchez to take you to the Sculpture Garden after the concert today?"

She shot Malena an angry look. "You told him? What about our confidentiality? I thought you never told."

"She didn't tell me anything," I said, redirecting her anger back at me. "I figured it out. Or at least part of it."

"What did you figure out?" she asked.

"That the message on the sticky note was for you," I said. "Yin knew that if he was missing, you'd be the one who'd have to replace him. You'd need to take his sheet music, which meant you'd get the message to look in the bridge. And then you were supposed to figure out that he would be waiting for you by the sculptures of the girls in the garden."

I stopped and all eyes were on her. She looked like she might cry, but she fought through it and said, "Why would I do that?"

And finally I had an answer to one huge question that had been eluding me. "Because you're Yin's one great friend. Believe me. I know how important that is to have. It's priceless." I stopped for a moment and gave a quick look at Margaret, who smiled back at me. "And what's so amazing about that is that nobody else seems to think the two of you have ever even spoken to each other."

For the first time she smiled. It's not that she was suddenly happy, but it was from the satisfaction of having fooled everyone and finally being able to gloat a little.

"Nobody knew," she said. "Not even Malena. That's part of what made it so special. You have to understand that no matter where I go or what I do, people are watching me, staring at me. Everyone who wants to be my friend has a hidden motive. You're proof of that." She paused for a moment to let that sting sink in. "And the same is true for Yin. Wherever he goes people are staring at him. Mrs. Chiang is always watching over him. So we have a lot in common. Then one day he slipped a note into my locker. His was right next to mine, so it was easy to do. In the note, he complimented my cello playing. It wasn't something basic like, 'you're good' or 'that was pretty.' He complimented me one musician to another, and coming from someone as talented as him, it meant the world to me. So I wrote him a note and put it in his locker. Slowly we became friends. Secret friends."

"How'd you communicate?" asked Margaret. "By passing notes in your lockers?"

"That's how it started. But we also came up with code names on Chat Chat and talked to each other on message boards."

"And then one day one of you discovered the secret passage that connected the practice rooms," I said.

She gave me a surprised look. "You found that?"

"I'm good at what I do. I even found the sticky goo on the trophy case. But I never could figure out what it was or why it was important."

"Cello rosin," she explained. "That was our signal. If one of us wanted to talk face-to-face, we'd just smear a little on the case. Then during practice we knew to sneak to the back hallway. When we met there we usually talked just about music or our crazy lives. It was the only time I didn't feel like a goldfish. The only time I felt normal."

I looked at the president and could tell he was sorry this was how his daughter saw her life. He asked her, "Did you know that he was planning to run away?"

"No," she said. "I just knew that he was unhappy."

"Why?" I asked.

"He found out they were going to move him to Berlin next month," she said.

"Who? The Chiangs?" asked Margaret.

"No, the Chinese government," she explained. "They like to use him to show off. Before he came here, he lived in Tokyo and Sydney. He thought the next move would be to go home and live with his family again. He only gets to see them two weeks every year. But then they told him he was going to move to Berlin and after that either Paris or Moscow. He was so discouraged."

"Wow," said Margaret. "That's a pretty grueling life for a thirteen-year-old."

"Did he tell you about the songbirds in China?" she asked.

"No," I said.

"He told me it's common there to keep songbirds as pets," she said. "Only, people don't just keep them in their houses, they take them to the park in little bamboo cages and hang them from branches where they sing for everybody. He said he felt like he was one of those songbirds."

Suddenly I realized something. "You gave him the baseball cap, didn't you? Because the oriole is a songbird."

"For his birthday," Lucy said. "And he gave me one for mine." She considered this for a moment. "You really are good at this."

Margaret shot me a smile.

"Anyway," Lucy continued. "He wasn't happy when he found out he was going to have to move again. So I told him that if they were never going to let him move back home he should just defect."

"Oh, Lucy, you didn't," exclaimed the president.

"What's 'defect'?" asked Margaret.

"It's when someone gives up their citizenship and asks for protection from a foreign government," explained Marcus.

"I was just joking," said Lucy. "But every now and then we'd talk about it like it was a possibility."

"Do you know what would happen if a celebrated Chinese citizen defected to the United States at the suggestion of the president's daughter?" asked President Mays. "Do you understand how big a deal that would be?"

"Yin said it would be a huge scandal and would cause problems for US-China relations," she responded icily.

"He's right," said the president. "They'd be furious at us and take all sorts of countermeasures. They'd blame me personally. Accuse me of putting you up to it to make them look bad."

"He also said that the US government would probably reject him."

The president hesitated for a moment before answering. "He's right. It would be too embarrassing for the Chinese government. It would cause way too many problems. If he asked for asylum the State Department would turn him down."

Lucy shot him an angry look and I realized how difficult it must be to balance the duties of being the president with those of being a father.

"Do you think he was planning to go through with it?" I asked her.

"I don't know," she said. "Lately I've gotten the sense that he's wanted to tell me something, but we haven't had a chance. We've been so busy getting ready for the concert, and all our methods of communicating have been cut off. First, I had to change lockers, which meant we couldn't pass any notes. Next Chat Chat went down, so we lost our message board. Then they put a camera up in the back hallway, so our meetings had to stop."

"So you had no idea he was going to disappear today?" asked Marcus.

"None," she said. "I didn't know anything was up until we were all in his dressing room and I saw the note about the bridge."

I ran through everything in my head one more time.

"Thank you," I said. "I'd like to apologize. I'm sorry that I misled you about who I am. I know it must be hard for you to trust people and I'm sure I made that more difficult. It wasn't intentional on my part."

She didn't respond, and after an awkward silence, Kayla spoke up.

"Mr. President, I understand why the State Department wouldn't want Yin to defect because it would embarrass

China," she said, "but wouldn't it look bad for our government to turn him away? A thirteen-year-old boy asks for help and we say no?"

"It would look terrible," he said. "Which is why it would be kept a secret. No one would ever know."

"Unless he made keeping it a secret impossible," I said, "by finding a way to defect that was too public to hide."

"You mean like disappearing in the middle of a big concert?" said Margaret.

"And then showing up at the White House with the first daughter," I added.

"It's a smart plan," said Marcus. "I imagine if he arrived here and asked to stay it would be much harder to refuse."

The president nodded his agreement. "That would change everything."

"So that was his plan," I said. "The songbird escapes his bamboo cage and takes flight. But what happened at the Sculpture Garden? Why wasn't he there when Lucy showed up?"

"Dad, you didn't do this, did you?" asked Lucy. "You didn't have someone pick him up and return him to the embassy."

"Of course not," he said. "I would never do that."

"Then what happened?" asked Marcus.

"Maybe we've gotten this wrong," said Kayla as she looked at her phone. "I think he might have been kidnapped after all."

"Why do you say that?"

"Because I just got a text from one of the members of the CARD team. They've received a ransom demand for Yin's safe return."

32.

The Ransom

"THIS DOESN'T MAKE SENSE," SAID MARGARET.
"If Yin ran away, how can there be a ransom demand?"

"There's no *if*," I said. "We know he ran away because he
hid the message in his composition. We found it. Lucy found
it. That meant he planned it ahead of time. And we know
that he followed through because we found his baseball cap
at the Sculpture Garden."

"Someone else must have figured it out too," said Lucy.
"Someone else knew that he was going to be there, and that's
where they kidnapped him."

I thought through the steps in my head and nodded my
agreement. "That makes a lot of sense. Maybe he ran away

planning to defect but was kidnapped before he had the chance." I looked over at Lucy. "You're pretty good at this too."

For a second I thought she was going to smile, but she didn't.

"Why would someone kidnap Yin?" asked Kayla.

"We don't have to know why," I said. "We just have to figure out who could've deciphered the message hidden in the music."

"Who else saw the note?" asked Kayla.

"The conductor found it and got me," said Malena. "After that it was Lucy and Mrs. Chiang. And then the FBI. And all of those people were at the Kennedy Center until the end of the performance. None of them could've been out kidnapping him."

"Was anyone alerted by phone?"

Malena and Marcus shared a look. "Mrs. Chiang called the Chinese embassy, but other than that we kept it a secret until the CARD team arrived," he said. "And I guarantee they didn't tell anyone."

"Nic the Knife says that the key to figuring out what's behind a kidnapping is to ignore everything except for the ransom demand and how it relates to the victim," said Margaret.

"Who's Nic the Knife?" asked the president. "And why were you speaking to him?"

"Actually, I don't think you want to know the answer to that," she replied. "But he's an expert, so I think it's probably good advice."

Marcus turned to Kayla. "What's the ransom demand?"

"I'll find out," she said.

She sent a text to the CARD team member and all of us waited anxiously for a minute until we heard the beep of a response. She looked down and started to read the reply.

"Wait," I said before she could. "I think I know what it is. I bet I can tell you the ransom demand."

She looked at it again and then at me. "I'll take that bet," she said. "There's no way you can guess this."

"The kidnapper is demanding the release of the West Lake Five."

She looked at me, shook her head, and then turned to Marcus. "Remind me never to bet against Florian."

"That's it?" said the president. "That's the actual ransom demand?"

"Yes, it is," she replied.

"Who are the West Lake Five?" asked Malena.

"A group of journalists being held in a Chinese prison for writing articles critical of the government," I explained.

"That's the group Henry Lu writes all the articles about," said Margaret. "Getting them freed is a big cause for him."

"That's right," I said.

"So Henry Lu's the kidnapper," she reasoned.

"Actually . . . no," I said. "I don't think so."

"But you've been suspicious of him the whole time," said Marcus.

"I know. And all the evidence reinforces it. He was at the zoo. He left the concert early. And now the ransom points to him too."

"Then why don't you think he's guilty?" asked the president.

"Because of what Nic the Knife said. Ignore everything except for the ransom and how it relates to the victim."

"Henry Lu wants the Chinese government to release the West Lake Five," said Marcus. "And the Chinese government would do anything it could to protect Yin. That makes sense."

"Except Yin wants to defect," I replied. "And that would be a huge story for Henry. He could make sure it was public. He could put pressure on the US government. He could embarrass China. It's what he was begging Yin to do when we were at the zoo. And it would be much bigger than helping the West Lake Five."

"Any chance they're in it together?" asked Malena. "Maybe that's how Lu knew he'd be at the zoo. Yin's the one who tipped him off."

"No way," said Margaret. "He was really shaken after their encounter. That wasn't acting."

"But everything you just said points to him," said the president.

"Right, because I think the kidnappers want us to think he's the one," I explained. "It's been part of their plan for a while and they've carefully set him up."

Margaret turned to me. "You know who did it, don't you?"

"I think so," I said. "Lucy gave me the missing piece of TOAST."

"Toast?" Lucy asked.

"The Theory of All Small Things," I told her. "It's how I put things together."

"And what did I give you?"

"Loki," I said. "It all started with Loki, and you told me who it was."

"The prankster at school?" asked Lucy.

"Yes," I replied. "You and Yin were secret friends and then suddenly all your methods of communication disappeared. Your locker got damaged. Chat Chat got hacked. The fire alarm was pulled. The pranks weren't done to disrupt school. They were done to disrupt your friendship. And once you know the motive, there's only one person who can be guilty."

"Mrs. Chiang!" blurted Margaret.

"That's right," I said. "She's the only one who connects to everything."

"But why would she do it?" asked Kayla.

"To protect her reputation and career," I said. "She and her husband were supposed to look after Yin. What would happen to them if he publicly humiliated the country? They'd get the blame, right?"

"No doubt about that," said the president. "Their careers would be over."

"And she couldn't let that happen," I said.

"Her room overlooks the lockers so it would have been easy for her to put glue in the locks," said Margaret.

"And as a faculty member she had access to Chat Chat," I said. "And she could have easily pulled the fire alarm without attracting attention because everyone was looking for a student. No one would've suspected a teacher."

"No one except for you," said Kayla.

"She watches Yin like a hawk; she had to know he was upset and looking for a way out," I said. "Her only hope was to control him until it was time to go to Berlin. Then he'd be someone else's problem."

"So she kept him from talking to Lucy," said Margaret. "But then she figured out that he might do something big at the concert."

"Which is why she needed Henry Lu," I said. "Yin didn't tip him off that we were going to the zoo. The Chiangs had someone do it."

"Remember they didn't go with us into the Panda House?" said Margaret. "They stayed outside. Because they knew Lu was going to be there."

"That's absolutely right," I said. "That ensured that we would be witnesses to him confronting Yin. And they already knew he was going to be at the concert because he'd arranged to get a press credential. Marcus, you said you saw him talking on the phone?"

"That's right."

"They probably had someone call him away from the scene to make him look suspicious," I said.

"And today Mrs. Chiang was there when we found the note and she's the one who made the call to the embassy," said Marcus. "Or rather to her husband at the embassy."

"Then her husband heads to the Sculpture Garden to keep Yin from meeting up with Lucy," I said. "And all the evidence points to Henry Lu."

"But we know that he's not guilty," said Lucy, getting into it. "So you can arrest the Chiangs."

"No, we can't," said Marcus. "First of all, they have diplomatic immunity, so we wouldn't be able to charge them.

But more important, we don't have any proof. The evidence all points at Henry Lu, and as carefully as they've planned this, I bet they have a way to make him appear completely guilty."

"Then we can tell the truth," she countered. "I mean, my dad could have a press conference and lay it all out."

"If the team investigating the kidnapping arrests Henry Lu, it will be an instant international story: An American who hates the Chinese government is arrested for kidnapping a Chinese citizen," the president said. "If we tried to follow that up by switching the blame to a pair of employees of the Chinese embassy, it would look like we're playing politics. They'd deny everything and use their immunity to keep from being prosecuted."

"Unless we can catch them in the act," I said. "None of that matters if we catch them with Yin."

"That'd be great," said Margaret. "I don't suppose you know where they are."

"Actually, I think I do," I said as I pulled out my phone, which I then realized had less than 10 percent power left. "My battery's dead. I need a computer. I need to search online."

"What are you looking for?" asked Kayla.

"A water tower with a picture of a giant crab on it."

33.

Marine One

IT WAS AN INTERESTING GROUP HUDDLED AROUND the computer in an office next to the Blue Room. There was the president, agents from the FBI and Secret Service, Margaret, Lucy, and me. And they were all looking over my shoulder as I made a simple search.

"There it is," I said, pointing at the image. "It's the same water tower that's in the background of the picture of Yin kayaking. The one we saw on Chat Chat."

"'Crisfield, Maryland,'" said Marcus, reading the caption. "'Crab Capital of the World.'"

"When we were at the zoo, he told us the Chiangs had a

cottage on Chesapeake Bay," said Margaret. "That must be where it is."

"I bet that's where they're holding him," I said. "If we can get there before the trap comes down on Henry Lu, then we can prove it's them."

"It would take about three hours to drive," said Marcus. "That might be too late."

"Isn't there an FBI field office nearby?" asked the president. "Or can't you alert the local police."

"About that," said Marcus, sheepishly. "We're freelancing a little bit here. We're not supposed to be working on this case. There's a CARD team that's in charge. We just happened to stumble across an alternate theory."

"But your theory is right," said Lucy. She turned to her dad. "Can't you just call the FBI and tell them?"

"No, honey," he said regretfully. "I can't interfere with a federal investigation. Especially one that involves my own daughter."

She was upset with him, so Marcus tried to help.

"We just don't have enough evidence," he explained to her. "This is all speculation." Then he turned to her father. "I'm sorry, Mr. President. In no way would I ask you to interfere."

"I appreciate that." He looked to Lucy, whose frustration

with him was growing, and I was tempted to offer him the peace medal for luck. "Although . . . ," he said, an idea forming. "I do happen to have a helicopter at my disposal."

"What?" I said, suddenly nervous.

"And if that helicopter was carrying a member of my staff to the town of Crisfield, Maryland, for White House business, I wouldn't have to know if there were any other passengers on board."

By now everyone was smiling but me.

"Really?" Lucy asked him.

"Really."

"What if we drove really fast," I suggested. "Maybe we could get there in two hours. That might be soon enough."

"You said you'd follow the clues wherever they led," Marcus teased.

"I think you even mentioned something about riding in a helicopter or a submarine if you had to," added Margaret.

"Those were hypothetical situations. I didn't think we'd actually have to use one."

"Too bad about that." She laughed. "You should probably sit near the window in case you have to throw up."

Ten minutes later Marcus, Kayla, Margaret, and I boarded Marine One, the president's helicopter. Joining us were Malena Sanchez, a member of the president's staff who had a "sudden emergency" to tend to in Crisfield, Maryland, and a last-second addition who demanded to come along, Lucy Mays.

We lifted off from the White House lawn and I sat in the middle seat, as far from the windows as I could get, and did my best not to look down. As we flew over the dark waters of Chesapeake Bay, Marcus and Kayla worked their phones trying to call in favors to get a possible address for the cottage.

"There are no Chiangs listed on the property records of Somerset County," Marcus said, frustrated, after he got off a call.

"And it doesn't appear that the Chinese embassy owns any homes along the Eastern Shore," said Kayla. "If we try to look any deeper we'll set off too many red flags."

"We'll have to figure it out on the ground," he replied.

"I don't get the Chiangs' plan," said Margaret. "Eventually they'll have to let Yin go, and when they do, he can say it was them."

"You're assuming he'll tell the truth," said Marcus. "I expect that right now they're trying to convince him it's in his best interest to tell an alternate story."

"Convince him how?" I asked.

"There are two ways," said Kayla. "Promise him something he wants, like a chance to visit home more often."

"Or threaten him with something he's scared of," said Marcus. "Like punishing his parents for his actions."

"They'd do that?" asked Margaret.

"Yes, they would," he said. "You'll know it's happened if the first thing out of their mouths is some variation of 'there's been a big misunderstanding.'"

Malena leaned over and asked, "How does Henry Lu work into this? At some point it will be obvious that he didn't kidnap anyone."

"Maybe," said Marcus. "But for now all the Chiangs need is a distraction. As long as the FBI's focused on him, they can keep working out their new story with Yin."

Throughout the conversation, Lucy never said a single word. She either looked out the window lost in thought or gave me the death stare. I felt terrible about everything but realized there was nothing I could do.

We landed at Crisfield Municipal Airport, three miles out of town, and were met by a driver with a large SUV big enough for us all.

"Where do we go first?" asked Kayla.

I had a sudden inspiration.

"Doughnuts," I said to the driver. "Is there a really good doughnut shop in town?"

"Are you serious?" said Lucy, finally breaking her silence.

"You really think this is the right time for an apple fritter or a cruller? What about Yin?"

"Not a chain," I said, ignoring her. "We need a mom-and-pop doughnut shop."

"There's Donut King on Bay Street," he said.

"Is it good?" I asked.

"Delicious," he said. "But I think it's closed."

"Doesn't matter," I told him. "Take us there."

Everyone gave me an incredulous look and Margaret asked, "Florian, what are you doing?"

"Finding the house," I answered. "Yin said it was near a great doughnut shop. I figured we'd start there and work our way out."

"I totally forgot about the doughnuts."

"I like this plan," said Marcus. He turned to the driver. "Feel free to exceed the speed limit as much as you'd like. I'll deal with the authorities."

"My pleasure."

Since it was a Monday night, there wasn't much traffic. And although the lights of an amusement park flashed along the waterfront, it didn't look like there were many tourists along the main strip. We passed some seafood restaurants and an ice cream shop before reaching the Donut King. It was closed but a neon sign in front flashed:

IT DON'T MEAN A THING IF IT AIN'T FROM THE KING.

Marcus pointed down the nearest street and told the driver to go slowly so we could look for the Chiangs' cottage.

"This still feels kind of impossible," Margaret said as we went down the block.

"Just keep your eyes open," I said. "And think about TOAST."

"First it's doughnuts, then it's toast," she joked. "This case is making me hungry."

We'd gone up and down three streets before I noticed the car.

"Look," I said, pointing. "A diplomatic license plate. The kind they give embassy employees."

Marcus gave me a proud slap on the back and told the driver, "Make a U-turn at the next intersection and park over there." He pointed at a spot two houses down and across the street. "Nice going, Florian."

"What's the plan?" Kayla asked.

"You go around back in case anybody makes a run for it," he said. "And I knock on the front door and hope someone answers."

"What about us?" I asked.

"Everyone else stays in the car," he said.

"No way. I didn't ride in a helicopter just so I could sit and watch," I argued.

"Besides," said Margaret. "If Yin's in there, he'll be less nervous if he sees us."

Marcus thought about this for a moment and begrudgingly said, "Okay. But you stay behind me."

We got out of the car and quietly moved toward the cottage, Marcus leading the way. We stopped at the carport and he put his hand on the hood of the car.

"Still a little warm," he whispered. "They haven't been here long."

Kayla slipped around the back while we followed Marcus to the front door. We could hear a man talking inside but I couldn't make out what he was saying. I wasn't sure if it was because it was muffled or if he was speaking a foreign language.

"I wish I knew for sure that it was him in there," said Marcus. "Because if it's not, this could turn out badly for us."

"Wait a second," said Margaret with a grin. She dug her phone out of her pocket. "I have Mr. Chiang's cell number. He had me text him my picture of Henry Lu."

Marcus smiled. "Why don't you give him a call?"

She dialed and seconds later we heard his phone ringing from inside the house.

"Nice," I said to her. "Very nice."

Marcus took a breath and went straight into action. "Open up!" he commanded, pounding on the door. "FBI!"

We heard some scrambling inside.

Marcus pounded again. "Jian Chiang, we know you're in there. We know Yin Yae's in there too. Open the door!"

Things were quiet for a moment until we heard a bolt unlocking. The door opened halfway and Mr. Chiang looked out at us, doing his best to block the view inside.

"Are you Jian Chang?" asked Marcus.

"Yes," he said coolly. "What seems to be the problem?"

"May we enter the premises?" asked Marcus.

Chiang thought for a moment and asked, "Do you have a warrant?"

"No," admitted Marcus.

"Then you can leave now," he said.

Chiang started to close the door, but I stuck my foot in the way and blocked it.

"Ooof," I grunted as it got squeezed in the process.

"Yin, are you in there?" Margaret called. "It's Margaret and Florian."

"Are you there, Yin?" I asked.

Suddenly Yin appeared from a back room, nervous and weary, but also curious. No doubt stunned to hear our voices. "What are you doing here?"

"We were worried about you," she said.

"We came to help," I added.

"Yin doesn't need any help," said Chiang. "Now move your foot."

He pressed against it harder with the door and I writhed in pain.

"Is he telling the truth, Yin?" Marcus asked. "Do you need any help?"

By this point Kayla had come around to the front door and was standing with us. Yin looked at our faces, thought about it for a moment, and shook his head. "No," he said sadly. "There was just a big misunderstanding." He looked at Chiang and then at us. "I got confused but Mr. Chiang has helped me figure everything out."

Margaret and I slumped. It was just like Marcus said it would be. They'd convinced him to tell a fake story.

"Now, if you don't mind," Chiang growled, "move your foot out of my door."

I wasn't sure what I should do and was just about to pull it back when Yin said, "Wait! What are you doing here?"

I turned to see that he was talking to Lucy, who'd come up from behind us with Malena.

"I got your message," she said. "But when I got to the

garden you weren't there." Then from behind her back she pulled out his Orioles cap. "You left this."

Yin looked at her and was clearly touched by the show of friendship. He reflexively moved toward the door to take the hat, but Chiang blocked his way.

"Yin," said Marcus. "Would you like to go with us?"

He hesitated as he weighed his options and then Margaret said the magic words: "Trust the river, Yin. Just let the current take you and trust the river."

Tears streamed down his face.

"Yes, please," he said softly to Marcus. "I would like to go with you."

34.
Without a Clue

"LISTEN TO THIS," MARGARET SAID, READING THE story on the *Washington Post*'s website. "'First daughter Lucy Mays saved the day as a last-second replacement when music prodigy Yin Yae got sick during intermission of a performance at the Kennedy Center for the Performing Arts.'"

She looked up at me astonished. "No defecting. No running away or kidnapping. Just a few quotes about how great the concert was and how well Lucy filled in."

"They said the story wouldn't come out," I told her. "I guess they knew what they were talking about. What does it say about Yin?"

She scanned the article until she found it. "'Yae's illness was attributed to exhaustion, and the thirteen-year-old wunderkind will recuperate indefinitely back home in Nanjing, China, where his parents are both music professors.'

"*Wunderkind*?" she said with a funny look. "I'm not sure what that is, but I think I want to be one."

"Trust me," I said. "You most definitely are."

Later that week, Yin stopped by to tell us good-bye. We were at Margaret's house practicing for the talent show, and he helped her make a few tweaks to the song.

"Are you happy with how everything turned out?" I asked.

"Very much," he said. "The president himself worked it out with the ambassador. I finally get to go home and be with my family again. I get to be normal."

Margaret laughed. "I hate to break it to you, Yin, but with your talent, you'll never be normal."

We all laughed.

"Everything worked out and I owe it all to you," he said. "Both of you and Lucy. Thank you so much."

"It was our pleasure," I told him. "I'm only sorry we won't get to hear you play anymore."

"Maybe someday," he said. "But before I go, I wanted to give you both something."

He reached into his backpack and pulled out a pair of Baltimore Orioles baseball caps.

"Here you go," he said. "Because now you are songbirds too."

Hat or not, I didn't exactly feel like a songbird two weeks later as I stood backstage the night of the talent show. Despite numerous practices, we hadn't been able to quite figure out exactly what I should do while she played.

"Ready to go on?" asked Margaret. "We're next."

I looked around and came to the quick conclusion that the auditorium at Deal Middle wasn't quite on par with the concert hall at the Kennedy Center for the Performing Arts. But it was still exciting, and appropriate for the level of "talent" I was bringing to the stage.

"I think I'm ready," I told her.

"Have you looked out into the crowd?" she asked. "It's packed."

We moved to a spot in the wings from where we had a good view of the audience.

"Our parents are sitting together," I said, pointing to the four of them, Margaret's dad ready to go with his video camera.

"And there are Marcus and Kayla," she said. "Fourth row center."

"Looks like a date to me."

"Looks like one to me, too," she said, and laughed.

Then she gave me a goofy smile.

"What?" I said.

"I keep waiting for you to notice something, but for a detective you sure do miss a lot of clues," she replied. "Look up there."

I looked into the balcony and saw a pair of people. They were just above the lights, so it took me a moment for my eyes to adjust so I could recognize the faces. It was Malena Sanchez and Lucy Mays.

"What's she doing here?" I asked. "She hates me."

Margaret shrugged. "'Hate' is a strong word. She was angry with you. But friends forgive each other. So maybe this means she's a friend."

"Imagine if the president's daughter became my best friend," I said.

She gave me a look—that Margaret look—and said, "I'm going to act like you never said that."

I laughed. "I mean, second best friend."

An eighth-grade magician finished his act and the stage manager signaled us to get onstage. We pushed the piano out to its position and Margaret sat at her bench.

"You know what friends do?" I asked.

"What?"

"They look foolish for each other."

"Does that mean you're going to do the interpretive dance?"

"Not that foolish!" I said.

Just then the curtain started to rise and the crowd applauded. The lights were blinding, but I wasn't worried about getting lost. I just listened for my best friend on the piano and reminded myself to go with the flow and trust the river.

Acknowledgments

There are so many people to whom I am indebted for this wonderful adventure in writing books for kids. First and foremost is the team at Aladdin, led by my editor Fiona Simpson and publisher Mara Anastas, who have created an ideal environment that is supportive and creative, understanding and collaborative. Joining them in that endeavor is a roster of Simon & Schuster all-stars that includes: Lucille Rettino, Mary Marotta, Christine Pecorale, Michelle Leo, Anthony Parisi, Carolyn Swerdloff, Jodie Hockensmith, Shifa Kapadwala, Laura Lyn DiSiena, Tricia Lin, Stephanie Evans, and Paul Hoppe.

This book is dedicated to my amazing literary agent, Rosemary Stimola, who is to writers what Tom Hagen was to Vito Corleone. (Although, unlike Tom, she's straight up Italian.) I'm so happy to be a member of the literal and figurative family that is the Stimola Literary Studio.

My quest for accuracy was greatly aided by principal James Albright and the wonderful faculty, staff, and students at Alice Deal Middle School. Also huge thanks to Taylor Hartley, Kim Peter Kovac, and the staff at the Kennedy Center for the Performing Arts, as well as Gail Samuel and the Los Angeles Philharmonic.

None of this would have been possible if it weren't for the incredible educators, librarians, and booksellers who fight the battle to get books into the hands of young readers. And it certainly wouldn't have been near as much fun without the friendship, counsel, and input of coconspirators such as Laurie Halse Anderson, Stuart Gibbs, Wendy Mass, Andrea Beatty, Donna Gephart, Liesl Shurtliff, Christina Diaz Gonzalez, Lisa Leicht, Kevin Sands, Tyler Whitesides, and the incomparable Suzanne Collins. Writers rock and I am so lucky to have a place among them.

Most of all, I am thankful for the family that continues to be the reason and inspiration for everything in my world. How lucky I am that I get to spend my life with you.

The mystery continues in Book 3:
TRAPPED!

Geek Mythology

YOU CAN'T JUDGE A BOOK BY ITS COVER.

If you looked at me, you'd see a twelve-year-old boy and think, *Seventh grader.* And, while that wouldn't be wrong, it wouldn't begin to tell you the whole story. For example, it wouldn't tell you that, in addition to doing homework and mowing the lawn, my list of chores typically includes solving cases as a consulting detective with the FBI's Special Projects Team.

And if you looked at the copy of Albert Einstein's *Relativity* that was checked out from the Tenley-Friendship branch of the DC Public Library nine days ago, you'd think, *Science book.* (Okay, first you might look at the picture of Einstein on the cover and wonder how he got his hair to look that way, but then you'd think, *Science book.*) However, you'd never guess that the book triggered an international incident involving a Russian spy ring, the theft of national treasures, a European crime syndicate, and a joint task force of the FBI, CIA, and National Security Agency.

And finally, if you looked at our plan to break into the Library of Congress, evade its state-of-the-art security system, and somehow find the single piece of information necessary to solve our case, you'd think my best friend Margaret and I were absolutely bonkers.

Okay, so sometimes you *can* judge a book by its cover.

The plan was totally nuts.

To be honest, it wasn't so much a plan as it was a list of nearly impossible objectives with no idea how to accomplish them. We knew it was bad. We just couldn't come up with anything better. We had to unmask a spy who'd spent decades as a deep-cover agent stealing U.S. government secrets. But more importantly we had to help Marcus.

Marcus Rivers was in charge of the Special Projects Team, but he wasn't just our boss, he was family. He was also an amazing agent who never once hesitated to risk his life and his career to protect us. It was our turn to return the favor.

At some point during the case, we slipped up, and the spy used our mistake to make it look like Marcus was guilty of theft, corruption, and espionage. Marcus, who'd spent a distinguished career fighting criminals, was now accused of being one.

Desperate times called for desperate measures.

"You're the mastermind," I said to Margaret as we approached the library. "What are we going to do?"

"Get inside, find the evidence, and prove Marcus is innocent," she said.

I gave her a sideways glance. "You have any specific details about how we should do those things?"

She shrugged. "I figured we'd just make it up as we went along."

Like I said, *absolutely bonkers*.

OBJECTIVE 1: Crash the "IT'S ALL ABOUT THE BOOKS" Gala at the Library of Congress

First we had to get inside the library by crashing a gala reception in the Great Hall of the Thomas Jefferson Building. When we arrived, there were about fifty people in tuxedos and gowns waiting to pass through security.

"How are we going to do this?" I asked.

"Clothes and confidence," answered Margaret, as if that were a complete sentence.

"What are you talking about?"

"I looked up 'crashing a formal party' online and it said the two most important things were clothes and confidence. You've got to dress like you belong and act like you belong."

Between my tuxedo and Margaret's dress, we had the clothes part covered. It was the confidence that had me worried.

"Speaking of clothes," she said. "Why do you have a tux?"

"Because it's a formal event," I answered, stating the obvious.

"No. Not, why are you wearing it. Why do you have it in the first place? What twelve-year-old owns a tuxedo?"

I couldn't believe it.

"Let me get this straight. You're giving me a hard time for having something we need?"

"I'm not giving you a hard time," she said. "I just think it's a little . . . unusual. Call me curious."

"Both my parents work in museums," I explained. "I've been dragged to more fund-raisers and exhibition openings than I can remember. They're usually formal events like this one, so I got a tux."

"Okay, that makes sense," she said. "It's also good news. Since you've been to a lot of these things you should fit right in."

"Well, there's one big difference between those events and this one."

"What's that?"

"We had invitations."

She gave me a conspiratorial smile and said, "You're not going to let a little piece of paper stop us from solving the mystery and saving Marcus, are you?"

She always knew what to say to get me to go along with her schemes. "No, I'm not," I answered. "Let's do this."

There were two lines with security guards manning metal detectors. Each also had a woman with a computer tablet checking invitations. One of the women looked to be in her mid-twenties and wore a black cocktail dress and very high heels. The other wore a longer dress with shoes that were nice but more comfortable. She also had a wedding band on her ring finger.

"The odds are better that the one on the right is a mom," I said. "That might mean she's nicer to kids."

"True," answered Margaret. "But the one on the left is more likely to think all kids are stupid."

"Good point," I said as we got into the line on the left.

During an FBI training session called "Outsmarting Your Opponent," we were taught that the biggest advantage you can have is for the other side to underestimate your abilities.

"When she asks for our invitations, we'll tell her our moms have them but are already inside."

"If our mothers are inside, then why are we out here?" I asked.

"That's where the 'stupid' comes in." Margaret suddenly adopted the voice of an airheaded middle schooler who spoke in endless run-on sentences. "I was talking to my friend Maddie about the party and the call kept cutting in and out so I started walking around trying to get better reception but it just got worse and worse so I went through a door and accidentally got locked outside. OMG, my mom is going to kill me if she finds out."

"Do you think people really think kids talk that way?" I asked.

"I'm counting on it," Margaret said.

"And why am I outside if you were the one on the phone?" I asked.

"You're my best friend. You go wherever I go."

"So we're both stupid."

"That's the plan unless you've got a better one," she said.

I took a deep breath. "Tragically, I don't."

We were about halfway through the line when she realized a potential problem. "Uh-oh."

"What?" I asked nervously.

"She'll probably want a name to check against the guest list. We'll need some TOAST help on that."

TOAST stands for the Theory of All Small Things. It was the method we used to read people and situations in order to solve cases. The idea was that if you looked for little details you could add them up to discover otherwise hidden pieces of information. At the moment we needed the names of two people who were already inside the gala.

"I got it covered," I said.

I pulled out my phone and started searching.

"What are you doing?" she asked.

"Looking on social media for any pictures tagged with that." I pointed to a banner that read, #ITSALLABOUTTHEBOOKS.

"Oh, that's kind of brilliant," she said as she did likewise.

Even though the party was barely an hour old, there were already dozens of photos to scroll through of people inside having fun.

"Find one posted by someone with an unusual name," I said. "It'll seem less likely that we made it up. Also, find out where they work in case that's included on the guest list."

By the time we reached the front of the line, we were ready to go. Margaret's airhead act worked like a charm; when asked, I became the son of a kid's book publisher named Mara Anastas. I even spelled it out for her so that she could find it on her tablet.

"See what I mean?" Margaret said as we walked through the entrance. "Clothes and confidence."

OBJECTIVE 2: Avoid detection while sneaking into the Library's secure area

It was amazing how different the Great Hall looked compared to when we'd come during normal hours. Multicolored lights gave it a party feel, and giant reproductions of famous book covers were hung as decorations. People mingled in clusters while a jazz quartet played on a stage.

A waiter walked past us carrying a tray of finger food, which caught Margaret's attention. "Ooh, those look delicious."

"We're working a case," I reminded her. "Not going to a party."

She gave me that Margaret smirk. "Actually, we're blending in at a party so that we can work the case. Besides, I'm starving."

She chased after the waiter, and I scanned the room. Now that we were inside, we needed to find the computer server. The library had an automated system that kept detailed records of its secure areas. If we could access them, we might be able to prove Marcus's innocence.When Margaret returned, she was carrying a little plate with two toothpick skewers of beef. "The waiter said it's called *bulgogi* and it's amazing," she said as she tasted one. "I think it's Korean."

"Is that one for me?" I asked, pointing to the untouched skewer.

"I thought you said we weren't at a party."

"I thought you said we were blending in."

She reluctantly held up the second skewer, and I snatched it before she could change her mind. It was mouthwatering.

"You're right," I said between chews. "We've got to track him down and get more."

"No, no, no," she said. "This is not good."

"What do you mean? This is absolutely delicious."

"Not the food," she replied. "Him."

She nodded over my shoulder, and I turned to see one of our suspects about fifteen feet from us. It was Alistair Toombs, the director of the library's Rare Book and Special Collections Division. Luckily, he was facing the other way. We'd already had a run-in with him and couldn't risk being seen.

We quickly worked our way to the opposite side of the room and tried to disappear into the crowd of people milling around chitchatting.

"We've got to find the server room fast," I said as I

studied the building's layout, trying to logically deduce where it should be. "It has to be cool and dry, which means it won't have any exterior walls. Humidity can seep through those. They'd also stay away from the lower basement to avoid potential flooding. As far as wiring . . ."

"I hate to interrupt your little Sherlock moment," she said. "But it might be quicker if we just follow him."

Next to the stage, a computer tech was making adjustments to the audio and lighting boards. He looked like he was just out of college. As soon as he was done, he took his tool kit and left.

"Change of plans," I said. "Let's follow him."

The guy led us back across the room before he got into an elevator labeled STAFF ONLY. After the doors closed, we rushed over to watch the display to see where he got off.

"Two floors down," said Margaret. "Now we're getting somewhere."

"Yeah, except we're not getting anywhere on that elevator. At least, not without a card key."

The call button was attached to a card reader.

"Not a problem," she said. "We'll just hang around here until somebody gets off the elevator. Then we'll slip in before the doors shut."

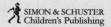 

WHAT IF INSTEAD OF JUST READING YOUR FAVORITE
BOOKS, YOU COULD JUMP INSIDE THEM?

STORY THIEVES

Molly Bigelow is NOT your average girl. She's one of an elite crew assigned the task of policing and protecting the zombie population of New York. *The Hunger Games* author Suzanne Collins says *Dead City* "breathes new life into the zombie genre."

From Aladdin • simonandschuster.com/kids

EBOOK EDITIONS
ALSO AVAILABLE